W9-BCB-131

## "All evening I've wanted to do this…"

Drake's lips then slid over hers, possessing her mouth. Ilona melted into him, her feelings running riot. Even if she had wanted to stop him, it was fast becoming beyond her power to do so.

Easing his mouth away, Drake murmured, "I knew it wouldn't take me long to soften that frigid manner. Am I to get my reward?"

Ilona frowned, uncomprehending.

"I've done my best for you this evening with my business acquaintances," Drake went on. "There should be enough work coming in to your agency to pay the rent for months ahead."

"You have my deepest thanks," she said quietly. "What more can I do to convince you I'm grateful?"

His fingers lifted her chin. "Surely I don't have to put it into words?"

**LILIAN PEAKE**
is also the author of these

# Harlequin Presents

186—A BITTER LOVING
190—THIS MAN HER ENEMY
198—NO FRIEND OF MINE
206—THE LITTLE IMPOSTOR
213—SOMEWHERE TO LAY MY HEAD
225—A GIRL ALONE
229—PASSIONATE INVOLVEMENT
316—NO SECOND PARTING
330—ENEMY FROM THE PAST
341—RUN FOR YOUR LOVE
353—DANGEROUS DECEPTION
384—A RING FOR A FORTUNE
407—A SECRET AFFAIR
424—GREGG BARRATT'S WOMAN
454—STRANGERS INTO LOVERS
474—ACROSS A CROWDED ROOM

and these

# Harlequin Romances

1778—A SENSE OF BELONGING
1831—MASTER OF THE HOUSE
1855—THE IMPOSSIBLE MARRIAGE
1868—THE DREAM ON THE HILL
1900—MOONRISE OVER THE MOUNTAINS
1944—HEART IN THE SUNLIGHT
2220—REBEL IN LOVE
2279—STRANGER ON THE BEACH
2404—PROMISE AT MIDNIGHT

Many of these titles are available at your local bookseller.

For a free catalogue listing all available Harlequin Romances
and Harlequin Presents, send your name and address to:

HARLEQUIN READER SERVICE
1440 South Priest Drive, Tempe, AZ 85281
Canadian address: Stratford, Ontario N5A 6W2

# LILIAN PEAKE

## day of possession

*Harlequin Books*

TORONTO • LONDON • LOS ANGELES • AMSTERDAM
SYDNEY • HAMBURG • PARIS • STOCKHOLM • ATHENS • TOKYO

Harlequin Presents edition published April 1982
ISBN 0-373-10496-0

Original hardcover edition published in 1978
by Mills & Boon Limited

Copyright © 1978 by Lilian Peake. All rights reserved.
Philippine copyright 1978. Australian copyright 1978. Cover
illustration copyright © 1982 by Tom Bjarnason Inc.
Except for use in any review, the reproduction or utilization of
this work in whole or in part in any form by any electronic,
mechanical or other means, now known or hereafter invented,
including xerography, photocopying and recording, or in any
information storage or retrieval system, is forbidden without
the permission of the publisher, Harlequin Enterprises Limited,
225 Duncan Mill Road, Don Mills, Ontario, Canada M3B 3K9.

All the characters in this book have no existence outside the
imagination of the author and have no relation whatsoever to
anyone bearing the same name or names. They are not even
distantly inspired by any individual known or unknown to the
author, and all the incidents are pure invention.

The Harlequin trademark, consisting of the words
HARLEQUIN PRESENTS and the portrayal of a Harlequin,
is registered in the United States Patent Office and in the
Canada Trade Marks Office.

Printed in U.S.A.

# CHAPTER ONE

'His secretary's away again,' said Mary. 'He's ordered flowers to be sent to her, as usual.'

Ilona sighed. 'He really must be in love with her,' she said. 'Every time she's away, he orders something to be sent. If it's not flowers, it's chocolates or perfume.'

'What wouldn't I give,' Mary sighed, 'to have a man like that besotted with me!'

Ilona gave a shrug. 'Do you really think he's all that wonderful?'

Even though it was a question, it was really also a lie. She knew exactly how she felt about Drake Warrick and it was a feeling she had no intention of telling anyone about, certainly no one with whom she worked.

There was something about the man that had her curling her toes every time she saw him. If he ever came into the typing pool and wandered around, as he sometimes did— which was surprising for the head of such a large organisation as Warricks, the timber importers—she would keep her eyes fixed firmly on her typewriter.

She refused to ogle him like the other girls, partly because it was beneath her dignity to do so but mainly because she knew that if their eyes ever met, he would, with his obvious knowledge of women, know exactly how she felt about him.

That particular morning was one on which he chose to go on the prowl. The door of the large office opened and the head of the firm came in. There was a moment's cessation of the pounding of typewriters, a few strangled sighs made their way into the silence, then the typing was resumed with, if anything, more energy than before.

Ilona was, to an onlooker, the only girl to remain outwardly unaffected by the appearance of the boss. No one, however, bothered to look at the quiet, brown-haired young woman who sat in the corner of the room.

The girls appeared as efficient as they always did, but to

Ilona's experienced ears the increase in the tempo of the typing revealed the flutters of excitement which they were experiencing at the presence of the man who owned the business. Not only that, they were feeling the strange kind of aura he carried around with him.

His height was formidable, his hair a deep brown and his eyes piercingly blue. All this, together with his proud bearing and dauntingly broad shoulders which were revealed to their greatest advantage by the excellently tailored suit he wore, combined to give him an irresistible magnetism.

That is, Ilona thought, eyes fixed firmly on the work she was copying, to those who wished to be magnetised. She had no such wish. She knew the dangers which that particular event would cause to her peace of mind.

She had seen her sister's best friend, Lucia, with whom she shared a cottage, rapturously in love and married to the object of that love. She had witnessed the slow disintegration of that marriage and Lucia's consequent heartbreak and descent into a decadent way of life. So Ilona had made up her mind that she would allow no man to wreak such havoc with her emotions.

The cottage was small, thatched and nearly three hundred years old. In the kitchen there was an ancient cooking stove. Water came from a tap outside. When she and Lucia bathed they had to heat pans of water and afterwards empty the bathwater away, throwing it on to the tiny, fenced-in patch which, for want of a better name, was called the front garden.

The landlord had offered to connect the cottage to the mains electricity and water supplies, but Lucia had refused, saying it was much more fun to live primitively. Living primitively, Ilona had often thought sourly, was indeed Lucia's way of life these days.

There were two bedrooms in the cottage. One was downstairs, leading out of the main living-room. The other bedroom, up a short flight of wooden stairs, Ilona had chosen to use as her own, thus leaving the larger downstairs bedroom to her sister's friend. Ilona had never regretted the decision to have the upstairs bedroom.

At least twice a week Lucia gave parties. Sometimes, in

order to get to sleep, Ilona would have to pull the bed-clothes over her ears in an attempt to shut out the noise. There were times when this ruse failed and the morning after such times, Ilona invariably arrived at work heavy-eyed and weary, as if she herself had taken part in the wild parties.

There were times when she had made mistakes in her work, mistakes which she knew were due to her tired state. When she tried to explain the situation to any of the managers for whom she worked—that it was the noise of a party which had kept her awake—the men would laugh ribaldly and refuse to believe her.

The situation was getting so out of control, Ilona was becoming desperate. She liked her job and did not want to lose it. On the other hand, she had no other place in which to live. Her parents resided abroad and the idea of sharing a flat with strangers did not appeal. At least her sister's friend was a known quantity, even if she had, as a result of disillusionment and desertion, grown wild in her ways. What Ilona did not know was how much longer her employer would tolerate her faulty work.

Footsteps approached along the gangway between the desks. The steps were firm and confident and Ilona knew to whom they belonged. Drake Warrick stopped beside her. She took a deep breath and held it. She stayed as she was, fingers poised above the typewriter keys. With the boss standing next to her and looking at her work, she dared not continue.

'Correspondence, Miss Bell,' said the man beside her, 'is spelt with two "r's", not one.' There was a pause and Ilona let her breath out slowly. 'Concerned, Miss Bell,' Drake Warrick went on, 'has a "c" in the middle, not an "s".'

Brown, troubled eyes swung upwards to meet the ice blue ones. 'I'm concerned, too, Miss Bell,' he said.

Was it coming now, Ilona thought, dismayed—that dismissal she had been dreading? And in front of all her colleagues? The cold blue eyes continued to hold hers.

'Too many late nights, Miss Bell?' he queried sarcastically. 'Too many parties, maybe?'

'I don't go to parties,' she snapped. She looked away,

conscious of having overstepped the bounds imposed by the employer-employee relationship.

He had looked as if he were going to reprimand her for her sharp denial, but appeared to change his mind. 'Come to my office, Miss Bell,' he said shortly.

Again her eyes sought his. Was this how he was going to do it—dismiss her in private? At least that would cause her less humiliation than within the hearing of her colleagues.

His gaze moved over her features, examining them as if he had never really studied a woman's face before. Then his expression changed from its detached, impartial assessment and his eyes mocked her anxiety. All the same, the ice did not melt. 'I'm not going to eat you,' he said, with a gleam of amusement. 'I need a replacement for my secretary, who is away ill.' He became abrupt and businesslike. 'Bring your notebook and pencil.' With that, he strode from the room.

As the door closed, the clatter of typewriters ceased. There was an incredulous silence. Out of all the girls he could have picked, he had chosen Ilona Bell! A girl who, in her own opinion, although not necessarily in others', had so little in the way of attractions to commend her that even Lucia's more lecherous men friends left her alone, except when they were half drunk. She could not even guess that it was her reserved, touch-me-not air which kept them at bay, and not her physical appearance at all.

Her hair was shoulder-length and brown, and caught back with a slide. Finely-pencilled eyebrows curved delicately and the large, intense brown eyes were further enhanced by incredibly long lashes.

As she made her way between the desks, Mary called out, 'Cheer up, Ilona. You're not going to your doom!'

Ilona smiled and shrugged, hoping that her attempt to appear uncaring had fooled the girls. Although other typists had in the past been called from the typing pool to take dictation from the owner of the business, this was her first time, and she hoped that her fear did not show.

She could not think why he had chosen her. Behind a desk and in his own surroundings, Drake Warrick looked even more formidable. There was about him an air of authority which daunted her. There was a pile of letters in front of him.

He motioned to them irritably. 'If Diane, my secretary, were here, I could have passed this lot over to her and she would have given the pile back to me reduced by half.' He sighed, but even that was abrupt. 'However . . .' He eyed her cynically and she felt a little like the mouse other people called her.

'Mouse' had been her sister's nickname for her, and Lucia had taken it up. Whenever Lucia used the expression, Ilona wanted to throw things. On the surface she might be quiet, but she knew that inside there was a tigress fretting to get out. But Drake Warrick, like everyone else, saw only the outward wrapping.

'However,' Drake Warrick continued, 'I'll have mercy on your lesser intellectual abilities,' the cold blue eyes taunted and dared her to answer back, 'and I'll deal with them all myself, even,' with a broad smile, 'the "Dear Sir, Thank you, Yours faithfully," variety!'

Drake Warrick dictated fast, but there was no doubt in Ilona's mind that she could keep up with his dictation. After a few minutes he paused and looked at her speculatively. She looked boldly back at him, pencil poised. He seemed to give a mental shrug and carried on. Had he been expecting her to complain, Ilona wondered, giving a secret smile.

'What's so amusing, Miss Bell?' Drake Warrick asked curtly.

Ilona coloured, her brown eyes momentarily dancing. Seconds later they sobered and their customary deep seriousness returned.

Drake Warrick studied her with a puzzled frown, then the words flowed again. Ilona wondered whether it was her imagination, or whether he had really speeded up the dictation. She was, however, able to cope with ease, even though he seemed to speed up even more, watching her closely, possibly hoping, she thought abstractedly, for a sign of a crack in her ability to withstand the onslaught of his fluent, highly technical phraseology.

Half an hour later, surfacing from the avalanche of words, Ilona noticed that the pile of letters in front of him had disappeared. Instead, a pile had formed on her side of the desk.

· Their eyes met and he regarded her steadily. 'They're all yours, Miss Bell.'

She did not, could not, move. She was mesmerised by those eyes, by the long fingers of his clasped hands, by the slightly unruly dark hair which set off his fine facial structure.

But despite his heart-tugging looks, she did not doubt that he could, whenever he wished, be utterly ruthless where women were concerned. She tore her eyes from his, and told herself she was being a fool. How could this man with, so to speak, the world of women at his feet, ever see her as anything but a piece of office equipment, to be switched on, utilised and switched off at any moment he might choose?

Having been lost in her thoughts, she had not realised that her employer had been watching her. 'I should be glad, Miss Bell,' he said with mocking amusement, 'if you would do your thinking outside office hours.' He became brisk. 'Not to mention outside my room. My time costs money, a great deal of money. Even yours as a typist is not exactly cheap. So——'

Ilona stood quickly. 'I'm well aware——' she began, then checked herself. His icy expression froze the words in her throat.

His hand came out. 'The door, Miss Bell.'

Head high, Ilona made for it. Thus, she thought rebelliously, am I dismissed from the great man's august presence.

The colour still stained her cheeks when she returned to the typists' room, a fact which the others noticed.

'Has he been getting at you?' Mary asked, sympathetically.

Ilona shook her head.

'Did he go fast?' asked a girl called Angie.

Ilona shrugged dismissively.

'He went so fast with me once,' Angie went on, 'that I had to ask him to slow down.'

'So did I,' said a girl called Joan.

'And me,' two others called out.

Ilona tried to shut out their chatter as she sat at her desk. No wonder he had seemed surprised at her failure to ask him to dictate more slowly! The session with her employer had, however, taken more out of her than she had realised. Suddenly her energy seemed drained and all she wanted to do was to cross her arms on her typewriter and rest her head on them.

She was suffering as usual from a shortage of sleep. The night before, Lucia had given yet another of her parties. At two o'clock, Ilona had given up trying to sleep and had sat for an hour reading a book. When, at three o'clock, the last guest had departed, Ilona had flopped down, exhausted, only to be awoken, less than four hours later, by the alarm clock.

Having breakfasted, Ilona had left Lucia in bed. In between parties, Lucia seemed to be having an on-off affair with her boss. This meant he was lenient with her. It also meant that she could arrive at work at whatever time she chose, provided it was before the lunch break.

As the bus took her from the clamour of the town to the peace of the north Essex village in which she and Lucia lived, Ilona felt the tensions of the day steal away, like thieves from a house whose occupants had been alerted by their noise. The tensions, like the thieves, went away empty-handed, leaving her sweet and clean. If only, she thought, staring through the bus windows at the wide-flung fields, I could live life my way instead of Lucia's ...

It was late May, and the village charity committee, of which Ilona was a member, were making arrangements to hold a fête. The vicar had offered the grounds of the vicarage, but Colonel Dainton, a tall, white-haired man with a military background of which he never ceased to remind his fellow-villagers, offered the use of the meadow which he owned as part of the estate attached to the large nineteenth-century mansion in which he lived.

The committee discussed the provision of food, the contents of the stalls, the competitions in which the children would take part.

'We must have a raffle,' someone was saying. 'A cake?'

'Let's try and be different this time,' Ray, a young man beside Ilona, suggested.

'I've got it,' the Colonel boomed, thumping the table, 'a woman, we'll raffle a woman!'

'It's a good idea,' said the vicar thoughtfully. 'After all, it is for charity. Now, let's think, who shall it be? The prettiest, the youngest among us?'

All eyes swung to Ilona. She pushed back her chair in an effort to escape. 'Please, for goodness' sake, don't look at me,' she pleaded.

'But, as the vicar remarked,' said a plump, middle-aged lady called Mrs Bryant, 'it is for charity, Miss Bell. Surely no harm could come of it?'

Ray urged Ilona down. 'You'd make the charity committee a mint of money,' he coaxed. 'Let's put a time limit on it. Let's call it,' he thought a moment, 'a girl for a day!'

Ilona returned to an empty cottage. She did not bother to light the oil lamp. There was such a weariness inside her that all she wanted to do was to sit in the old rocking chair and look out across the fields, lifting her eyes to dwell on the glorious sunset colours which were scrawled across the sky as if put there by the superbly inspired hand of an artist genius.

If only, she daydreamed, rocking gently, it was always as peaceful as this! If only Lucia would tire of this primitive way of living and move into the town. Then the cottage would be mine, she reflected with a smile. She closed her eyes, enjoying the to and fro movement of the rocking chair.

She yawned, thought, 'I really must be tired, although it's only just after nine o'clock ...' She was drifting off, then the rocking chair was still.

Mr Warrick's work! The words stampeded into her semi-conscious state, trampling over the half-formed dream that was just beginning. Ilona sat up and attempted to drag herself from the rocking chair. It was no good. Sleep had already got to work on her limbs, relaxing them so much that they flatly refused to do her bidding.

Her mind had savoured the sweetness of sleep and, liking the taste of it, wanted more. She sank back, her head found the dent she had made in the cushion and she slept again.

It was half an hour to midnight when the crowd burst into the pitch-dark room. There were shouts and laughing threats and curses as feet tripped and hands groped.

A lighter flicked, its flame was lifted to find a clear path to the oil lamp—and someone called out, 'Good grief, what's this, Lucia? A ghost from your doubtful past? No, it's not. It's a girl. My word, she's a beauty!' The voice was male, the words ran into each other.

'Oh, God!' a young woman sighed. 'It's Ilona, the girl I share with. What's she doing down here? Come on,' Ilona's arm was shaken, 'up to bed, like a good little girl.' Over her shoulder, Lucia said, 'She doesn't approve of my way of life.'

Ilona, wakened so roughly from a deep sleep, let her arm fall where Lucia dropped it.

'If she's going to bed,' said the man, whose voice sounded vaguely familiar to Ilona, 'let me be the one to take her there. If you don't see me till morning, Lucia . . .'

'Try it, Ron,' said Lucia, with scorn, 'just try it on the sweet, puritan little sister of my friend, and see how far you get.'

'*I'll scratch your eyes out!*'

The words shot into the sudden silence and the group stared open-mouthed at the girl who had spoken, sitting stiffly upright, her hands gripping the chair arms.

The lighter flame was lifted higher, moved in a slow circle around Ilona's face. The hand holding the lighter shook a little. The face above it was florid and full and heavy-eyed. It belonged to Ron Bradwell, one of the men for whom she had worked. He was, like herself, an employee of Warricks. There, however, the resemblance ended. He was much higher in rank than herself. He was, in fact, the personnel manager of the company.

Ilona had never liked him. He was well-known for his extra-marital activities, as one of the other managers had called it. He had, on a number of occasions, taken the various secretaries and typists to dine and afterwards——? That was anyone's guess.

He had, on occasion, asked Ilona to go out with him. It was, he had told her, her air of innocence that had challenged him—something no other girl of his acquaintance possessed. She had always answered his invitation with a polite 'no', at which he had always shrugged resignedly. But there had been a malicious look in his eyes which had worried her.

He was not shrugging now. 'So you'd scratch my eyes out, would you, my beauty?' He caught her arm and hauled her from the chair.

Someone had put a match to the oil lamp, giving a yellow glow to the room.

'Leave me alone, Mr Bradwell,' Ilona said, endeavouring to stay calm. 'I'm not a sleep-around girl.' She shook herself free of his hold.

'I could give you a lesson, darling, one you'd never forget.'

'If you're that frustrated, Mr Bradwell,' Ilona said between her teeth, 'try going back home to your wife. You've got a beautiful wife, Mr Bradwell, and two lovely young children. I've seen photographs of them on your desk.'

He could find no words with which to answer the criticism. Instead, he reached out again and caught her arm, jerking her so that she staggered.

'Leave me alone, Mr Bradwell,' Ilona repeated, her temper simmering. 'I find you revolting in the extreme. You repel me. Everything about you disgusts me!' Her eyes blazed with challenge, as she saw that each one of her accusations had gone home.

His hand lifted and made contact with her cheek with such force that it sent her flying. As she fell to the ground her head hit the corner of a table. As consciousness fled, she heard herself cry out, but what the words had been she did not know. Moments later she came round and she found she was stretched full-length on the floor.

There was a thudding pain at the side of her head. She felt dazed and ill. Someone helped her to a chair. The face of Ron Bradwell loomed large and menacing, but the party, she realised, was going on around her. No one, it seemed, apart from the man who had hit her, took the slightest notice of her.

'It's Warrick, isn't it?' Ron Bradwell was saying, leaning over her as she lay back in the chair. 'It's Drake Warrick you've fallen for! You cried out for him as you fell.' He watched the frown that formed between her brows.

'You didn't know, did you,' he pressed, 'that you called out his name?' He shouted above the din. 'Lucia, your friend's sister's in love with her boss. But unlike you, she keeps it all to her innocent little self. Going to have an affair with him, darling?' he asked Ilona insultingly. 'Follow in Lucia's footsteps. Let him make love to you, then he'll forgive you everything, even your typing mistakes.'

There was no energy left within Ilona to retaliate, no strength to deny the assertion. Anyway—the drowsiness was creeping up on her again—wasn't it partly true that she loved Drake Warrick? No, she thought, slipping into an unhealthy kind of doze, not partly true, wholly true. She had to face it. She, Ilona Bell, loved her employer Drake Warrick.

Unconsciously her lips moved and, although she was unaware of it, once again his name slipped from her on a sigh. Somewhere not far from her face, came Ron Bradwell's exultant laugh.

# CHAPTER TWO

When the scream of the alarm bell woke her, she found she was in bed. Someone must have carried her upstairs to her room. She was fully dressed.

Ilona rolled on to her front and tried to burrow into the pillow, but she had to face facts. In a few moments, despite her throbbing head, despite the bump which had swollen to the size of a minor mountain in the night, she had to get up.

There was the day to face. She stiffened and her finger nails dug into the pillow. *Mr Warrick's work!* Feeling this way, how could she hope to hand him perfectly-typed letters? How could she hand him *any* letters? Her brain and her fingers would be so out of phase she was sure that not for a single moment would they come together and blend in complete harmony.

If she attempted to explain, would Drake Warrick believe her? In the circumstances, she thought, rolling out of bed, it was a pity that the bump for which Ron Bradwell had been responsible did not show, and also that headaches were invisible. They would have been evidence which even Mr Warrick could not ignore.

At mid-morning, the telephone rang in the typists' office. 'For you, Ilona,' said Mary. 'The big bad boss himself. Watch your step—he's in a mood.'

Ilona picked up the receiver, pushed back her shoulders and said, 'Yes, Mr Warrick?'

'Will you bring my letters in, please.' It was not a question. His receiver hammered down. No chance to tell him, I'm only halfway through. No chance to say, I've done my best to finish them, but it was no use.

As she returned to her desk, the other girls looked at her pityingly. 'You're the first in,' said a girl called Sarah. 'He's always worst with the first one. He must be missing his secretary.'

One of the girls laughed meaningfully. 'In more ways than one!'

Ilona collected the letters she had typed. There was no time to read them through and correct any mistakes. There was nothing in her appearance, either, which might have softened his heart and coaxed him to forgive the errors. The kitchen mirror had shown her in painful detail that morning exactly how she looked, how lack of sufficient sleep had dulled her eyes and her reactions.

As she entered, Drake Warrick threw down his pen and leaned back. The blue eyes had a coating of frost sufficient to make her shiver even if her legs had not already felt weak and her head full of something which resembled dense autumnal fog.

Her employer looked her over from the top of her brown hair to the tan-coloured sandals. But, it seemed, he was unmoved by the shadowed eyes and the droop of the shoulders. He was, as Mary had warned, in a mood, black and threatening.

His hand came out for the letters, which he flipped through. Expressionless eyes lifted to hers. 'The rest?'

'I haven't typed them yet, Mr Warrick.'

'I said distinctly that I wanted them by mid-morning.'

Her head ached and there was a persistent throbbing in the bruised area which had crashed against the table when Ron Bradwell had hit her. 'I'm not feeling very well this morning, Mr Warrick. I——'

He interrupted curtly, 'Since you've spent half the night taking part in a semi-orgy, I'm not surprised.'

Ilona frowned. 'Semi-orgy?'

He looked deceptively relaxed, lifting his hands and linking them behind his head. 'Why aren't you honest with me, Miss Bell?' he drawled. 'Why don't you admit you're suffering from a hangover after too much self-indulgence, a too-prolonged appeasement of your—appetites?'

Still bewildered, Ilona asked, 'Indulgence? Appetites?'

'Yes,' he rasped, 'and to such an extent that you're incapable of tackling any work which requires complete concentration, such as transcribing shorthand, and typing letters I've dictated, with the high standard of accuracy I require.'

It had not taken him long to find some errors. His

finger moved over the first two letters, pinpointing mistakes on three or four lines.

His anger, which had all the time been simmering just beneath the surface, began to bubble like water in a kettle midway to boiling point.

'If your private life,' he grated, 'has a detrimental effect on the work you do to earn your living, and for which, if I may say so, you are generously paid, then your private life must be radically changed.'

Ilona frowned again. Private life? What 'private life' did she have? Nothing more questionable than being a member of the village charity committee, the enjoyment of reading, of listening to music ... It read like the information given under 'hobbies' on a job application form!

She put a hand to the bump at the side of her head. Why did it have to throb so? 'Mr Warrick, don't you understand——'

He said nothing, made no move of encouragement or reassurance that he did indeed understand.

'The—the girl I share a cottage with gave a party last night,' she faltered.

'Ah,' he said, his face set, 'now we're getting the truth.'

'It's not the truth,' she cried, 'not the "truth" you mean. What you're thinking is wrong. Things happened and I——'

'So,' he unhooked his arm from the back of the chair, 'you didn't attend this party she gave?'

'That's not the point.' She was afraid now, afraid of the meaning he was reading into her evasions.

'You haven't answered my question.'

'Yes, yes, I was at the party, but against my will. You must believe me——'

His lips curved in a slight smile. His eyes grew even colder. 'I'm glad you've decided to be honest. You see,' his hand reached for an internal telephone, 'I have a witness.' He dialled.

Ilona knew that it was Ron Bradwell's extension number. 'Look, Mr Warrick, I can explain——'

'Don't bother. My personnel manager will fill in the details.' He flashed her a sardonic smile and said, 'Ron? Come in again, will you?'

'Again?' So Ron Bradwell had already been in there pouring poison into his employer's ear, telling him heaven knew how many lies ... The man came in, his air jaunty and confident.

'Hi, darling,' he said to Ilona. 'Yes, Drake?' Surely that air of assumed innocence didn't mislead Drake Warrick into trusting him?

'Miss Bell now admits she was at the party.'

'Yes,' Ron Bradwell stroked his chin and looked at Ilona, 'I didn't think she'd hold out against you for long. Anyway, there were more than enough people there to testify to the truth.' He said, grinning broadly, 'How's the head, darling?'

Ilona turned on him. 'Stop calling me "darling"! It's a beautiful term of endearment. You're desecrating it.'

He smiled spitefully. 'She's a fighter, Drake. You should try her for yourself.'

Drake regarded her through narrowed eyes. 'You surprise me, Ron. I would never have thought of Miss Bell as being anything but virtuous and untouched by man.'

'Which,' replied Ron Bradwell, 'shows how deceptive appearances can be. She's great, Drake, once you get her going. You know what they say about the quiet ones ...'

Furiously Ilona confronted the personnel manager. 'How did your wife greet you, Mr Bradwell, when you eventually got home and crawled into bed? Did she hold out trusting arms and welcome you?'

In trying to crush him, she discovered to her cost she was wasting her time. 'I didn't go home to bed, darling. You of all people should know that.'

Ilona looked from one man to the other. She had been caught in a trap of words and innuendoes so cleverly set that it had shut tightly on her before she even realised she had rushed headlong into it. The two men exchanged glances.

Man-language, she fumed, a silent interchange of meaningful looks which put a woman in her place as indisputably as if she had been thrown to the ground and violated.

'What is this, Mr Warrick?' she queried, lifting a hand to her throbbing head. 'Are you putting my integrity on trial? Is Mr Bradwell the prosecutor and you both the jury and the judge? Am I to have no chance to defend myself?'

Drake Warrick frowned, moved a paperweight and started to speak.

Ron Bradwell, guessing that his employer's sense of fair play might be asserting itself, broke in with false sympathy, 'What's wrong, darling? Is that bump on your head troubling you?' He smiled malevolently. 'I shouldn't have hit you so hard, should I?'

Wide-eyed, Ilona stared at him. He was admitting he had hurt her?

'You hit her, Bradwell?'

'Yes, Drake,' Ron Bradwell said easily, 'and she loved it.'

Ilona rounded on him. 'You're lying and you know it! You're slandering me, Mr Bradwell, and if I had a more reliable witness to the fact than our employer here——'

Eyes black with anger, Drake half rose as if to come round the desk and seize her. Instead, he lashed out with his tongue. 'You're fired, Miss Bell.'

'But, Mr Warrick, what have I done? Spoken the truth, that's all.'

'The truth? Is that what you call it?' He made a dismissing movement. 'I've taken as much of your abuse as I can stand. Collect your things, go to accounts and get a month's salary in place of notice and get off my premises!'

He dialled and said 'Accounts? Wait a minute.' With scant patience he watched Ilona walk slowly across the room. At the door, she turned and looked at him, unable to prevent the sudden tears from brimming over. 'If this is what you call justice, Mr Warrick, then I hope I never have to have any kind of dealings with you again.'

He gazed steadily back at her, waiting for her to go.

As Ilona opened the cottage door, Lucia was swaying gently in the rocking chair.

Ilona frowned. 'What are you doing at home?'

Lucia drew on her cigarette and released the smoke. 'I had such a filthy hangover, Colin let me have the day off.' As realisation dawned, Lucia stared. 'You're hardly late home yourself. Lost your job?' she joked.

'Yes,' Ilona hurled at her. 'Because of the mistakes I made in my work and all because I was tired through not sleeping. Because of your miserable parties!'

'Darling little mouse,' Ilona gritted her teeth at the term, 'how can you blame last night on me? You stayed down here voluntarily.'

'I——' Ilona stopped. What was the use of arguing with Lucia? Or anyone, for that matter. Hadn't she argued earlier with her ex-employer and his manager? And where had that got her?

She climbed the stairs to her room.

'How are you going to pay the rent?' Lucia called after her. 'You're not going to live here rent-free.'

'I can pay you for next month,' Ilona answered wearily. 'Mr Warrick gave me a month's pay.'

'M'm, generous,' said Lucia, 'considering you were sacked for being incompetent.'

Ilona opened her mouth to deny the statement, but snapped it shut. It was true, wasn't it? If she hadn't made so many typing errors, not only in his letters but in work given to her by other men he employed, she would still be in the office at her desk with all the other girls. But there hadn't been anything wrong with her shorthand speed. Even the other girls had complimented her on her ability to keep up with the boss's dictation. And even Drake Warrick himself had seemed surprised.

Ilona sat on the bed and punched her pillow. It wasn't fair, it just was not fair! Later she went downstairs to get herself some lunch. Lucia was in her own bedroom, grooming her hair. It was long and a rich brown and she combed it lovingly.

Ilona stood in the doorway. 'Want some lunch?'

'No, thanks. I'm going out. I'll call Colin and get him to give me a meal.'

Alone, with lunch eaten and cleared away, Ilona stared out of the cottage window. She was listless and depressed. There was something missing from her life, and it did not take long to work out what—or rather who—that 'something' was.

She sat in the rocking chair and stared into the large and empty fireplace. She must remember to fill the big vase with flowers and put it in the hearth.

It was impossible not to brood on the manner of her dismissal. Two men ganging up on her, one telling the grossest lies, the other not only believing him, but also, most mortifying of all, accusing her of incompetence, when she owned certificates to prove how efficient she was.

No, she had to be honest. Lately, she had not been efficient. But—and this was what hurt the most—it had not been caused by her inability to do the job, but had been the fault of circumstances out of her control.

Lucia still had not returned when Ilona went to bed that evening. She had sat in the rocking chair but found herself drifting into sleep. Afraid that there might be a repeat of events of the evening before, she shook herself awake and went upstairs. Exhausted as she was by the day's unhappy events, when her head finally hit the pillow, sleep came at once.


Daylight brought a return to consciousness and memories of the day before: the quarrel with her employer, the dismissal by him from her job, the sense of hopelessness that followed.

She flung the bedclothes aside. As her feet felt for her slippers, she thought, Why am I hurrying? I haven't a job to go to. There's the whole day in front of me with nothing to do. The thought of the empty, useless hours appalled her.

With a sigh she washed and dressed. The cold water brought to her face and body a tingling anticipation, even if her mind remained blunted and unresponsive.

Lucia would probably still be in bed, she decided, even though it was gone ten o'clock. Colin Hardcastle, Lucia's employer, would again forgive her for arriving late at work. Pulling on an old shirt and jeans, Ilona bumped down the stairs in her low-heeled shoes. If she woke Lucia, what did it matter?

In the bread bin she found two rolls, spread them with butter and honey and carried them on a plate into the living-room.

Lucia's bedroom door opened. It seemed she had breakfasted, because she was dressed in outdoor clothes. Following her out of the room was Colin Hardcastle, her employer. Ilona, about to snap off a piece of roll with her sharp white teeth, paused and sat, open-mouthed. She had known Lucia was in the middle of an affair with Colin. She had, indeed, spent many nights away from the cottage. But never before had she so blatantly displayed her relationship with him. He had never, until now, stayed overnight with her in the cottage.

'Hi, Mouse,' said Lucia, full of the joys of living. 'Colin, as you know from the other night, this is Ilona, the girl I share with.'

'Hi,' said Colin. 'Come on, Lucia, break the news to her gently.'

Ilona chewed slowly on the half-eaten roll, wondering what was coming.

It came, like a bucket of cold water thrown in her face. 'I'm leaving,' Lucia said bluntly. 'I'm going to live with Colin.'

The remaining piece of roll hit the plate. 'But,' said Ilona aghast, 'he's married!'

They both burst into laughter. 'When was she born, Lucia,' Colin asked, 'yesterday? Or the day before?'

'If it's any comfort to you,' Lucia said, 'Colin's getting a divorce. Before we tie another knot—*if* we do—we're going to make darned sure we don't make a second mistake.' She turned. 'Come on, Colin. Time we went to the office. Ilona,' Lucia turned back, 'I'm leaving some of my clothes. Colin's going to buy me some better ones, aren't you, darling? So,' she looked Ilona up and down, 'if you want to pretty yourself up, *if* that's possible, you can have the pick of my wardrobe.' Her hand lifted carelessly. ' 'Bye, little mouse. See you again one of these days.'

Lucia had reached the door.

'But,' said Ilona, dazed, 'what about money? What about the rent? Food——'

'You'll have to pay that all yourself, won't you?'

'How? I haven't got a job now.' She didn't add, Thanks to you. What good would it have done? 'So where's my money coming from?'

'Frankly, Ilona,' Lucia shrugged, 'I just don't care any more.' She swept out of the cottage.

Ilona spent the afternoon washing, scrubbing and polishing. It seemed to be the only way in which she could use up her excess energies.

As she worked, she thought about her problems, both

immediate and long-term. Since her first requirement was to find some means of earning money, she decided that the following day she would go to the town's employment agency. There was one thing of which she was only too well aware—she would never be able to replace the employer she had lost.

The thought of the man brought a picture of him into her mind. It was not easy to accept the idea that she would never see him again. It was, in fact, impossible to discipline her mind so that she did not even think about him.

As she stared across the rutted track which ran past the front of the cottage, the outline of the window became a picture frame. Enclosed in its rectangular shape was a face which had become so familiar it was almost as if it were part of her.

She had seen the face remote and cool on the opposite side of a desk; aloof and slightly sardonic as it had gazed down at the letter in her typewriter. She had seen it furious and cruel as the man had dismissed her from her job. With a physical effort she dragged herself to the present and started searching for food for her evening meal. What was the use of thinking about the man? For the rest of her life, he would be as out of her reach as the stars in the clear night sky, no matter how brightly they shone.

It was while she was toasting a piece of bread in front of the coal-burning cooking stove that she heard a noise that sounded like a knock at the door. Fleetingly, her subconscious mind told her it was Lucia returning from work. By the time she remembered that Lucia was not coming back, the visitor had found the latch and entered the cottage.

Fearing an intruder, Ilona straightened from her crouching position and hurried into the living-room. It was indeed an intruder, but he was no stranger. Still holding the extended toasting fork with the slice of bread attached, she stared at Drake Warrick.

He was dressed as if he had come straight from work.

'What are you doing here?' she challenged. 'And how did you know where I lived?'

'Company records. And by asking the way. You seem well-known locally.' He regarded the old-fashioned toasting fork. 'Are you going to attack me with that?'

'After the way you've treated me, I don't see why I should welcome you in my home.'

He half-turned. 'I'll go if you insist.'

How could she maintain the pretence of objecting to his presence when he was the person she most wanted to see in the whole world? 'You're here now. You might as well stay.'

It seemed the remark had been lukewarm enough to affect him, because his eyebrows lifted. She held her breath. He did not go, and she released the breath slowly.

He eyed the browned slice of bread on the fork and inhaled. 'Toast—I love the smell. It's something you miss when you live my narrow, sophisticated kind of existence.' She did not move. 'There's nothing quite like the aroma of bread being toasted in front of a real fire.'

There was no way out. She had to respond. 'Are you——' Ilona wished her heart would stop bounding like a dog overjoyed at its master's homecoming. 'Are you inviting yourself to share my supper?'

He looked at the toast, he looked at the girl holding it. 'Will you take pity on a man with a gaping hole in his stomach?'

Involuntarily her eyes dropped to that part of his anatomy. It was as flat and muscle-hard as the most experienced athlete could wish for. His jacket was pushed open by hands thrust into trouser pockets and she saw the dark leather belt inserted through the loops of the waistband.

It rested on his hips and the tautness of the material which he himself was creating emphasised his masculinity in a way that set a match to her feelings and had the warmth flooding her cheeks.

Slowly she lifted her eyes and looked into the smiling depths of his. 'Well? What's the verdict?'

'You mean about feeding you?'

'That. And about whether I pass as a representative of the male of the species.'

'I refuse to answer that.' She turned away. 'All right, you can stay for a meal. I possess too much compassion to turn you away from my home in the way that you turned me out of my job.'

He pretended to wince. 'Bull's eye. Dead on target!' He

removed his jacket, loosened his tie and said, 'Thanks also for telling me to make myself at home.'

'I'm sorry,' she said indignantly, facing him, 'but you did walk into the cottage uninvited. *And* ask yourself to a meal. You really expect the impossible, Mr Warrick.'

'Agreed,' he grinned. 'I'm a perfectionist, which is, when all's said and done, the same thing. And, I'll say it to save you the trouble—I'm ruthless, exacting and insensitive. What's more, I won't rest until I get my own way.'

He looked down at her, hands in fists on his hips. She could not help smiling. In such a mood he was irresistible, and even as Ilona walked away, she felt the pull of him sucking her back into his magnetic field.

He stood, arm upraised, to rest against the kitchen doorway. A piece of hair fell over his forehead and he ran his hand over his head, pushing the strands back into place. 'Is there anything I can do?'

Ilona shook her head. 'It's a small kitchen. It really isn't big enough for two. Anyway,' she looked up from her crouching position in front of the bars of the roaring fire which heated the stove adjoining it, 'you're so big you'd get in the way.'

'Thanks for that,' he said, but strolled in just the same. He bent down and opened the ancient stove door. 'What's this for?'

'Cooking food.'

'You don't mean it!' He indicated a circular lid over the fire. 'And that?'

'Cooking things in saucepans.'

'What's for supper tonight?'

'I wasn't expecting visitors,' she answered uncertainly, 'otherwise——' She shrugged. He'd have to take it or leave it. 'I'm going to melt some cheese and spread it on the toast.'

He looked around. 'Where's the tap?' He frowned. 'No tap?'

'Outside.'

He put a hand to his head. 'Primitive is hardly a strong enough description. Prehistoric might be more accurate!'

'I love it here,' she responded defensively. 'It restores one's sense of values. When I come home, I find myself again. The world takes its proper place in my life.' She stood, having finished toasting the bread, and looked up at him challengingly. 'In a place like this you can leave behind all the terrible things going on in the world. No sitting down and watching on a television set night after night the spectacle of man's senseless inhumanity to man.'

The dark eyebrow above her lifted sardonically. 'Would the lady speaker like a soapbox? Unfortunately, I can't provide a platform, but——' with his foot he hooked an upright chair from under the table, 'maybe this will do?'

'You think what I've been saying is something to joke about?'

For a moment his eyes grew serious. 'No, I don't. What I do find surprising is that you share my sentiments exactly. After this,' he looked around at the stark simplicity of the cottage interior, 'I hardly dare contemplate allowing you to put even the tip of your classically straight no-nonsense nose into my apartment. Without doubt, you'd label my way of life decadent.'

She gave him a fleeting, provocative smile. 'If you really do live up to the standards which your wealth puts within your reach, then yes, I would.'

He bowed mockingly. 'I'm duly reprimanded, ma'am.' His smile, as she turned away, had her heart hammering. Drake Warrick's charm was as devastating as his anger, and she wished he had not come to disturb her peace.

In a saucepan she melted cheese, milk and butter and spread the bubbling mixture on the buttered toast. In a tin were some small iced cakes she had made. These she arranged on a plate, together with some peanut butter cookies. Drake's eyes followed her every move.

'I've seen women do many things before,' he commented, 'but until now I've never watched a woman cook a meal.'

Ilona smiled up at him, tucking a piece of straying hair behind her ear. 'Not even your girl-friend?'

He glanced at her quizzically, started to speak, changed his mind and said, 'Which one?'

Nonplussed, she looked down at the dish in her hands, then stared up at him, 'Your secretary, for instance.'

The blue eyes into which she gazed cooled by twenty degrees. 'Let's leave Diane out of this.'

All Ilona's muscles tensed. She recognised that for the first time in her life she was experiencing jealousy. 'Why? Is she so special?'

He answered quietly, 'You heard what I said.'

Everything that had seemed so pleasant and sweet had gone sour. She made for the kitchen. He followed. In a glance she saw that in another lightning change of mood, his good humour had been restored. Relief swept through her and she gave him a dazzling smile. He reached out and lifted her chin, looking his fill into her brown eyes. A hand on her shoulder drew her towards him.

The kiss seemed inevitable, yet when it came it took her by surprise. There was in the touch of his lips a kind of tender sensuality. Their very softness provoked in her a tingling awareness of feelings which until then had remained sleeping within her.

A hand fastened round her waist, the other stroked her hair. Her arms, which had hung loosely at her sides, lifted to settle about his neck. His gentleness was disarming her, yet even as her acquiesence to his dominance increased, she knew that beneath the tenderness there was a streak of uncompromising toughness. She knew it because, to her cost, it had been this which had unleashed itself upon her when he had fired her the day before.

When he finally lifted his head, she saw that the gentleness which had seduced her into yielding to the demand of his kisses was missing from his expression. The brown eyes which gazed up at him with a bold innocence did not melt the hard core of coolness in his.

He released her and, finding nothing adequate with which to fill the ensuing silence, she turned to pick up a plate of food, handing it to him. He lowered himself into the rocking chair, while Ilona chose to sit on the floor near the empty fireplace.

She put her plate down on the circular woven grass mat which covered the worn patches in the carpet. With difficulty she had regained her composure after a kiss which had meant so much to her, yet which apparently meant no more to him than the test-tasting of untried lips. She had needed the silence that followed to steady her reeling world.

She watched Drake secretly. He looked so right leaning

back in the chair, his mind as relaxed as the driving restlessness of his body would allow. He was there, eating with
her in peace and harmony—however temporary that harmony might prove to be.

He had refused her offer of a knife and fork, so they ate
with their fingers. His refusal to accept the tools which went
with a more civilised way of living surprised her. Had she
misjudged him by picturing him as being constantly sur-
rounded by the refinements of modern life? Was it her
subconscious mind which refused to admit the possibility
that he might well have the ability to adapt to simplicity,
throwing aside with ease the shackles of luxury living?

When he had finished, he put down his plate and let his
head rest against the chair back as if his appetite had been
completely appeased.

'Coffee, Mr Warrick?' Ilona asked.

'No, thanks.' He rocked back and forwards for a moment
or two, then said a little edgily, 'My first name's Drake, so
will you drop your formal method of addressing me?'

She answered slowly, 'I don't think I want to.'

'You don't *want* to? After your response to my kiss, I
could surely be forgiven for believing that you'd like our
relationship to progress a hell of a lot further than kissing?'

It was impossible to answer 'You're wrong,' because what
he had said was true, so she attacked from a different angle.
'We're worlds apart and if you were honest, you'd admit it.
Our aims in life could hardly be more different.' Her eyes
lifted and searched his, but his eyes were hidden by the
spreading shadows of evening invading the unlighted
cottage.

'Carry on, Madam Speaker,' he commented sardonically.
'You have all my attention. What, in your opinion, is my aim
in life?'

'To make as much money as possible,' she answered
promptly, 'mainly for your own benefit.'

'Thanks.' He added dryly, 'What's yours?'

'To—to live as simply and unpretentiously as I can
manage. And——' As she thought about what she was
going to say, she realised how conceited it would sound to
him. All the same, she went on, 'And to help others in every
possible way. For no reward.'

'Noble aims indeed.' He stood, tightening his tie and thrusting hands into pockets. 'Long may you live up to them.'

He looked down at her as she curled at his feet. His eyes narrowed broodingly and she became painfully aware of how carelessly she was dressed. The old shirt had been patched under the arms. The top button had pulled free. The jeans were dusty at the knees and threadbare and mud-stained at the edges.

Was he comparing her with his blonde secretary-girl-friend, the woman whom he pampered as if she were his mistress, sending her flowers and perfume even when she left him high and dry without secretarial help? Was he remembering Diane's sophistication, her carefully made-up face, her breathtaking figure? Then was he comparing her with the slim, long-haired, brown-eyed girl down there on the mat, a girl with a piquant face and whose clear skin bore not even a touch of cosmetics, and who was addressed as 'mouse' by anyone who wanted to annoy her?

It was no use trying to read his expression, so she tried to turn away his scrutiny. 'Why did you come here?'

'This morning your friend Lucia Wood called me at work. You were desperate for a job, she said. She was worried—on her own behalf, no doubt—because you wouldn't be able to pay your rent. She accused me of being a heartless swine for firing you on the spot instead of giving you reasonable notice and allowing you time to get other work.'

So Lucia had tried to help her, after all!

'Which means that you came this evening because a guilty conscience drove you here?'

'Now you're being as impudent as your friend.' His tone was mild. 'I told her that, first, since I was the boss, I could hire and fire who the hell I liked. Second, since I hadn't even had the pleasure of meeting her, she had a damned cheek to talk to me in such a way.'

She waited for him to continue, but he was silent. 'Did she say anything else?'

'No. Was there anything more for her to say?'

So Lucia hadn't told Drake that she had left the cottage. She shook her head. 'Then she rang off?'

'She did.'

'Well, Lucia was right. You did fire me unfairly——'

He said curtly, 'I repeat, it's my business whom I fire, and why I fire, an employee.' The blue eyes had dropped in temperature, making her shiver.

It seemed to her that she was entertaining two men. One of them was the head of a large and fast-growing organisation. The other was a warm-blooded, very masculine man called Drake Warrick.

'All the same,' she rallied, 'you took away my only source of income.'

There was a long pause while he contemplated her bent head. 'Want a job?'

The question startled her. 'You mean—you mean my old one in the typing pool?' Did she really expect him to say, 'No. As my temporary secretary'?

He did say 'No,' but followed it with, 'As a receptionist at the enquiries desk in the entrance lobby.'

She uncurled herself and stood. 'You've got so little faith in my ability to be an efficient shorthand-typist you're actually offering me a job which doesn't involve it?' The fire was back in her eyes. 'Didn't I *tell* you the mistakes I made were due to Lucia's parties?'

He answered coldly, 'Judging by the things Ron Bradwell told me about your behaviour the night before last, it seemed you joined in that party voluntarily. So isn't it a little hypocritical of you——?'

'*Hypocritical?*' she stormed. 'Ron Bradwell was lying, *and* he'd had too much to drink. I was there by accident because I was so tired——'

He frowned and shook his head. 'Tired, yet you went to the party? If you're going to invent excuses, at least let them be plausible.'

'How *can* you believe the word of a man who ill-treated me in the way he did?' Her hand lifted to touch the bump, which even now felt large.

Drake pushed her hand away and felt it for himself. 'Is that what Ron Bradwell did?'

'Yes. It's gone down a little. It was much larger—and painful.'

He seemed puzzled. 'There must have been a reason. You didn't by any chance provoke the man?' he asked sarcastically.

'Not really. I only told him that I found him revolting and disgusting and—and that everything about him repelled me. It wasn't really provocation, because it was the truth.'

Drake threw back his head and laughed.

'Anyway,' Ilona went on, 'whatever I might have said last night I didn't really mean, because—well, I didn't know completely what I was saying.'

'So,' he smiled, 'despite the fact that you called out for me as you fell, or so Ron said, you don't feel anything for me—anything at all?' His voice softened. 'And despite our kiss just now, when you didn't exactly tell me to go to hell, but even seemed to want more?'

She could not tell him how she wanted his arms wrapped about her again, wanted him kissing her and touching her ... There was Diane, his secretary and his woman.

'No, nothing at all,' she lied. 'In any case, I'll never feel anything for any man, not after seeing what happened to Lucia. We've known her for years. She's an old friend of my sister's. I watched her marriage disintegrate, taking her happiness with it after she married the wrong man.'

'Meaning that I'd be the "wrong" man?'

She could not lie to him again, so she affected a shrug. 'The right man, maybe, for a woman with glamour, beauty and poise, but not for someone like me, a—a——'

'Mouse?' he finished. He moved towards her and pushed his hands under her hair, lifting it from the back until it formed a crown across the top of her head. 'A mouse, according to Ron Bradwell with the temper of a tigress, and the acid tongue of a shrew.' His voice softened again. 'A mouse with the most enormous brown eyes,' he lowered his head and his lips touched each closed eye, 'lashes so long they tremble as I breathe on them. A mouth that issues a silent invitation each time a man sets eyes on it ... Tell me, Miss Bell,' he was back in his boss's skin and his blue eyes took on a coolly probing look, 'how could I ever have overlooked you on my frequent prowls round that typing pool?'

'I was right at the back of the room. You never came that

far—except once, and that was the other day, when you saw me. But,' she whispered, 'I didn't overlook you.' Then she maltreated her lower lip at what she had said.

'So,' he gloated, releasing her hair and seizing her shoulders instead, 'Ron Bradwell was right. "She's in love with her boss," he said.'

'No, no!' she cried, desperate to convince him. 'Anyway, you aren't my boss any longer, are you? And——' as he was about to interrupt, 'and I told you I'll never feel anything for any man, not after what happened to——'

'Lucia.' He let her go and looked around. 'Where is she, by the way?'

Ilona summoned a shrug. 'Out somewhere with a man friend.' To her relief, he did not ask who the man friend was. He wandered into the kitchen, looking about him and shaking his head.

'Unbelievable! Absolutely empty of the accessories of modern kitchens. No dishwasher——'

'I wash the dishes by hand.'

'No washing machine.'

'I wash the clothes by hand.'

He turned and his eyebrows lifted. 'In cold water?'

'I heat it on the stove.'

He looked at the ancient, but shining, cooking range. 'Which you heat with coal.' She nodded. 'Where's the coal?'

'In a shed round the back.'

He looked thoughtful, moved from the kitchen and glanced up the stairs. 'No——?'

She laughed. 'In a smaller shed round the back. There's no back door, so you get there through the front door.'

'You don't mean it?' He disappeared outside. A few minutes later, he returned. 'My God!' was his only comment.

'I've seen worse,' she said defensively.

'You have?' with mock surprise.

'At least it's a chemical one.'

'The joys of back-to-nature living!'

'I love that kind of living.'

'As you've said before.'

There was a crunch of wheels on the rutted track outside. A blue van drew up behind Drake's car and a young man slammed the driver's door. His once-white tee-shirt was grubby. His jeans were mud-stained, telling of long hours spent working on his father's farm.

Drake followed Ilona's eyes and looked out at the young man. 'Good grief,' he commented, 'is this the lover of the lover of the joys of back-to-nature living?' He glanced quickly at the interior of the cottage. 'Yes, he'd fit in admirably with these primitive roughly-hewn surroundings.'

She turned on him. 'Will you quit denigrating where I live?'

Drake's smile was cool. 'It wasn't denigration. It was the truth. Snap.'

Ilona knew that he was referring to her comment about her accusations which had moved Ron Bradwell to hit her.

She shifted her ground. 'Well, will you stop mocking my friends? He's no layabout—he works hard for his living. He's recently graduated in agriculture.' Ray Hale was walking up the garden path. 'His father's a farmer, and Ray works for him, hence the mud. The result of honest toil, Mr Warrick.'

He looked down into her accusing eyes. 'My apologies, Miss Bell,' he said softly as the latch lifted. 'The young man is lucky to have you defending him so staunchly.'

'Hi, Ilona,' said Ray, stepping inside. He slipped a friendly arm round her waist. 'How's things?' He looked enquiringly at Drake. The introduction Ilona made was strained.

Drake had become the aloof, cool-eyed man who had, until yesterday, been her employer. Ray, whose nature was normally open and extrovert, greeted him pleasantly, however.

'Come in,' Ilona invited warmly. Anything, anyone to relieve the tension which entertaining Drake Warrick had caused.

Ray looked at Drake, who remained where he was by the window, leaning back against the sill, ankles crossed, arms folded. His whole aspect was one of a detached but interested onlooker. His sophistication and self-confidence made Ray who, like Ilona, was in his mid-twenties, look like a gauche, teenage boy.

'I won't keep you a minute, Ilona love,' said Ray. His last word had been no endearment. It was spoken, as anyone who knew Ray Hale was aware, as part of his personal speech pattern. But Drake Warrick did not know Ray. Consequently to him, the young man's use of the word 'love' meant exactly what it implied—that Ilona was his 'love'.

'There's a meeting about the summer fête the evening after next. Seven prompt. Okay? And Colonel Dainton said to tell you not to forget your promise.'

'If it's about the raffle, Ray——'

Ray smiled. 'That's what he meant. "A Girl for a Day". We all agreed, didn't we?'

'It's a good title, Ray,' Ilona's voice was strained, 'but——' How could she speak openly in front of Drake who, although he was closely inspecting his nails, was also listening intently. How could she say, I can't do it. One of the other girls, perhaps, but not me ...

Drake's eyes glinted. 'Sounds interesting. Who's "The Girl"?'

Ray caught her hand and held it high. 'This one. She'll raise a good bit of money from the men, won't she?' He grinned. 'I'm going to buy a handful of tickets myself. Don't know what I'll do with her if I win her, though.'

'Ray, please—tell Colonel Dainton I——'

'That you'll keep your promise,' he broke in decisively. He was at the door before she could remonstrate.

The silence after he had gone was broken by the revving of the van engine, and the bumping of the wheels over the uneven surface.

'So,' said Drake, 'Miss Ilona Bell, known to her friends as "Mouse", is going to sell herself for the price of a raffle ticket. "A Girl for a Day". Now,' rubbing his chin, 'what would I do with a girl who was mine for a day?'

'Nothing,' she snapped, incensed by his interpretation of the situation. 'It was only meant as a joke. It's for charity. And I'm not "selling myself".'

His eyebrows lifted. 'What would you call it? A cut-price offer? Bargain of the year?' He inspected her physical assets, item by item. 'Speaking personally,' he said, 'I wouldn't waste my money.'

'Frankly,' she answered furiously, 'I wouldn't want you to. I'd be standing there in dread, in case they drew your ticket from the hat!'

She glowered at him. He looked coolly back at her.

Contempt crept into his eyes. 'Is this one of your "noble aims"? To help others, in "every possible way"? Especially men, because in a raffle where the prize is a woman, it would have to be men, wouldn't it?'

'*You* called my description of my aims in life "noble". And anyway, it was simply an idea to boost charity funds, which is what the fête's all about. There's nothing sinister, no immoral motive. It's not a new idea. It's been done before ...'

'Methinks the lady doth protest too much,' he quoted sarcastically.

'Think what the blazes you like, Mr Warrick!' she shouted. 'You're really no better than Ron Bradwell. *And* you'd be quite capable of hitting me, just as he did.'

Hands on hips, he came forward. 'Yes, if you provoked me enough. Any man would.' His hands grasped her upper arms, bruising the flesh.

The pain from his fingers was such that her control snapped. She twisted violently, freeing herself, groped behind her to the table, found something hard—it was a plate— and lifted it to hurl at him.

He leapt at her, prised her fingers from the plate and put it down. Then he found her wrists, pushed them behind her and put them into one of his hands. Thus caught, she was helpless. He had mastered her at the height of her anger.

But the anger did not subside. It shook her from head to foot, making her tremble as if the very ground underneath was shaking. 'Just like a man,' she flung at him. 'Lose a battle of wits and resort to violence!'

'You call our conversation a battle of *wits*? My dear girl, intellectually speaking, it was like babbling baby talk.' He tightened his grip on her wrists. 'And you call this violence? My word, you've got a lot of learning to do about men. This is like playing with a kitten compared with my hidden muscle potential.'

He looked down at her and she met his eyes unflinchingly. The look in his underwent a subtle change. The more she became convinced of his sudden alteration in intention, the more the uncertainty grew in hers. The tremble of anger changed within her to a tremble of apprehension, then, alarmingly, to expectation and anticipation. She felt herself being propelled forward. Cunningly, he used her own trapped wrists to manoeuvre her towards him.

With a slowness that provoked, maddened and excited, his mouth came down, hovering within a breath's touch until she nearly cried out for the feel of his mouth on hers. The moment his lips made contact, it was as if a match had been struck and the flame flared, large and burning.

He did not release her hands. Instead, with his left arm he swung her sideways so that she was bent back over it and helpless. His lips moved over hers, placing small kisses all around them, moving to her chin, her throat, finally making their way back to capture her mouth entirely.

At last he freed her wrists and in a movement that was quite beyond her control, she found his shoulders, the back of his neck, his hair, running her fingers through it convulsively, finally wrapping her arms across his neck.

His arms caught her to him and she became aware of the effect she was having on his body. Knowing of his desire aroused hers to a greater pitch and she clung, even though she sensed the climax of the kiss had passed and that he was easing her from him.

'Now I know it all,' he drawled, looking down into her flushed face.

She frowned, not understanding the caustic note. All her love had been there in her response, in the kisses she had returned, in the way she had yielded herself to the demands of his lips. Hadn't she made it plain enough? How much farther did a girl have to go with a man to let him know without any shadow of doubt how much in love with him she was?

'Know what?' she asked.

'How it is you can put yourself up for sale to the highest bidder, covering your act of wantonness by saying it's all in the name of charity.'

If he had hurled her from the top of a tower he couldn't have inflicted greater injury. Was that how he saw her expression of love for him? As wanton and shameless?

'Good grief,' he moved away as if he could not bear to be near her, 'your boy-friend must either be unbelievably gullible, or generosity itself when it comes to sharing his lady love's favours with other men!'

Ilona was too puzzled to retaliate as she would normally have done against such an insult. 'Boy-friend?'

Drake folded his arms and his eyebrows lifted sardonically. 'Forgotten him already?'

'You're not talking about Ray Hale?'

'Who else? He called you "love". He held you round the waist and you let him.'

'But—but that's Ray. He calls everyone—every girl or woman—"love". It doesn't mean anything to me. Don't you believe me?'

'I don't believe you. I could see the way he looked at you.'

'You imagined it.' How could she convince him he was wrong? She still had not recovered from that kiss. On her mouth the pressure of his lips lingered. Her heart and body still cried out to him to hold her again, to let her show him again how deeply she loved him. And this time she would leave him with no doubts as to where her affections lay. 'If Ray really were my boy-friend,' she said, 'how is it that he can contemplate without protest my spending a day with another man?'

'Practice.' She shook her head, not understanding.

'Judging by your reaction to my approaches to you just now,' he said, finding his pockets, 'he's no doubt had to harden himself to your periods of unfaithfulness.'

'How dare you accuse me of double-dealing with a man when you're guilty of that with another woman?' She started shaking again as anger took hold. 'Why don't you get out, Mr Warrick?' she said between her teeth. 'Why don't you go to your beautiful blonde secretary-stroke-girl-friend and seek in *her* arms the complete fulfilment I denied you?'

For some reason Ilona could not understand, Drake seemed to be angry, too. 'I'll do that,' he answered, going to the door, 'I'll do just that. Thanks for the food. Thanks for the passionate interlude. I'll pay for them both by buying a ticket for the charity for which you're so willing to sacrifice your self-respect, integrity—and body!'

He rammed the door into place behind him.

# CHAPTER THREE

When Ilona awoke next morning, she lay in bed attempting to adjust to the empty day ahead. As she pushed back the covers, she reached for her diary and made a note of the committee meeting the following evening. Then she gave herself a quick, all-over wash with cold water, shivering a little, but glowing after the brisk rub-down.

While eating her breakfast, she scribbled some figures on the back of a used envelope. After adding them up, she was able to see in black and white the exact state of her finances.

On paper, the amount looked reasonable. Considered in relation to her outgoings, and the fact that she did not know where the next few weeks' wages were coming from, it was not a large sum. Even when added to her savings, the amount looked pitifully small.

Her first need, she decided, was to find employment. Over a crisp white blouse she buttoned a blue summerweight pinafore dress. She slipped her feet into white sandals and found a matching handbag. She was ready to catch the bus to town.

With the cottage door locked behind her, she walked along the track, joining a narrow country lane. Turning right into this, Ilona eventually met the main road and waited at her usual bus stop.

Clouds that had gathered, obscuring the sun, released a light and unexpected shower of rain. Ilona retreated to stand under a tree, wishing she had brought an umbrella. A large and ancient car pulled up at the kerb. The vehicle might have been getting on in years but, like its driver, it was in excellent condition.

'Hallo, my dear,' boomed Colonel Dainton, leaning across and winding down the passenger window. He did not seem surprised to see Ilona there at that hour of the day. His world was a small one, bounded by the limits of the Dainton Hall estate.

'Going to town?' The Colonel did not wait for an answer. 'Just come from there myself, otherwise I'd have offered you a lift. Haven't changed your mind, have you, about the fête? About you being the prize in the raffle?'

'Well, I——' Ilona began.

'No, of course you haven't,' said the Colonel. 'All in a good cause, isn't it? Just a bit of fun. Not the first girl who's raffled herself!' With a booming laugh he lifted his hand and went on his way.

Ilona shrank farther into the shelter of the trees. It was really raining now. She was caught by the weather, just as surely as she was caught by the promise she had never really made. Whatever people might say or think about her—and she was sure they did not all have twisted minds like Drake Warrick—she could not back out now.

Another car drew up at the kerb. She recognised this one, too. Like the other it was well looked after, but unlike the other, it was new and expensive, not only in looks, but in fact. The driver, however, did not in the least resemble Colonel Dainton.

He was brown-haired with hard blue eyes and a cynical mouth; a caustic tongue, and ruthless in his dealings with incompetents, as she knew by experience. With hands that could give pain or caresses; with lips that could inflict insults or imprint unforgettable kisses. A man to love or fear—or both.

Like Colonel Dainton, he leant across and wound down the window. Like Colonel Dainton, he called out to her. But there the resemblance ended.

'If you're going to town, I'll give you a lift,' Drake Warrick said.

Her reply was to turn up the collar of her jacket and huddle nearer to the trunk of the tree.

'Get in out of the rain,' he persisted impatiently.

'No, thank you. I don't want a lift from you.'

'I'll get you into this car,' he said, 'even if I have to carry you kicking and screaming into it.'

'Go ahead!' she retorted, with a pretence at defiance.

He drew in his lips, checked in the rear-view mirror, opened his door and started to get out.

The rain began to pour down and Ilona realised what a

mess she would look when she arrived at the employment agency. 'Don't bother,' she called. 'I'll get in.'

Drake closed his door and stretched across to push open the passenger door. Ilona ran to the car and almost fell into the seat.

He looked at her and gave a twisted smile. 'What was that little show of defiance in aid of?'

'What did you expect?' she snapped, 'after what you've done to me.' She pulled a tissue from her pocket and mopped her face.

He released the handbrake and they drove on. 'Tell me,' he said, his smile sardonic now, 'what have I done to you?'

'Well,' she searched around in her mind, 'first you fire me from my job. Then—then you attack me physically,' she rubbed her wrists to remind him. 'After that you—you kiss me as though you own me body and soul——'

He laughed loudly at that.

There were other things—she just had to remember. 'Then,' she said, 'you insult me by accusing me of selling myself in aid of charity. Finally,' her head swung round, 'you accuse me of unfaithfulness to my boy-friend—a non-existent boy-friend!'

'Quite a list, isn't it?' he commented with a smile. The car came to a stop at traffic lights just outside the town. 'But if your behaviour prompted me to do or say all that, how can I be blamed?'

'Well, first of all you shouldn't have fired me without warning me in advance——'

'So now you're giving orders to the boss,' he remarked coldly. The traffic lights changed and they moved on.

'No, I'm not. But at least you should have been humane enough to have given me the chance to prove myself. I'm a *good* shorthand-typist,' she burst out.

'So good that I've received complaint after complaint from the managers for whom you worked.'

'But surely,' she cried, 'you understand by now that was because I couldn't sleep, because of Lucia's parties.'

'If it's so bad it interferes with your work performance,' he said crisply, 'then, since you're the one who suffers, you should set about coming to terms with the situation. Either that or leave.'

'You mean find somewhere else to live? No, thanks. Not even to save my job would I leave my cottage and my village.'

'Then you have no alternative but to accept the consequences.'

'Are you always so callous towards your employees?'

Her remark was intended to annoy but he remained unmoved. He said at length, 'Why didn't you tell me yesterday that your friend had left home?'

She glanced at his profile, which was serious and remote. 'How did you find out?' she asked.

'Ron Bradwell told me.'

Of course, she thought, Ron Bradwell would be the link between them. 'I suppose,' she said sourly, 'that he went to a party in her boss's apartment?'

'It seems so. Which is where, I believe, she's living now?'

'Yes,' Ilona said dully.

'Where do you want me to drop you?'

'Anywhere in the town.'

'Can't you be more precise?'

If she lied, it would only waste time walking to her real destination. 'The employment agency.'

He turned at a crossroads and said, after a pause, 'Do you want your job back?'

Her heart leapt. More than anything she would like to walk into the typing pool at Warrick's head office and talk to all her friends again, before settling down to work.

Then she recalled the last time he had offered to take her back. 'No, thank you,' she replied offhandedly, 'work at the enquiries counter just doesn't appeal.'

'I meant your old job. Your desk is still empty. Your leaving has left us one short in the office.'

Pride overrode her common sense. 'Blame yourself, Mr Warrick. I didn't resign. I got the push, as they say. This time,' the car drew up in front of the agency, which occupied shop premises, 'I'm going for a secretaryship. Which means that I place a higher value on my abilities than you do. Which also means,' she flashed him a defiant look, 'that I'm ambitious.'

He stared straight ahead and she wondered if he was listening or whether his mind had wandered to his work.

'That's all wrong in your eyes, isn't it, Mr Warrick? An office worker as *incompetent* as I am should know her place. She shouldn't consider herself good enough to move into the boss's domain.'

'There are ways, Miss Bell,' he said, coldly furious, 'of refusing a perfectly sincere offer to reinstate you in your old job. You have chosen the wrong way. I withdraw my offer. And if you answer me back again, I'll turn around and drive into the country, open that door and dump you in a ditch.'

He leant across her, uncaring that his arm and shoulder pressed against her breasts and that his thigh came into intimate contact with hers, and opened the door. He waited, eyes ahead, body rigid, until she left the car.

When he was a speck in the distance, Ilona wilted, defiance gone, self-reproach and hopelessness taking its place.

The interview at the employment agency was thorough and brisk. Ilona was given a form to complete with details of her educational background, her past working experience and the names of two people to whom application could be made for references of her capabilities and character.

Ilona could, in fact, think of only two people—the headmistress of her old school and, since she had worked for only one firm since leaving that school, Warricks, the timber importers.

When she wrote the name Drake Warrick, owner and chairman of the company, she was filled with misgivings. What would he say about her? Surely, she reasoned, he would not be petty enough to allow their bad personal relationship to prejudice his business judgment?

The woman interviewer looked the form over and said that it seemed satisfactory. Then she asked the most awkward question of all.

'Why, Miss Bell, did you leave Warricks?'

Ilona knew she should have been prepared. Since she could not say, 'I was dismissed by the boss himself,' she had to think quickly.

'Because—because ...' She searched feverishly for a

reason. 'Because I was in the typing pool and felt I was getting nowhere.'

The woman thought for a moment, then said, 'A reasonably acceptable answer, I suppose.'

She flicked through some papers, selected a few and pushed them across the desk. 'Which of these appeals?'

After some consideration, Ilona said, 'This one.' It was a request from a firm of furniture manufacturers for a personal secretary to one of the directors. The money was good, the hours convenient.

'I know that firm,' the woman said. 'Like Warricks, they have high standards.' She picked up the telephone. 'I'll get you an appointment.' After a brief conversation, she covered the mouthpiece and asked, 'Could you go straight away?' Ilona nodded and the woman wished her luck.

As she made the journey to the factory, Ilona could not deny that she was nervous. However, the personnel manager seemed approachable and he said, after a brief discussion about her past office experience, 'If you will go through that door, my assistant will give you a shorthand test.'

The assistant was young and her smiling welcome helped to ease Ilona's apprehension. The girl dictated fast, although not as fast as Drake Warrick. Ilona coped well, both with the dictation and the typing of it.

The young woman seemed pleased with the result and went through to the personnel manager, who called Ilona in. 'Subject to your references being satisfactory,' he said, 'we are prepared to take you on to our staff. Thank you for coming, Miss Bell. We'll be in touch.'

Ilona spent the afternoon cleaning the cottage. She enjoyed herself so much it was almost, she told herself with a smile, as if she were trying to scrub away Lucia's presence —the discord between them, the clash of personalities and, most of all, those terrible parties.

That evening she took the large tin bath from a hook on the outside wall, brought it into the living-room, cleaned it thoroughly, then filled it with hot water poured from pans. She lay soaking for a while, closing her eyes and pretending she was in a luxurious bathroom.

Then she came out of her dream, told herself that the simplicity of the cottage was all she ever really wanted, stood up and scrubbed herself. It was as if she were cleansing herself of the humiliation of her dismissal from Warricks, of Drake's insults and more important than anything else, his meaningless kisses and caresses.

However, when she stepped from the bath, reached for the towel and looked down at herself, remembering where Drake had touched her, a wave of longing went through her, a tidal wave which engulfed all reason. She knew, then, that no matter how much she might try to rub away the feel of his touch and of his kisses, she could never erase the love which, no matter how much they might clash, would be with her for the rest of her life.

The meeting of the charity committee the following evening was shorter than usual. The Colonel had another appointment which he was anxious to keep.

The main topic was, of course, the charity fête. The agenda did not contain many items, but, to Ilona's amusement, as she scanned the list and reached number five, she found that she was listed under that item. 'Raffling Ilona,' it said, with breathtaking simplicity.

It was all right for them, she thought, for Colonel Dainton with his white hair, apple-plump cheeks and supreme self-confidence; for Ray Hale, with his ebullience, his quick-thinking brain, his long, thin frame.

They didn't have in front of them the ordeal of seeing people buying tickets to spend a day with them. They didn't have to worry about being pleasant and full of smiles and looking attractive to please whoever had 'won' them. To the committee, she was just an item on the agenda. To the girl who was that 'item', it was a nagging worry she would gladly be without.

'We must tell the press about raffling Miss Bell,' said the Colonel. It was a statement and not to be queried. He was still the Colonel, although many years had passed since he had retired. They were his army, and members of an army did not have the audacity to question the orders of their commanding officer.

All the same, Ilona trembled inwardly. None of the others had protested and if she had dared to raise her voice in protest, she would have been sat upon—probably liter-

ally!—and the thought of being squashed, even figura-
tively, by someone of Mrs Bryant's proportions was too
formidable to be contemplated. So she remained silent.

'I'm going away for a couple of weeks,' Mrs Bryant said,
'but as soon as I return, I'll send in an appropriate paragraph.'

Ilona wondered ruefully just what Mrs Bryant would consider 'appropriate', and wished she had the writing of it
herself.

Five minutes later, the meeting ended. The Colonel hurried away and the others did not linger. Except for Ray,
who turned to Ilona and said,

'Let's go out somewhere, you and me. I've got a bit of
extra money in my pocket—I took it out of my bank account to buy myself a new transistor radio but changed my
mind. Come on,' he seized Ilona's hand, 'where shall we
go?'

Ilona did not care and, as she got into the van, said so.
She insisted, however, that wherever it was, she would pay
her share. After protesting, Ray agreed. At first the van
would not start. Ray got out and inspected the engine, ad-
justing some connecting wire, and the engine started.

'That's a relief,' he said. 'It's been giving trouble lately.
I keep telling my father we need a new van.'

Ilona said, looking down at herself, 'I'm not dressed for
much more than a beefburger and chips at a snack bar.'

'Hey,' said Ray, inspecting his boots, 'you're right there.
How about me taking you home to change and I'll do the
same, then I'll pick you up in about half an hour?'

Ilone said that suited her fine and within five minutes she
was opening the cottage door. Her choice of clothes was
simple. There was no need to dress up to please Ray. His
tastes were simple, too. Their relationship was easy and
friendly with no emotional complications.

When he called for her, she was wearing an embroidered
peasant-style cotton blouse with a low rounded neckline
and a swirling black skirt. Around her neck she had clasped
chunky white beads. Her hair fell loosely to her shoulders
and was held back from her face by a white slide.

Ray had put on a clean shirt and added a tie. If Drake

Warrick saw Ray now, Ilona thought, he could not jeer at his appearance as he had before.

'I've never seen you looking so grand, Ray,' she said with a smile and following him to the van.

'Thanks,' said Ray, plainly pleased. 'It's the new fashion —looking tidy! Anyway, I'm taking you out, aren't I, and that's special.'

Ilona was touched, and squeezed his shoulder as they stood by the van.

'Sorry I haven't got a Rolls to drive you in,' Ray said. 'Nor even a Mercedes-Benz, like some good-looking guy I found you entertaining in your cottage the other day.'

'That was my ex-boss. And I didn't invite him. He found me preparing my supper and as good as asked to share it.' It was the partial truth, and, to Ilona's relief, Ray accepted it.

'Anyway,' said Ray, 'you're looking pretty good yourself.'

He was holding the van door open for her and Ilona smiled her thanks at his compliment.

'Sorry about the farm smell, not to mention the dried mud,' he commented, as they bumped along the track to join the road.

'What smell? What dried mud?' asked Ilona, closing her eyes playfully.

'That's what I like about you,' Ray responded. 'Most girls would wrinkle their noses and find a handkerchief, not to mention the rude remarks they'd make about "that's the trouble with spending an evening with a farm labourer".'

'You're certainly not that! You're a graduate in agriculture. Anyway, why should I object to the smell of honest-to-goodness manure, and a few bits of mud? It goes with what I love best—back-to-nature living.'

Ray laughed and drew into the forecourt of a large hotel. Its name, The Falcon, was illuminated in neon lighting. Ilona stared at the floodlit hotel façade. 'We can't go in there, Ray!'

'Why not?' He paused in the act of opening the van door. 'I told you, I've got some extra cash. Why not spend it on the prettiest girl in the village?'

Ilona laughed. 'It's a *pretty* compliment, Ray, but you know it's not true. What about Andrea Hirst?'

Ray coloured a little but shrugged. 'She's nice enough to look at. But,' Ilona guessed that he was searching for something derogatory to say because he could not often persuade the girl to go out with him, 'but she hasn't got— well, what you've got.' He tapped his own head.

'Be honest, Ray. Intelligence is not the main reason a man goes out with a girl, is it?' He coloured again and smiled.

Ray made no attempt to hide away his farm van and Ilona liked him the better for that. It was plain that he experienced no feelings of inferiority in relation to the relatively wealthy crowd with whom they were about to mingle —and why should he? His father owned a small but flourishing farm which one day Ray would take over from him.

He locked the van, saying, 'Hope it starts all right when we leave. I'd hate to get my best suit covered in grease.' As he led her up the steps and into the entrance lobby, his personality changed into that of a more poised and worldly young man. It was plain that he was well able to hold his own when it came to mingling with those who maybe possessed a little more money than he did, but certainly less brain power. He had, after all, obtained a first class degree in his subject, agriculture.

On each table candlelight danced inside a bulbous cover of deep red glass. Scarlet lamps hung low from the ceiling, creating an atmosphere made for lovers. Ilona suppressed a sigh. 'I'm not really ungrateful to Ray for bringing me here,' she thought, 'but I wouldn't be human if I didn't wish that the person at my side was not just my friend but the man I loved.'

Where was he? she wondered. More important, in whose company? She was swept by a wave of despondency so unexpected and enervating, she touched her fingers to her forehead.

'I hate to tell you this, Ray,' she murmured, 'but I'm not very hungry.'

She managed a smile to placate a disappointed escort, only to find a look of something like relief on his face. Maybe, she thought with amusement, he had decided to buy that transistor radio after all and needed that money in his pocket.

'Okay,' said Ray cheerfully, 'let's go to the bar over there. We could have a drink and a sandwich or two.'

The bar was semi-circular and occupied most of one wall of the dining room. Above the glasses and the upturned bottles and the chromium ice buckets, golden lamps shed their light. Ray helped Ilona on to a stool, then sat beside her to her left, his shoulders hunched, waiting for service.

The white-jacketed man behind the bar was just about to attend to them when he noticed two people entering and making for the bar. As they took their place, the attendant's attention was switched at once to the newcomers.

Neither Ilona nor Ray looked round. Instead, Ilona sighed and Ray's hunched shoulders rounded even more, expressing his disgust.

'Anyone would think,' said Ray quietly, 'royalty had just arrived.'

'Diane,' said the man, 'what will you have?'

Ilona's hands, clasped loosely on the counter, tightened and pressed painfully into the knuckles. Her head swung left towards Ray and she mouthed in dismay, 'No, it can't be!'

'It is,' Ray whispered back, and his head indicated the golden-tinted mirror which ran the length of the wall behind the barman.

One glance was enough. Beside her a man was pushing himself on to the stool, a tall man, with dark-brown hair and a long straight nose, whose rounded chin jutted stubbornly, whose lashes were long above shrewdly discerning eyes.

The mirror threw back the dark-suited powerful shoulders, the lemon shirt and diagonally-striped tie; the confident set of a proud head on those shoulders, the relaxed good manners as he consulted the snacks menu with the help of his companion. And what a companion she was!

Ilona recognised Diane Ayrton, despite the fact that she looked paler and slimmer than when she had passed her in the office corridor. She was the private secretary of the man beside her, to whom he sent gifts during her unexplained absences from work.

Who could forget such a woman, with her slender grace and, her almost childlike trusting smile? There was a strange tranquillity about her to which a man in a position of management and who shouldered countless responsibilities would turn with eagerness after a long day's work. Although the thought was like a bullet screaming into her brain, Ilona told herself she could not blame Drake Warrick for loving the woman.

Ray leaned sideways and whispered, 'We can't go on ignoring them, love. He knows we're here. He must have seen us the moment they came in.'

'Let him speak to me first,' she hissed back.

A shoulder brushed her arm. A thigh made fleeting contact with hers as the man on her right turned his stool so that he could see both herself and her companion. He must, Ilona thought angrily, have hearing as keen as an eagle's eyesight.

'Miss Bell,' said Drake Warrick, as if they were distant acquaintances instead of two people who had kissed with a demanding passion, entwined in each other's arms. He looked at Ray and nodded. 'Mr Hale.' He put his hand on Diane Ayrton's arm and said to Ilona, 'Miss Bell, no doubt you've met my secretary. Diane, Mr Hale—Ray Hale?' Ray nodded. 'A friend of Miss Bell's.'

Diane smiled. It was a sweet smile, devoid of any kind of animosity. Ilona thought with surprise, I always did like Diane. Why, even now, when I love the man who loves her, don't I hate her?

## CHAPTER FOUR

'MISS BELL——' Drake Warrick's formality grated. 'Mr Hale—can I get you both a drink?'

'Please,' said Ray, 'let this be on me——'

'Next time, maybe,' Drake said, and asked them what they would like.

With their drinks on the counter in front of them, there was a small silence. It was Drake who broke it. 'Are you dining here this evening, Miss Bell?' He turned towards her and she saw that his eyebrows were raised, giving him a cool, detached air.

She wanted to shout, Stop Miss Bell-ing me! I'm the girl whose cottage you came to, whose meal you shared, sitting in the rocking chair while I sat at your feet. Am I so insignificant to you that you don't even recall your visit, let alone holding me in your arms?

'We were, but——' How could she say, I lost my appetite when I thought of you ...

'We decided to have a snack at the bar,' Ray broke in.

'Sounds fine,' said Drake. 'Diane?'

'Count me in,' said Diane. 'I'm not——' A small frown appeared, only to melt into a smile. 'Very hungry,' she finished, flashing a look at Drake. It contained a message which Drake received and decoded immediately.

Ilona watched them by way of the mirror. She thought miserably, They share the understanding of a couple with years of happy marriage behind them. No wonder the interlude with me in the cottage of discussion and kisses has, for Drake, gone beyond recall.

'So,' said Drake, 'since we're all agreed, do you mind if we join you, Mr Hale?'

'Not really, I suppose,' said Ray, his down-to-earth bluntness overriding the pleasure usually expressed in such circumstances.

'What about you, Miss Bell?'

Ilona looked at the man beside her, saw his mocking

'admit I've won' smile and nearly shouted, 'No!' She looked beyond him to his companion, with her strangely luminous beauty, and felt a curious compassion for the woman. She said politely, 'Yes, that would be nice.'

'Good,' said Drake. 'I suggest we order, then move to more comfortable seats.' He took up the menu again. 'Diane—salad? Or sandwiches?' Diane shared the menu, and their two heads together, their two cheeks almost touching, gave Ilona a pain in the pit of her stomach.

Together they selected their choice of sandwiches and passed the menu to Ray. Ilona, imitating Diane, moved closer to Ray. He did not seem to object to her nearness. In fact, he turned and smiled encouragement. He breathed deeply against her cheek and said, 'M'm, lovely perfume. Better than a farm smell!' and Ilona burst out laughing.

'That's just like you, Ray,' she commented. 'No sentiment, no poetry. What you might call "gut realism".'

'Thanks,' he said dryly, looking at the others who were smiling. 'Just call me "muck-raker", love, and be done with it! Son of the soil, that's me.'

'And none the worse for it,' said Diane, leaning forward and speaking across Drake and Ilona, 'if I may say so.'

Ray coloured and smoothed his hair exaggeratedly. 'Why, thanks, Miss Ayrton. If I've got your approval, then I didn't spend three years at an agricultural college for nothing!'

'Make it Diane, Ray.'

Drake Warrick looked at Ilona. 'Now it's your turn, Miss Bell.' At her frown, he added, 'Unless you want me to go on calling you——'

'Ilona's the name, as you're quite aware, Mr Warrick.'

Ray nudged her. 'Hey, you're among friends, love. Drop your barriers for the evening. No one's going to push you around—not with me here!'

He had made her smile and she tried to relax. The cynical smile on her ex-employer's face did not help, however. 'M-make it Ilona,' she paused and gave him a rebellious look, 'Drake'. She hoped she had made it plain to him that the taste of his name in her mouth was not pleasing.

But he was not the kind of man to be put down, especially by a mere girl and one, moreover, he had summarily dismissed from his employment.

He leant sideways and whispered, his lips skimming her ear, 'That sounded very sweet—Mouse.'

She shivered involuntarily at the touch of him and drew back. He had angered her by using the mocking nickname Lucia so often used when intending to irritate. But before she could retaliate, a girl behind the bar asked what they would like to eat.

Having given her their order, they moved, taking their glasses with them, to a long, low table with two-seater couches grouped around them. Surprisingly, Ilona found herself with Drake beside her, while Ray, of necessity, placed himself next to Diane. He did not seem displeased. There was something about the young woman that aroused a man's instant interest. Diane, however, gave no obvious encouragement, but she had so many attractions working for her there was no need.

'I understand,' said Diane, starting the conversation, 'that you live alone, Ilona, in a tiny thatched cottage. Or so Drake told me. You've been there, Drake, haven't you?'

Drake's half-closed eyes came reminiscently to rest on Ilona. 'Yes, I was fed with bread which had been held on the end of a long fork and toasted by glowing coals to a smoky, golden brown. It was spread with melted cheese and——'

The sandwiches they had ordered were brought to the table and placed in front of them. 'Ah,' said Drake, 'it's just as well. I was talking myself into a gnawing hunger!'

As they ate, Drake pursued the subject of Ilona's home. 'Question this girl about her way of life,' he said, motioning to Ilona but directing his words to Diane, 'and she gets herself on to a mental public platform. It's almost as if,' the look he gave Ilona taunted now, 'she feels guilty about the primitive conditions in which she lives and this puts her on the defensive.'

'*Defensive?*' Ilona erupted. 'Why should I have to *defend* the way I choose to live? I wouldn't give up my cottage,' she went on, 'not even for a fortune. I've got privacy of mind as well as body. I recommend it, Mr Warrick.'

His hand came down to cover hers. 'Drake's the name,' he said softly.

Taken aback, she made herself say, 'Drake.' Why was speaking his first name as difficult as swimming against the tide?

She persisted, 'When I close the door of my cottage I shut out the world.'

'Is that a good thing?' Diane asked with a frown.

'There's many men at the top of their particular tree,' said Ray, 'who'd envy you. I know quite a few who would.'

'You sound, Ilona,' said Diane with a smile, 'as if you don't like the twentieth century.'

'Not all that much,' Ilona replied, with a faint, answering smile. 'I think that in the so-called "civilised world" we've imprisoned ourselves by gadgetry and put ourselves into a kind of scientific solitary confinement.'

'Tell us more,' Drake drawled.

So he wasn't convinced? She turned to him. 'In my opinion—for what it's worth in the eyes of Mr Drake Warrick——'

'So fierce she looks!' he commented with deep amusement.

She would *make* him take her seriously! 'In *my* opinion,' she repeated, 'we've given in to the technological invasion of our homes to such an extent that we simply can't believe that a world exists outside the bastions of our dishwashers and washing machines and central heating and air-conditioning and all the rest. In fact, most people plunged into living my way would be utterly lost.'

'That's true,' said Ray.

'I think we've finally overdone it,' Ilona finished. 'We've lost the basic ingredient of a really happy life—our peace of mind.'

There was a long silence, broken by the chatter of those around them, by the pouring of liquid into glasses, by the endless coming and going of guests.

Ilona held on to her empty glass, feeling it, smoothing it with her palms like a blind person learning the shape of an object by heart. Ray broke the silence.

'Don't you ever wish you had running water inside the cottage? Or an electric cooker? Or a bathroom?'

For a long moment Ilona thought about the question. 'Well, to be honest, I sometimes find myself reaching for a switch. Or wishing fleetingly that there was a tap in the kitchen. Only in the winter, though, when I have to put my coat and boots on just to go out to the tap in the garden.'

Her quick look at the man beside her dared him once again to smile in triumph at her momentary reaching out for just a little of what the twentieth century could offer. But his face was impassive.

'As for electricity,' Ilona said to Ray, 'what frightens me is that, if it was connected, everything that goes with it would inevitably follow.'

'Such as?' Drake asked casually.

'Well, a refrigerator, washing machine and so on. But worst of all, a television set.'

Ray rose, indicating the empty glasses. 'My round, Drake. What's yours?' He asked them all in turn and went to the bar.

A short silence followed, then Drake half-turned towards Ilona. 'You're condemning television now?'

The mockery was back and her colour rose with her annoyance. 'Yes, I am.'

'But why?' Diane asked, genuinely interested.

'Because——' Dared she speak her mind with Drake smiling so cynically beside her? 'Because I think a great deal of the terrible wrongdoing in the world is motivated by it. Because I think it corrupts and dehumanises——'

'Wow!' grinned Ray, returning to the table with the drinks on a tray. 'She's really in full spate!' He handed round the drinks and as Ilona took hers, Drake said sarcastically,

'Do you really think you should? Won't the alcohol in it corrupt and defile you?'

In a movement which was vengeance and rage and retaliation rolled into one, Ilona lifted her glass, drew it back the better to propel its contents forwards—and found her wrist imprisoned by a hand which shot out in a reflex action so fast her eyes could not trace its path.

With his other hand, Drake removed the glass, then he let her go, throwing her wrist away. 'Don't give me your self-righteous lectures, your high-handed, sanctimonious hypocrisy!'

Bewildered, Ilona faltered, 'What are you talking about? Everything I said I meant sincerely.'

'Is that so? In that case, you must be the biggest humbug around. If you want us to believe in your sincerity, then tell me how you can reconcile what you've been saying with what you're intending to do?'

'How's that?' asked Ray, frowning.

'What I'm trying to say is, how can your g——' Drake looked from Ray to Ilona and back, 'how can Ilona, with her high-flown, slightly overbearing idealism, allow herself to be put up for sale as she intends to do at some fête or other next month? She's just been pontificating about the corrupting influence of television, yet even without one, she herself has been corrupted sufficiently to offer herself as a prize in a raffle——'

'Hold on a minute, Drake,' said Ray. 'It is for charity, after all.'

'And that makes it good and clean and high-minded? Tell that to the lecher who rubs his hands with pleasure when his ticket's drawn out of the hat and he anticipates a day of unbridled passion with——'

'Will you be quiet!' Ilona cried. 'You're exaggerating, and you know it. Any man who won a girl in a raffle for charity wouldn't dream of——'

'No, little mouse, he wouldn't *dream*. He'd act. A whole day with Miss Ilona Bell, and he'd waste it on walking round the town, wining her and dining her—and afterwards, a chaste kiss, saying, "Thanks for the memory"? You really believe that? You must be kidding!'

Ilona looked to Ray for help, urging him with her whole being to refute Drake's statement and support her contention that any man who won would act like a perfect gentleman. Her heart sank when Ray said,

'She can't back out now. The programmes have been printed. We're distributing them in a day or two. Anyway, you don't want to back out, do you, Ilona?' To her relief, he didn't wait for an answer. 'The whole committee's relying on her to bring in the largest sum of money ever. Incidentally, it was Colonel Dainton who thought of it.

He's one of the old school. He wouldn't risk a girl's reputation, as they used to call it. And the vicar supported the idea, didn't he, Ilona?'

'Very touching.' The words were murmured close to Ilona's ear and she doubted if the other two heard them.

She turned on Drake, her lower lip escaping her teeth and trembling. His slightly cruel smile was intended to provoke her to retaliate yet again, but she was silent.

For the rest of the evening, she spoke as little as possible. Diane looked at her now and then with a touch of pity. Ilona did not think her spirits could sink any lower. At last she looked pointedly at her watch and Ray took the hint. As they rose to go, Diane suggested to Drake that they should do likewise.

A waiter handed them their coats and they left the hotel. They left behind not only the bright lights but also the warmth. The evening was chill and Ilona wrapped her coat about her.

Drake's car was parked nearby. With an arm about Diane's waist, he led her to it, helping her into the passenger seat. Ilona turned her back on them. She could not bear to witness Drake's protectiveness towards the woman he so plainly loved and, moreover, placed above all others.

Ray called to Ilona to get into the van. He had shown no such politeness to her, but she couldn't blame him. After all, she was not the girl Ray loved—if, indeed, he yet loved anybody.

As she got into the van, Ray sighed heavily and tried once again to start the engine. 'Getting old, that's the trouble.' He smiled briefly. 'The van, not me.' He tried again. The engine spluttered and died. 'Won't be long—I hope.' He got out and lifted the lid of the bonnet.

'Want some help?' Ilona's pulses leapt at the sound of Warrick's deep voice.

'Can't get a thing out of her,' Ray answered, only the lower half of him visible in the lights around the hotel car park.

Drake stood watching for a moment, then asked, 'Got a flashlight?'

'In the van,' Ray directed, 'on the floor near Ilona.'

Drake opened the van door and glanced at Ilona, who

had turned up the collar of her coat. Then he bent down and groped around Ilona's feet. Two hands came to rest round her ankles, lifting them to one side.

'Oh!' she exclaimed at once, trying with a show of indignation to conceal the alarmingly pleasurable response his touch had aroused.

He emerged with the flashlight in his hand and a broad smile on his face. 'Pardon me, lady, for taking such a liberty, but your slender ankles were in the way.'

'It's all r-right.' Her teeth had started chattering. 'S-sorry. N-no heating in here.'

He gave her a considering look, went away, handed the light to Ray and returned. 'This might be a long job. Go across and wait in my car. Diane's there——'

'No, thank you.' She was immediately sorry because the note of distaste in her voice had sounded so ungracious.

'What's wrong with my car? Too fine for your tastes?' He was angry now. 'Too much *technological gadgetry* for your simple needs?' He shrugged dismissingly. 'Suit yourself. Sit here and shiver——'

Her legs swung to the ground. Her hand caught his arm. 'Drake, I should like to sit in your car.'

He gave her a long, penetrating look. 'Diane will let you in.'

Ilona tapped on the passenger window and Diane's head turned. She stared, as if her thoughts had been far away, then she smiled. 'Can I come in?' Ilona mouthed, and Diane comprehended at once. She turned and unlocked the rear door.

As Ilona settled in the back of the spacious car, Diane said, 'Van gone wrong?'

'Won't start,' said Ilona, trying to stop shivering. 'Might be a long job, Drake said.'

'Oh, dear. Then I think I'll come and join you at the back. There's more room to relax.' A few seconds later she was beside Ilona. They talked generalities, then fell silent. Diane's head went back and she closed her eyes.

'Aren't you feeling well, Diane? Can I get you something?' Why, Ilona wondered, did she feel so compassionate towards this woman, when she was so obviously Drake's——

'I'm all right,' said Diane. 'Thanks. It's just that—well, now and then I slip back into the past.'

In the subdued lighting from the lamps outside, Diane's face with its classic beauty, looked white and drawn. Ilona did not speak. It was for Diane to choose whether or not she would proceed. It seemed she wanted to.

'I just can't forget Larry.'

Ilona frowned. A man she had loved and lost? A brother, maybe?

'We were only married two years when he died. It was a Saturday morning about ten days before Christmas. He'd gone out to buy me a present.' There was a short pause. 'He never got there. The roads were icy. Another car skidded, hit him head-on.' Her voice sank to a whisper. 'He didn't have a chance.'

'I'm very sorry, Diane, I didn't know. At the office we called you *Miss* Ayrton.'

'Which is what I wanted.' She smiled wanly, then sighed, closing her eyes. She murmured some words and Ilona strained to hear. It sounded like, 'It won't be long now.'

When Drake bent down to look in the car window, saying, 'Hi there, you two,' Diane's eyes flew open. A bright smile swept away the hopeless look and Ilona realised what those half-whispered words had meant. *It won't be long before Drake and I are married.* How better to forget the sadness of the past, Ilona thought with some bitterness, than by marrying a man who was madly in love with her?

Drake smiled at Diane, and the smile slid, easily and just a little mockingly, to Ilona. Two women under his spell. If he but knew it, he could take his choice and no matter whom he chose, she would go at his call.

He got into the driving seat and Ray sat beside him. 'What's happening?' Ilona asked.

Ray half-turned. 'Drake thinks the battery's flat. It's needed replacing for some time, but I've kept putting it off. Now it's really let me down. I've told the hotel I'll call a garage tomorrow and they'll come and fix it.'

'I'm taking you all home,' said Drake. 'Any objections?'

Yes, thought Ilona. 'No,' said the others. 'It's good of you, Drake,' Ray remarked.

'That's okay. Now, let me see. I'll drop Diane first, then Ray, and Ilona last.'

It was the voice and the decision of a man who was un-used to having his statements questioned. Which, Ilona thought, was presumably why no one challenged the order in which he intended delivering them to their doors. And which left her until the last!

Having escorted Diane to her apartment, Drake dropped Ray. Ilona watched his disappearing figure for so long that Drake remarked sarcastically,

'You look as though he's abandoned you to an unknown and terrible fate.'

He had read her mind so correctly she stammered, 'D-don't be silly. Do you think I'm afraid of you?'

'Yes,' he returned coolly, and she was glad she was in the back of the car and that he could not see her clenched hands.

Even though Ilona told Drake not to bother, he drove along the bumpy track to the cottage door. And even though she told him, Thanks, she would be all right now, he got out and accompanied her into the cottage. Flus-tered, she said, 'I'll light the oil lamp,' but his hand came out and caught her arm.

He turned her to face him, pulling her close. 'You were very quiet towards the end of the evening. There's some-thing wrong, isn't there?'

She wished she could see his face. She wished he had let her light the lamp. There was only the moon's pale light creeping in the window and it shone directly on to her own face, keeping his in shadow.

There was something wrong, but how did he know? She could fence and say, 'If there is, what is it to you?' In-stead, she stayed silent.

'What's wrong, girl?' The tone was so tender, the pale outline of the face above her so neutral, the darkness of the hair lightened by the moonlight reminding her so forcibly of the shadowed handsome features a breath's distance from hers, that her body melted and yielded to the pres-sure of his arms.

It had been beyond her control. Darkness had destroyed the barriers, dispersed the restraints. Whether he had intended to kiss her, or whether she had invited the kiss, she would never know. All she did know was that the sweet familiarity of his lips seeking and finding hers released a knot of tension inside her which she did not even realise was there.

When his hands ran down to her hips, pressing her body to him, making her overwhelmingly aware of his masculinity, she knew that, since the last time she had been in his arms, the days had dragged interminably. With strong fingers he turned her head first one way, then the other, his lips skimming her ears, making her tingle and turn expectantly back to him. But, with an action which betrayed his reluctance, he held her away.

'I think,' he said huskily, 'you'd better light that lamp.'

She remembered Diane and thought, Of course, he's exercising restraint. But why, oh, why did he kiss me? Why didn't he drop me here at the cottage first, then he would have had Diane to himself. How stupid! she reproached herself, slipping from his arms and walking to the window. When he leaves here, he'll go to her.

'There's no need to light the lamp. I'll keep away from you.'

'You've just remembered your boy-friend?' It was not sarcasm, it was a simple question.

'My boy-friend? Ray?' Why should she deny it? He had Diane, so why should she not have Ray? Her answer was a deep sigh. She pushed aside the net curtains and gazed at the moon riding high in the sky.

'You haven't told me what's worrying you.' The voice was nearer. He was closing the gap again and she gave a shiver.

'It's—well, it's the raffle. I'm not the part, am I? Not the right sort of girl.' Because it was dark, she could confide her deepest fears. 'I won't know how to act, what to say, how to make a man pleased he—he "won" me. Before the day's past, he'll want to ditch me. I'm not the kind to puff up a man's ego by gazing into his face and hanging on his arm, making him feel like a king for a day. Which is how a man should feel when he's "won" a girl.' She whispered, 'I don't know what to do.'

He joined her at the window. 'Shall I come to your aid? Help a girl in distress?'

'In what way?'

'I know a man, a silversmith. I could get him to make a silver rose bowl.'

'You'd pay all that money to get me off the hook?' Her heart throbbed painfully. Was there a deeper meaning behind his offer? Was it not Diane for him, after all?

There was a long silence, then she felt his shoulder shrug against hers. 'Put it down to the fact that I hate seeing a fish floundering helplessly on the end of a line.'

Her heartbeats steadied. How easily a woman could fool herself over a man! 'There's no need to pity me,' she replied tonelessly. 'I may be floundering now—like your poor fish—but on the day, no doubt I'll find a way of living up to the winning man's expectations.' She felt his arm muscles tense as they pressed against hers. 'I've got everything else a woman's got. No doubt I'll learn how to use them in the time between now and the fête. I'll take a few lessons from Lucia——'

'So you're refusing my offer? You'd prefer to cheapen yourself, give yourself away to a man, all for the price of a raffle ticket? And when he starts struggling with you for what he'll most certainly call his "rights"—after all, he paid for the privilege, didn't he—you'll claim that it was all done in the name of "charity"?'

Drake moved away. Moments later the lamp was lit and the room glowing softly. But there was nothing soft about his face. The angles of anger gave a rigidity to his jawbone, a thin line to his lips.

'And you talked like a puritan this evening about the evils of twentieth-century living! You had the audacity to talk of television's corrupting influence?' He looked around. 'No television, yet you're as corrupted as the next man—or woman. In fact, underneath all that façade of innnocence, you're nothing but a cheap little tramp!'

'I can't let them down,' she cried, but he was at the door, opening it and slamming it shut.

# CHAPTER FIVE

NEXT morning Ilona received a letter from the firm of furniture manufacturers. They regretted to inform her, the letter said, that they were unable to offer her the position of director's secretary for which she had applied. It had been offered to another applicant. They thanked her, however, for her interest.

There was a tight pain under her ribs. She would have liked the job. She was sure they had been impressed with her speed test, and that they had liked her, too. She sighed and tried to be philosophical. There was, it seemed, always someone better than oneself, no matter how hard one tried!

A bus journey took her back to the employment agency. The woman she had seen earlier in the week had been informed of Ilona's failure to be given the job.

'We've had another one in this morning,' Miss Houston, the interviewer, told Ilona. 'Secretary to the manager of an insurance company.' She looked up, her eyes encouraging. 'Like to try it?'

'I'll try anything,' said Ilona, and took the paper bearing the address.

There was an interview, which was again followed by a test, given by the manager himself. He dictated slowly and precisely and Ilona passed the test with ease. 'Well,' said the youngish, slightly balding man, 'I find you suitable. We'll take up references and let you know. Personally, I think you're the best of all the girls who have applied so far.' He rose, shook her hand and said he hoped he would see her again.

With a light step, Ilona left the building, bought herself a coffee and a cream cake—a rare luxury for her—at a self-service restaurant and went home. During the afternoon, which she spent tidying Lucia's old room, Ray called.

'We're going out in a group this evening selling programmes for the fête. Coming?'

Ilona agreed and arranged a time for Ray to call for her in his van, which was once again in working order. The outing was a success, thanks mainly to Colonel Dainton who, once on a doorstep, would not take 'no' for an answer. He talked until even the most reluctant person put money into his hand. His pile of donations, when they arrived back at Mrs Bryant's house, was larger than anyone else's.

Another sales drive was arranged for later in the month, then they parted, pleased with their evening's work.

The following afternoon the rent collector called. Ilona was aware that he came every month, asking for the rent in advance, but she herself had never seen him as she had always been at work. Since he arrived during the morning at the time when Lucia was usually eating her breakfast, it was she he dealt with. It was Lucia, also, who was the official tenant of the cottage.

That morning the man, called Mr Elson, looked surprised as Ilona opened the door. 'Mrs Wood in?' he asked.

'Er—no, she's——' Ilona checked herself quickly. She had seen the rent book in his hand. As far as this man knew, Lucia was the sole occupant of the cottage. In fact, Lucia had often said she did not know whether the landlord's agreement allowed her to share the place.

'Mrs Wood's out,' Ilona told him.

'Oh.' The man rubbed his cheek with the end of his pencil. 'When will she be in?'

'I—I'm sorry, I don't know. I'm—I'm just a visitor.'

'I see.' The man frowned. 'Well, she owes a month's rent.' He told Ilona the amount and she gasped inwardly. It would take all her savings, plus the month's salary Warricks had given her. With that gone, what then? Surely, when the next demand came, she would have found another firm to work for.

'I'll call again,' Mr Elson said, and went away.

When Ilona received a letter from the insurance company telling her that her application to join their office staff had been unsuccessful, she was shattered. The interview had been so satisfactory. After the first shock of rejection had passed, puzzlement followed and then a growing anger.

Somewhere along the line, someone was telling lies about her work. On each occasion all had gone well until, it seemed, references were taken up. Pushing away her unfinished breakfast, she ran a comb through her hair. She pulled on a waist-length jacket, dismissed her old pants and shirt as of no consequence and ran to catch the bus into town.

She knew where she was going. She also knew exactly who the target of her attack would be. No matter how many barriers were put in her way, she would batter them down.

Barriers were, indeed, put in her way. Mr Warrick was busy. Mr Warrick had a meeting to attend and had no time ... frantically calling after her fast disappearing figure as she raced up the stairs came the faint words, 'Mr Warrick is dictating to his secretary ...'

If *that*'s all he's doing, Ilona thought, then as far as I'm concerned, he's free. Reaching his floor at last, and without pausing for breath, she hurtled along the corridor until she was in the executive section of the building. Taking two or three deep breaths—not to give her courage, but out of sheer necessity—she raised her hand, used her knuckles and walked in.

Her first reaction was surprise that Drake Warrick was not surprised. The girl at the enquiries desk must have rung to warn him. Her second reaction was one of annoyance that he did not rise to greet her, a fact which told her without words that his contempt of her had not diminished.

Mistakes in her typing—even though they had been due to circumstances beyond her control—and 'selling herself', even though it would be in aid of charity ... What other reasons did he need to justify giving her bad references?

At her noisy entrance to his suite of offices, he had merely looked up, eyebrows raised. Then he had continued signing the letters which Diane, who stood beside his chair, took from him one by one.

He said, eyes still on his work, 'You've been told by Cheryl, at the enquiries desk, that I'm busy. Diane,' with a warm, intimate smile at his secretary, 'when you've disposed of those letters, come back, will you? I have more dictation to give you.'

She nodded, returning his smile, which she then transferred, with a touch of pity, to Ilona. And was it I, Ilona thought ironically, who only the other evening in the hotel car park was pitying her?

When Diane had gone, Drake said coldly, 'I've told you, I'm not available for discussions, interviews, heart-to-hearts, call it what you like, *I'm not available*!' His fist hit the desk.

'You are at this moment, Mr Warrick. And what I've got to say won't take long.'

'Won't it, indeed?' The coldness in his eyes almost caused her to hesitate, to turn and leave, but his next words revived the fire which had not been quite put out by the ice in his voice. His hand stretched towards the telephone. 'I could have you thrown out of the building—just like that.' He clicked finger and thumb. He dialled.

She ran across the room and grasped his wrist. For a moment, they froze, eyes clashing, breathing checked. Then, with his other hand, Drake gripped Ilona's wrist. His intention, she guessed, was to remove hers, so she held on all the harder, even sinking her nails into his skin. His teeth came together with the pain and, like hers, his grip tightened, bringing tears to her eyes.

He prised her fingers away and contact between them was broken. He looked at his wrist, stood up and held it out. 'Blood—you little bitch!' He swung round to her side of the desk, towering over her and catching her shoulders. 'I should throw you bodily out of this building for that!'

Her head tilted backwards, searching his eyes. 'I'm sorry,' she breathed, 'I'm sorry.' I love you, she wanted to shout. Don't you know I wouldn't really hurt you for the world? Don't you remember how the other night you kissed me in the moonlight, how you once shared my meal, how many times you've held me close?

Are you really as emotionally cold inside as you seem to be on the surface? Is Diane the only woman you will *ever* allow to penetrate your barrier, to whom you'll show any tenderness, even though she's never really forgotten her late husband, so that, side by side with her memory of him, any man, to her, must inevitably come second?

'Will you get out of my office?'

She ran her tongue swiftly over her lips. 'Not—not until I've had my say.'

Diane came in, saw the anger, the merciless grip of Drake's hands on Ilona's shoulders, and said, 'Shall I come back, Drake?'

'What? Yes, yes.' He threw Ilona from him. 'I'll give this girl five minutes.'

Diane left and Drake half-sat on his desk, handkerchief to the blood-marks which Ilona had inflicted. 'I should have remembered your vicious streak,' he said, eyelids drooping. 'Well, one minute's gone. Get on with what you came to say.'

'All right, I'll come straight to the point. I accuse you of sabotaging my career.'

'Do you indeed? On what grounds do you base that statement?'

'Experience. You know I'm trying to find employment, because you gave me a lift to the agency one morning. Well,' her chin rose, 'I had two good interviews and the tentative offer of two jobs, subject to references. When those references were taken up—naturally I'd given your name as one of them—I was mysteriously turned down. It's happened not just once, Mr Warrick, but twice. Now, deny if you can that you're deliberately denigrating me in the references you give.'

He looked her over, taking in her warm cheeks, the straining shirt beneath the open jacket, the tight-fitting, dusty jeans; examining the curve of her hips and the slim length of her legs. Ilona steeled herself to tolerate the scrutiny and kept her head high.

Having looked his fill, he smiled, but without amusement, more with a touch of sensual pleasure, and Ilona tingled with a mixture of anger and humiliation.

However, when he spoke it was not of personal matters. 'When references are given on members of staff, whether past or present, what is written or spoken about those individuals is strictly confidential.'

'So you admit you've been saying bad things about me!'

He met her stormy eyes coolly. 'I fail to follow your logic.'

'You said——'

'That references are strictly confidential. That's all.'

'But,' she went on bewilderedly, 'why am I not getting the jobs when the people who interview me and test my proficiency are so pleasant to me and encouraging about the prospect of the job being mine?'

He studied her for a moment, and he was every inch the detached, eminently successful owner of a flourishing business concern. 'Any requests for references which might be addressed to me are opened by my secretary and passed automatically to the personnel manager.'

'Ron Bradwell!' she exclaimed, aghast. That explained everything. So her future prospects for a job were in his malicious hands!

Drake nodded, his leg swinging slightly, his hips as they supported him on the desk lean and sensual, his straight back revealing the firm slimness of a waist which was spanned by a brown leather belt. He stood, walked about the room, turned and said, 'Yesterday, I had a call from an—insurance company, wasn't it? I answered their questions.' He came to stand in front of her, the jacket of his suit draped over his pocketed hands.

'What did you say?' she whispered. He was silent. Goaded by the impersonal gaze above her, she burst out, 'So you told them about my mistakes—which you *knew* were caused at the time by circumstances beyond my control——'

'I told them, Miss Bell, if you want the truth and can take it, that according to my experience of you which, on an employer–employee basis, was small, that on the surface you were quiet, rational and tractable. But—I had to be honest—there were times when your private life got out of hand, to the detriment of your work.'

'So you did attack my integrity! You did cast doubts on my personality, in spite of the fact that you said you knew little about me apart from work. You lied to me.'

He gazed at her steadily.

She had not even begun to reach him! 'Whatever mistakes I've made while in your employment were caused by a situation forced on me.' Her voice grew unsteady. 'Nothing I said made any impression on Lucia. I was so tired it was like sleep-walking sometimes, yet I didn't stay away from work like some people would have done. Maybe,' bitterly, 'it might have been better if I had. If I hadn't been so stupidly conscientious and had caught up on my sleep instead, at least I wouldn't have made those mistakes. Thanks to you they're still haunting me, even though you don't employ me any more.'

He remained stiff and unmoved in front of her.

'Don't you *understand*?' she cried.

He continued to gaze into her brown, moist eyes, wide with appeal. Still he did not speak.

'How am I going to pay the rent if you don't let me get a job?' Her whispered pleading did not even scratch his implacable surface.

'Apply for unemployment benefit, Miss Bell. Ask for social security payments to help you pay the rent. This is a civilised country. Officialdom may be daunting and pernickety and at times, maddening, but it does its best not to let people starve.'

'How can you insult me like that?' she whispered, her eyes large with disbelief. 'I have confidence in my abilities even if you haven't. You're denying me, on totally false grounds, the right of every human being, that is, the right to work.'

'Stop putting my name on the application forms as one of your referees.'

'I can't,' she cried. 'Yours is the only firm I've worked for since I left school at eighteen.'

'Well, well. So you've been here all that time.' His detached amusement maddened her. 'I must have watched you growing up. And without even knowing it!' He reached behind him and switched on the intercom. 'Diane, come in now, please.'

He was dismissing her! His sarcasm had driven her to her limits. His unrelenting attitude, his complete lack of compassion or sympathy for her plight, drove her beyond them.

She rushed forward, hitting him with her body. She reached up and gripped the lapels of his suit and pulled at them until they almost tore. She clenched her hands round his upper arms and tried to shake him, but it was as if he were carved in stone. Finally, she hit his chest with the palms of her hands, like someone trying to batter down a locked and bolted door.

'You *must* give me a break!' she shrieked. 'You must help me instead of gunning me down behind my back with your lies about my character.' She broke down and sobbed, her cheek against the chest she had just battered, her tears dampening the silky fabric of his shirt.

She would have got more comfort from the hard earth in a parched field. Although her arms had crept round his waist, in an instinctive and spontaneous endeavour to remind him of the times when he had cradled her unresisting body, his hands stayed in his pockets. She might just as well have been embracing the trunk of a tree.

At the moment Drake said to Diane, 'Show Miss Bell to the door,' Ron Bradwell burst in.

'What the——?' He saw Ilona's clinging arms. 'Oh, touching!' He noted Drake's stony face. 'Good God, is the lady trying the oldest trick? What's she after—reinstatement in the company?' Drake must have motioned to him because Ilona felt Ron Bradwell's hands trying to disengage her from Drake.

She lifted her head, jerked her arms free and swung round. 'You keep away from me, Mr Ron Bradwell! And keep your filthy hands off me, too.'

The man backed away, lifting his arm in exaggerated self-defence in front of his face. 'All right, all right, so the lady's mad. What about?'

'I'll tell you what about. About giving me bad references!'

A comforting, feminine arm came round her shoulders. 'Calm down, Ilona,' Diane said, leading her into the corridor. 'Life's too short for recriminations and fruitless quarrels between fellow human beings. It's a jungle, the world of business, a ruthless, heartless jungle.' They stood outside Drake's office. The door remained open. 'You've just got lost in it, that's all, my dear. It will pass. Everything will work out.'

Diane comforting her—Diane, the woman she should hate, but could not. 'Thanks, Diane,' Ilona said haltingly. 'It doesn't solve any problems, but it's a bit of philosophy I'll try to remember.'

Drake's door closed, but she was not alone. Diane had gone. Ron Bradwell had taken her place. Ilona began to walk away, drying her tears and wishing her cheeks were not so flushed. Ron Bradwell followed, then she remembered his office was along the same corridor.

As they reached it, the door stood open. Ron Bradwell pushed her inside and stood with his back to the door. 'So you want me to give you better references?' He walked towards her. 'What'll you give me, darling, if I do?'

'Give you?' she said disgustedly. 'I'd like to——'

'Ah,' he held up his hand, 'think before you speak, sweetheart. Give me what you were offering Drake.'

'I was offering Drake nothing.'

'No? It looked to me as if you were offering him the full works.'

'Yes, with your one-track mind, it would look like that.'

'Come now,' his arms caught her, taking her by surprise, and she was pulled close, despite her struggles, 'just think. With my help—there's a kind of grapevine among firms——'

'Yes, I know. The "old boy network", I think it's called,' Ilona sneered. 'Just pick up the phone——'

The door opened. 'Ron, has Ilona gone?'

Ilona pulled away and stared, frightened, into eyes which were at first startled, then filled with contempt. 'She didn't get far, did she?' Drake sneered. 'Having failed to get round me, I assume she's now in the process of trying the same tactics on you.'

'You're dead right, Drake.'

Ilona put her hands to her ears. 'Will you both be quiet? Will you stop using me as a verbal football, kicking me around between you?' She swung round to Ron Bradwell. 'You're a miserable liar!' She turned to Drake. 'You're a callous, unfeeling, unforgiving brute!'

'So she doesn't like us, Drake,' Ron Bradwell jeered. She swept past them both to the door. 'Watch out, lady,' Ron called after her, 'one of us might win you in a raffle. Then what will you do?'

'Ray, what shall I do?'

It was the following evening and they were sitting at the

table in Ilona's living-room. She had told Ray everything—
about her interviews and subsequent rejections, about her
violent quarrel with Drake Warrick, and about the unwelcome and malicious attentions of his personnel manager, Ron Bradwell.

'The rent collector called the other day,' Ilona said.
'Ray, I've just got to do something about getting a job and
some cash. I'm a good typist, I *know* I am——'

'Hold on,' said Ray, 'I've got the local paper in the van.
Let's look through the classified ads and see what we can
find.' He was back in a few moments and spreading the
paper over the table. Together they studied the 'situations
vacant' columns, but there were few for secretarial work.

'Hey, look,' said Ray, 'Mrs Bryant must be back from her
holiday. Here's a paragraph about the fête.' He read,
' "One of our committee members, Miss Ilona Bell, has
kindly consented to allow herself to be the first prize in
our raffle. Miss Bell will be prepared to spend a day with
the winner, most probably a man. Lucky man! Miss Bell is
a thoroughly nice girl, with very high morals, and no wife
need have any fears where Ilona is concerned, should her
husband be the winner." '

Ray made a gulping noise with his throat and put a hand
to his head. ' "Thoroughly nice girl. Very high morals," ' he
quoted. 'All quite true, but what a way to sell a woman!'

Ilona winced. 'Selling herself.' It echoed Drake Warrick's
sentiments exactly.

'I'm glad,' she said defiantly. 'At least whoever wins
won't expect——'

'A night out,' Ray interrupted jokingly.

'That's right,' said Ilona, returning to studying the advertisements.

Ray folded his arms and leant on them on the table. 'You
might—just—find one of that type wished on you, love.'
Was he, too, now entertaining doubts? It seemed not, because when Ilona said,

'Ray, I'm worried. Isn't there any way I can get out of
it?' Ray answered, with urgency,

'Not at this stage, love. The programmes are being dis-
tributed, tickets sold, the press informed and even the
paragraph printed here will attract a lot of attention.'

Ilona's heart sank. She watched Ray's fingers running once again down the 'jobs vacant' column. 'I'll just have to go back to the agency and ask if they've got a post for a junior, something like a filing clerk . . .'

'Hey, wait a minute.' Ray caught her arm. 'Did you say agency? Why not start one yourself? A typing agency, I mean, where you advertise for work, do it at home and send it out again?'

'Ray,' Ilona's eyes shone, 'that's a wonderful idea!' Then she glanced round. This was, as Ray had said, a home—a home, moreover, with none of the modern amenities to be found in even the most modest of today's living accommodation.

'No good, Ray. No typewriter, to start with. No desk, no——' she looked around again, 'electricity.'

'You're making difficulties. Basically all you need is a typewriter. You don't need electricity for that.'

'What about things like duplicators? Photo-copiers? What about tapes and cassettes which people send in to be typed?'

'Buy a hand-operated duplicator. And if you can't type work dictated on to tapes, you must say you can't.'

'There's something else,' said Ilona. 'The little question of money. What do I use to buy the equipment? I've got a bit put away in the form of savings, but I need that to live on. Warricks gave me a month's salary in place of notice, but I need that to pay the rent.'

'Look,' said Ray, 'the rent's not your responsibility, it's Lucia's. She may have moved out, but her name is still on the rent book, isn't it?'

Ilona nodded. 'In the landlord's eyes, she's the tenant. I don't even know if I'm supposed to be living here. When Lucia went to live with Colin, she said it was up to me to pay the rent.'

Ray forcibly expressed his exasperation.

'You see,' Ilona said despondently, 'it's stalemate. Everywhere I go there are stone walls I just crash into.'

Ray thought a moment, then said, 'Look, love, don't take it the wrong way, but—would you borrow some money? If I offered to lend you some—at least to buy yourself a typewriter——'

Tears came into Ilona's eyes. 'You're very sweet, Ray, but I couldn't.' She put her hand over his for a moment. 'You see, I've just realised—it's not only lack of money. Anyone running a typing agency needs a telephone. It's absolutely essential.'

'The cottage along the road—that's got a phone. I've seen the wires running to it.'

'Mrs Macey, yes, she's on the phone. She's very pleasant, and nearly always in. She might help ...'

'Better and better. Tomorrow, get yourself a typewriter, some typing paper and carbons—you know what's needed. Then sit and wait for the work to come rolling.'

'I'll have to advertise, maybe a few times before I get any response. That will cost quite a bit.'

'I'm willing to bet it won't take as long as you think. Good secretarial assistants aren't all that easy to come by. Got a piece of paper?' Ilona tore a sheet from a notebook and Ray found a pen. 'Let's draft an ad and I'll phone it in tomorrow morning. I'll tell you the cost and you can put a cheque in the post to the newspaper. Okay?'

Together they wrote, re-wrote and wrote again. When Ray left with the final draft of the advertisement, he said it would catch everyone's eye and simply could not fail.

Ilona smiled at his enthusiasm and wished she could share it.

The cost of typewriters so astonished Ilona when she gazed around the shop in town, she nearly abandoned the whole idea.

To buy a new machine would take more money than she would dream of borrowing from Ray. When the salesman saw that he was about to lose a customer, he produced two or three reconditioned machines which were, he said, in excellent working order. Since she had to eat to live, and work to eat, Ilona had little choice but to buy one.

The typewriter, although in a case, was heavy but, determined not to be beaten, Ilona carried it home on the bus. She had bought some stationery, too, and, lifting the machine to the table, spent some time practising. Later in the day, Ray called. He too tried out the machine, typing with one finger and amusing Ilona with the errors he made.

'Now,' she said, 'it's just a matter of waiting for the advertisement to go in.'

He looked a little awkward and said, 'Hope you don't mind, love, but I handed it in at the newspaper office very early this morning. I paid for it, too, because if I did, they said, they might get it in the ads column by this evening.'

Deeply grateful, Ilona thanked him and when she asked how much the advertisement had cost, he tried to evade the answer. However, she insisted on knowing and paid in cash.

'Independent little girl, aren't you?' There was a flash of a young man she had never encountered. To her, until that moment, he had always seemed like a brother, but his tone was anything but brotherly at that moment. It caused her to gaze at him and colour a little. It also worried her because she was afraid—afraid that if the deep friendship between them should be broken by the creeping in, on his part, of a feeling more meaningful, they would have to stop meeting. And there was no doubt about it, she would be the loser.

She tried to avert a crisis by joking. 'Yes, independent now and for ever. Freedom from men's slave-making ways, that's my aim in life!'

He laughed and the meaning of her reply was not lost on him. 'You win,' he said. 'So far, no farther.' He took her hand. He was so gentle—why couldn't she like him in that other way? She knew the answer, of course, but she could never tell him, or anyone, about how she felt about Drake Warrick. 'Friends, love?'

'Friends, Ray,' she answered, smiling with relief.

Ilona went shopping for food next morning, buying carefully to find the cheapest prices.

As she walked home from the village, she thought, Maybe the postman's been with the second mail delivery of the day. And if he had, maybe there were replies to her advertisement, requests for letters to be typed, short stories or articles, even, from freelance writers ... But there was nothing waiting for her on the mat when she opened the cottage door.

As she sat in the living-room drinking her morning cup

of coffee, she saw her neighbour, Mrs Macey, passing by on her way home. Ilona ran to greet her. As they walked towards Mrs Macey's cottage, Ilona explained the idea she had had of running a typing agency and asked Mrs Macey if she would object to taking telephone messages for her.

Mrs Macey invited Ilona in. Ilona refused the offer of coffee, saying she had just drunk a cup. With a touch of anxiety, she awaited Mrs Macey's reply. So much depended on it.

Her neighbour did not let her down. 'I'm only too willing to help you, my dear, in that respect and any other way. I could even give you a spare key in case I should be out and you wanted to make a phone call yourself.'

'And,' Ilona reciprocated, 'I'll give you my spare key just in case the postman calls with a parcel too bulky to push through the letter box.'

Mrs Macey said, as Ilona left, 'I expect you realise that if I should be out, there will be only my little cat in charge of the house, and he wouldn't be able to answer the telephone!'

They laughed together and Ilona thanked Mrs Macey sincerely for her help.

It was late in the afternoon when the rent man called again. He was of medium height, thin and wore a pinched look, although the day was bright and sunny.

'I've called to see Mrs Wood,' he said. 'Is she around?'

'Oh.' What excuse could she use this time? 'She's—she's out,' Ilona said truthfully. 'Still—still at work.'

The rent man frowned. 'That's funny. She's been in other times at this time when I've called. She told me once she gets home from work just after four.' He scratched the back of his neck with his pencil. 'She keeps funny hours, but——' He frowned. 'It's a bit odd, this business.' His small eyes took on a suspicious glitter. 'You're still here, aren't you? Staying here for a bit, you said.'

'That—that's right.'

'A long stay, is it?'

It was no use. She would have to admit the truth. 'I'm—I'm living here, you see. I——'

'Sub-tenant?' He shook his head. 'Not allowed under the

terms of the landlord's agreement. Only the tenant can live here. Furnished place. Could get her out any time he wanted.'

Ilona's anxiety did not escape his notice and his suspicion grew. 'She's not here, then? One month's rent in advance, that's what's owing.' He thrust his face closer to Ilona's 'Curiouser and curiouser, as Alice in Wonderland said. Done a flit, has she?' he persisted. 'Gone off with someone else?'

'I'm afraid she has.'

'Man, eh? It's always a man these days. Well, miss, she's the tenant here and if she's gone ...' He shook his head slowly. 'There's not much I can do for you. Mr Moorley, the landlord, said that as soon as this cottage was vacant, he wanted to sell. And the tenant's gone, so it's as good as empty from the landlord's point of view. See what I mean, miss?'

'Oh, but—Mr Elson, if I have to get out, I've got nowhere to live. I'd be without a home. Mr Elson,' she summoned up her sweetest smile, 'please, *please* try to persuade the landlord to let me stay. I'll find the rent somehow. If I give you the rent each month and you don't tell him, and we pretend Lucia—Mrs Wood—is still here——'

A thought struck her. 'After all,' she added coaxingly, 'she's left a lot of her things behind. You know, clothes and—and things. *I think*,' far more confidently than she felt, 'that it won't be long before she leaves the man and comes back.'

It was, of course, a blatant lie. Ilona knew that Lucia had been growing weary of their primitive way of life and had been looking for a way out, and Colin Hardcastle had provided it.

'M'm.' Mr Elson considered the appealing brown eyes and pale face of the girl in front of him, a face which was beginning to take on the pinched look he habitually wore. 'Bit like Alice in Wonderland yourself, aren't you, miss?' Had she touched a chord of sympathy? 'Got a daughter myself about your age. Wouldn't like to see her turned out homeless on the streets.'

So the man was human! 'Oh, Mr Elson,' she put her hand on the sleeve of his raincoat, 'thanks, thanks a lot!'

He shrugged, perhaps embarrassed by his own show of humanity. 'Can't keep it from him for ever, you know. Best if you keep looking out for something. Mr Moorley's out of the country at the moment, but he's due back before long. But you have that money for me, miss, otherwise——' he made a horizontal movement with his hand through the air, 'it's out, miss, as far as you're concerned. You've got no legal hold on him at all, you know that?'

She nodded, knowing it only too well.

A day or two went by with no response to her advertisements. Then one evening, Mrs Macey ran along from her cottage.

'A phone call, Miss Bell. Someone with a bit of work for you.'

It was a local freelance journalist wanting two articles typed. Could she do it? Ilona had the greatest difficulty in restraining her cry of joy. When the price of the work was settled, the man said he would put the articles in the post immediately, and could he have them the moment she had done the work?

'I'll have them back to you by return,' Ilona promised eagerly.

Having kept her promise and posted the articles by return, she sat back and waited for the account to be settled. It had not occurred to her that that would not be paid by return, but it was not.

Some letters were posted to her from an elderly lady— she had told Ilona her age in an accompanying letter, as a way of explaining the almost indecipherable writing. Again the typed letters were posted back to her by return and again the long wait for payment.

By then, the writer had paid his bill and, looking at the cheque, Ilona came to the conclusion that this trickle of money was no answer to the problem which never left her thoughts—that of paying the month's rent, already overdue.

Although more work arrived from the writer, and one or two letters from a company too small to employ a typist, it was nothing like the avalanche of work Ilona had hopefully imagined would come her way once the advertisement had appeared in the local newspaper. She had forgotten the many other small typing agencies already in existence.

The third time the rent man called, she ran upstairs to hide. She curled up under her bed, in case he possessed a key, and listened terrified to the repeated knocking. When at last there came a thud of receding footsteps, followed by a bicycle being ridden away, Ilona emerged, fluff-covered and dishevelled, and shaking with dread.

It was impossible to go on like this. If she delayed any longer, she would lose not only the sympathy of the rent man, but her home. There was only one solution: she would have to go cap in hand to her former employer and ask for her job back.

# CHAPTER SIX

THINKING of quelling her pride and biting the dust of humiliation at the feet, so to speak, of the man who had not only fired her but had, on countless occasions, insulted both her integrity and her capabilities was one thing. Putting the thought into action was very much another.

Maybe the dust would not taste so bitter if she called him on the phone. It was not easy getting through to him, but at last she found herself talking to Diane.

'He can spare a few moments, Ilona,' Diane said. 'Is that enough?'

Ilona assured her it was. A short silence followed, then a curt,

'What do you want?'

Nothing to encourage, everything to make her want to apologise for troubling him and ring off. 'Oh—er—Mr Warrick, it's——'

'I know who it is. I said, what do you want?'

A sophisticated, self-confident, experienced woman would have said, 'Drake darling, I've got an awful problem, and only you can solve it for me.' Lucia would have purred, 'Sweetie, you're a wonderful guy and I love you. I need some money fast. I haven't a job, but I know you've got one waiting for me.'

Ilona Bell said, in little more than a whisper, 'A little while ago you asked me if I wanted my job back. I said "no". But now I do.' She gulped and pleaded, 'Please, Mr Warrick, can I have it back? Can I come and work for you again?'

'My God,' was the sarcastic answer, 'that was one hell of a swallow. That pride of yours must have stuck going down! The answer's "no."'

Ilona's voice rose. 'Oh, but Mr Warrick, *please*! You see, I must have a job, and quickly. You wouldn't let me get one through an agency because you gave me bad references. So the least you can do is give me back——'

'There's nothing to give back. Your job's been filled.'

'No job?' she whispered, horrified. 'But—but how do I pay the rent?'

'That's your problem.'

'A whole month's rent,' she went on, 'and I've got to have it at once. I can't put the rent man off any longer. He keeps calling on me, Mr Warrick,' she was crying now, 'and today I hid from him, because he said if I didn't pay I'd have to go. And if I have to get out,' she was sobbing uncontrollably, 'I'll be homeless. I'll be sleeping in the fields, I'll——'

'You're tearing my heart to pieces, Miss Bell,' was all the answer she received. 'What do you really want from me? A cheque to the value of one month's rent, for a girl who gives me full permission to fondle her like a lover and when I stop, asks for more? Then, when she doesn't get it, runs to another man's arms?'

'What other man?' she asked, bewildered.

'Ron Bradwell. I can tell you this, sweetheart, if you want me to hand over the rent for you to pay, you'll have to give me a heck of a lot more than a few kisses. You'll have to give me the key to your cottage, so that I can come—and now and then go—whenever I like.' The ramming of the receiver into place almost deafened her.

Before leaving the telephone booth, Ilona dried her eyes. For some time she walked, finally making for home. There was only one way out. Lucia would have to come to her aid.

It was about nine o'clock in the evening when Ilona arrived at Colin Hardcastle's house. It was modern, of reasonable size and without a great deal of character. There was nothing to distinguish it from its neighbours except perhaps the front garden. It was concreted over, with only a small semi-circular area of earth left in which to plant bulbs, although nothing appeared to be planted there. It was plain Colin was no gardener, which gave him one thing, Ilona thought, approaching the front door, in common with Lucia—besides the only other thing which had brought them together.

If she had arrived any earlier, they would have been in the middle of their evening meal. Lucia would then have told her, without mincing her words, how unwelcome she was. Arriving later, Ilona found that the inevitable was happening. The large number of parked cars outside should have warned her—there was a party.

Although she had guessed that this might be the case, Ilona had not bothered to dress up. She was not an invited guest. She intended to talk to Lucia in the hall or even on the doorstep, so what would have been the use, she had asked herself, of changing out of her tee-shirt and dark blue pants, old and faded though they were, if she did not mean to stay?

The door was opened by a stranger, a bearded young man wearing, to Ilona's astonishment, not only a shirt, but also a tie! Lucia was indeed moving in different circles now she had come to live with her boss.

'Hi,' said the young man. 'Enter in the name of Colin and Lucia. I don't know who you are, but it doesn't matter. All are welcome.'

She stepped inside and the door was closed. The volume of music which emanated from the record player grew louder. It seemed to come from a room at the rear of the house.

'I'm Ilona, Ilona Bell.'

The young man frowned. 'Bell? Bell? That rings a bell!' He laughed at his own joke, and Ilona joined in, not wishing to embarrass him by a failure to respond to his good humour.

'Please,' she lowered her voice, 'could you find Lucia and tell her I'd like a word with her? Please say it's urgent. No,' as the young man motioned her towards the music, 'I'd rather stay here, thanks.'

The young man shrugged and disappeared into the back room. Moments later he re-emerged. 'She says she's all tied up—with someone you know.' Of *course* I know Colin, Ilona thought irritably. 'She says come and join the party.'

'Look, I *must* talk to her somewhere——'

'Ilona, *darling*!' Lucia came into the hall, wearing a long coffee-coloured dress which left little to the imagination. She was not alone, and her companion, whose arm she clung to, was not Colin Hardcastle. It was Drake Warrick.

His clothes were no more of the casual variety than Lucia's. His suit was, no doubt in his estimation, suitable only for office hours. Nonetheless, its cut could not be faulted, the cloth faintly striped and of excellent quality.

'You?' she breathed, gazing at Drake.

'Yes, Mouse,' said Lucia, 'your ex-boss, no less. I had a bet with Ron that he wouldn't come, but he did.'

'He must have been hard up for entertainment,' Ilona commented acidly, defying the cold blue eyes that had not changed in their ability to turn her knees to water and disconcertingly, the blood to boiling point in her veins.

'I'll dismiss that double-edged and feline remark as one that's chucked between one female friend to another,' Lucia commented coldly.

'Where's Colin?'

'Still working. And——' she smirked spitefully, 'don't dream up anything between your ex-employer and myself, because I'm still faithful to my lover. So far.' She flashed a glance at Drake, but he ignored it.

'Where's Diane?' Ilona asked Drake and trying, like Drake, to ignore Lucia's blatant hint.

'At home, I guess,' Drake drawled. 'Since she's off work again——'

'Again?' There was surprise as well as query in Ilona's voice. The last time she had seen Diane, she had looked all right. Then she thought, If his secretary's away . . .

He must have traced her thoughts by her expression. 'Nothing doing, Miss Bell. The agency's already supplied me with a temporary replacement.'

Ilona swung from him. 'Lucia, I must talk to you.'

'Talk away.'

'Not—not in company.' Her glance would have sent any other man retreating, but Drake Warrick stood his ground.

'Drake darling,' said Lucia, 'promise not to listen.'

His eyes flickered, but otherwise he did not respond, except to release himself from Lucia's hold. Realising there was no way in which she could send him away, Ilona tried to pretend he was not there.

'Lucia, you've *got* to help me.' Out of the corner of her eyes she saw Drake slip his hands into his pockets. 'The rent man called.'

'M'm, I thought he might,' Lucia murmured, smoothing her skirt to her hips.

'He's called two or three times, Lucia.' Ilona's voice wavered. 'He knows now you're not living there, but he's promised not to say anything to the landlord yet—he's abroad at the moment anyway—if I can produce the usual month's rent in advance.'

'Well,' Lucia's eyes met Ilona's coolly, 'you've got a bit of money saved up. You told me.'

'Not now, not any more. That's the point. I've—well, I've spent it, you see.'

'On food, you mean?' Lucia's eyes widened in disbelief. 'Good grief, living alone must have sharpened your appetite. When I lived at the cottage, you hardly ate enough to keep a sparrow alive.'

'No, not on food. On——' She did not want to tell Lucia. 'On other things. So you see——'

'What things?'

Lucia plainly had to hear the truth. 'Well,' Ilona tossed a poisonous look at Drake, who stood a little apart, aloof and detached, 'since somebody ... somehow ... was stopping me from getting another secretarial position, I made the decision to create my own job. I decided to set up an agency. Ray put some ads in the paper, and I bought a typewriter and filing baskets and so on. That's where my money's gone. So now you know.'

'Which is why you want me to pay your rent.' The flat, emotionless tone in which Lucia spoke made Ilona's heart sink. Put that way it sounded as if she were asking for charity.

'Well,' Ilona rallied, 'you're still the official tenant. Your name's on the rent book——'

'And you're living there illegally. You could be thrown out any time.'

'You know that, and I know that. And the rent man knows it, too. Unless I produce the money——'

'Which you won't get from me.'

Ilona paled. 'So you won't help? You'd rather see me put out on the streets ...?'

'You can stop your whining, Mouse. You won't get round me that way. Out of the kindness of my heart I invited you to live in the cottage, thinking that before long you'd find a

place of your own. Can I help it if, when I decide to quit,
you're still there?'

'You know what you are, Lucia Wood?' Ilona retorted,
her voice rising. 'You're an irresponsible, utterly selfish,
hard-bitten, immoral bitch!'

With that, she rushed to the front door, wrenched it
open and flung herself down the path to the gate. Without
looking she raced across the road, uncaring whether or
not there was any traffic approaching and reached the other
side to the accompaniment of squealing brakes and a
stream of invective from furious drivers.

She hurtled on, passing people who stared, disregarding
where she was going. Footsteps seemed to be coming up
behind, but she did not slow down to look. A hand caught
her arm, swinging her round. Drake Warrick stared down
at her. He breathed deeply. His eyes, no longer cold, blazed
with anger.

'What the hell did you figure you'd do to yourself?
Sacrifice your life for the sake of a month's rent? Then
we'd all feel sorry for you and spend the rest of our lives
plagued by guilt that we did nothing to help in your hour
of need?'

'Oh, go away,' she said through her teeth, trying in vain
to shake off his hand, 'and take your sarcasm and cynicism
with you!'

'You won't escape from me that easily,' he said, sliding
his hand down to hers and forcing her fingers apart so
that they entwined with his. He turned her, despite her
protests, to retrace their steps. Soon they stood beside his
car and he raked in his pocket for the keys.

'I'm not going anywhere with you!' she snapped.

'Not even home?' He unlocked the passenger door,
opened it and bundled her in. He bent to fasten the safety
belt across her. His arm pressed against her body, as it had
once before, but she pretended she was not even conscious
that he had touched her.

They drove in silence into the countryside. He made no
mention of what had taken place between herself and
Lucia. Instead, he told her, 'At the weekend, I'm giving a
party.'

She groaned. 'Not you, too!'

'All right, I should have phrased it differently. I have invited to my house a number of friends. You can rest assured that they bear no resemblance to those of Lucia. They're mainly businessmen, like myself. They will be accompanied by their wives, which means that everything will be completely respectable. I'd like you to come.'

'No, thank you.'

'I might well be able,' he went on, ignoring her stiffly-spoken refusal, 'to put some work your way. Some of them run small businesses and their office staff is small. Occasionally, they have letters or documents to be typed urgently, which their over-burdened secretaries can't manage to do in time. If I tell them about this new agency of yours, I'm sure they'll be delighted to utilise its services.'

In listening so intently to Drake, she had not realised they had arrived at the cottage. He braked, switched off the engine and the vast country silence crept into the car.

At last she asked, her harsh voice shattering the peace, 'What's the matter? After your abuse of me on the telephone this afternoon, has your conscience got the better of you? Are you trying to kiss me better?'

'If that's an invitation,' he reached out and turned her roughly, his hands gripping her shoulders, 'I'll accept it with pleasure.'

She was jerked across the space which separated them and she tried to pull away, saying, 'No, no, I meant the invitation to the——'

His mouth covered hers possessively. At first she struggled against him, but when his hands pushed aside her jacket and began slowly to caress her body, she felt herself yielding and softening and returning his kisses.

It was not until the crunch of footsteps and the beam of a flashlight warned of the approach of someone walking their dog that Drake's hold slackened and he put her from him.

Until the man had passed they sat like statues. If only Drake would speak, she thought. He had stirred her passions to life and she wanted to say 'Here's the key to my cottage, Drake, just like you said on the phone. Come when you like, and please—stay.' But it would all be based on the few kisses which had passed between them in the short time that their relationship had become more intimate—although, she thought, that was not really an accurate description.

Where was the intimacy in a few kisses and caresses? In bitter and damaging quarrels? It was not even friendship they shared, and most certainly not love, not on Drake's part anyway. Yes, she thought, as a sigh escaped her, I love him, but what's the use?

'That money you need,' said Drake, and she thought his voice sounded tired. 'Since Lucia's left you high and dry, I could lend it to you.'

'No, thanks,' Ilona answered, her voice tense. 'I wouldn't take a penny from you. After all, in return for the favour, I'd have to give you my key, wouldn't I, the key to my cottage, the—the key to my——' she took a deep breath, 'to my body. That's the only language you understand, isn't it, the only form of thanks that would satisfy you for such a magnanimous gesture.' She opened the car door.

'So you'd rather be made homeless than accept help from me?' His voice sounded dead.

'Yes. But I won't be made homeless. Someone's already offered to lend me money, someone I—I like, someone I respect.'

'Which implies that you don't like—or respect—me.'

She was silent.

'I suppose it's your boy-friend, Ray.'

'You suppose right. And for your own private information, he won't ask for the key to my cottage in return for the loan. Nor are we living together, sleeping together, or anything else people of my age might do these days. We're just friends, real friends. And when you're up against it as I am, Mr Warrick, one gets to know who one's real friends are. Goodnight, Mr Warrick. Thanks for the lift and for the offer, although it had strings attached.'

As she watched the car drive away, tears rushed into her eyes.

It was while she was having breakfast that Mrs Macey came hurrying along to tell her she was wanted on the phone.

A gentleman, she said, as they walked back together. 'You never know, he might have some work for you, dear. How's it going?' she asked kindly. 'Getting plenty to do?'

'Not too bad, Mrs Macey,' she answered, 'not too bad at all.' Which, Ilona thought, going to the telephone, was a slight exaggeration.

'Ilona Bell here,' she said breathlessly, 'Bell's Typing Agency. Can I help you?'

'No,' came the curt voice. 'It's taken you a long time getting here. How far away is your place from this?'

Her heart, having initially sunk at the thought that it was not an offer of work after all, began to rise in alarming leaps and bounds. 'A good few steps,' she answered waspishly. 'You should know, you've been here.'

'So how do you think you can run a successful typing agency with someone else's telephone?' She did not answer. 'That party—er—my apologies,' with sarcasm, 'that reception—does that please you?—I'm giving at the weekend. Are you coming?'

'I—I haven't decided.'

'I said I might be able to put work your way. Call it,' she could almost hear the cynical smile, 'a business appointment, if you prefer.'

She thought, The effect of the advertisements seems to be wearing off. I can't afford to keep putting them in the local newspaper. I must find work in order to live. If I can find it by socialising with those who could provide it ...

'I'll come. Thank you.'

'Eightish,' he responded crisply. 'Please dress. And you can take that whichever way you want.' With which acid comment he rang off.

Ilona called at Ray's father's farm—she knew she was free to do so at any time. His mother, rounded face, rounded figure, welcomed her with a smile. 'Ray's in the parlour, dear, struggling with the accounts. You know your way, don't you?'

Ilona thanked her and nodded. She also knew that Ray's mother would like nothing better than to welcome her as a daughter-in-law. In that, she was afraid she would have to disappoint her.

Anyway, Ilona thought as she made her way through the rambling farmhouse, Ray was not ready for marriage. He'd told her so a number of times, when they had each discussed their own careers. He would be content to have a girl-friend or two for some time to come.

The world was a big place, he'd said, and was beckoning, as it did to so many young people these days. Before he settled down, he had often told her, he wanted to get a few thousand miles and a great many countries under his feet.

He looked up as Ilona put her head round the parlour door. It was a small, cosy room with a round, polished table at which Ray was working. He stood and said how pleased he was to see her. His father was out somewhere in the fields. His mother busy in the kitchen.

'I know you've come for help. You've got that look in your eyes.'

'Oh, dear,' she laughed, 'am I really as transparent as that?'

'Only in times of emergency.' He invited her to take a seat at the table. 'I suppose this is one of them?'

She nodded. 'I wouldn't have come, Ray, but—well, I've tried everything else.' She couldn't be entirely honest and admit that she had turned down an offer of a loan from her former employer.

'How much?' asked Ray, getting out his cheque book. 'The month's rent?'

Ilona nodded. Ray already knew the amount. She had told him the evening they had discussed her future plans.

Later, his mother brought in a tray of coffee. As she shared it with them they chatted about the fête and, inevitably, the raffle. Ilona told Mrs Hale of her fears about this event but Mrs Hale laughed, telling Ilona not to worry.

'You never know, it might be our Ray who wins you, and you'd be quite safe with him!' Mrs Hale gathered the cups and took them to the kitchen.

Ray made a face at this motherly comment and Ilona rose to leave. As Ray saw her out, she said, 'I can't thank you enough for the loan. Just as soon as I can, I'll pay it back.'

'Don't be in a hurry. I may not be rich, but I'm certainly not poor. By the way, there's more where that came from, if you need it. Remember that, love.'

'You're so sweet, Ray,' said Ilona, and quite spontaneously reached up to kiss his cheek.

His cheeks reddened and he said, 'If I'd know that was coming my way, I'd have lent you more, then you might have made this your target.'

He touched his mouth and waved her off.

When Mr Elson called next day, Ilona handed over the rent with a bright smile.

She had gone to the bank and taken out the necessary amount in cash. It was, she decided, safer to do this than to write a cheque which, since Lucia was the legal tenant, should have carried her signature.

It was plain that Mr Elson did not care in which form he was given the money, as long as it was put into his hands. 'It's just as well you're giving it to me now,' he said. 'The landlord's back early from abroad and if I hadn't got your rent, he'd have wanted to know why, and I'd have had to tell him the whole story. But I'll keep quiet, miss, as long as I can.'

As he went away, he called out, 'Won't be long before the next lot of rent is due.' And that, thought Ilona, closing the door, was a warning, no doubt about it.

Work, in the form of letters and documents, was coming through the letter box in slowly decreasing amounts. It was plain that having to rely on the telephone of a busy neighbour was insufficient for the requirements of a typing agency. With increasing frequency, in letters which accompanied the work, were comments like,

'I tried to contact you by telephone, but there was no reply.' Or, 'Since I wished to give verbal instructions to you in the typing of my thesis, and I was unable to speak to you on the phone, I was forced to send it to another typing agency who were more readily available than you seem to be. However, I should like the enclosed two letters typed as soon as possible.'

Two letters, when it could have been a thesis! With its length, it would have brought in much more money. Yet she knew that, even if the telephone were installed, she could not afford to pay for it. It was a vicious circle, and she wondered if she would ever find a way out of it.

As the week had passed, she had come to look upon Drake's party as her salvation. If he had known, she thought, how he would have crowed, especially after her initial refusal.

The day on which the party was held was a Saturday. Only an hour or two before she was due to leave, Ilona still had not decided what to wear. She searched in vain among her own dresses for something suitable, but she possessed nothing sufficiently formal for the occasion. She wondered, gazing out of her bedroom window, what Drake's home was like.

When she thought of the kind of people who would be present, she grew nervous. They would be Drake's friends, a closed circle, company in which Lucia would have felt at home. If only she did not have to go, if only she did not need the work Drake had promised would come her way ...

It was necessary to make a good impression. Since she had no suitable dress, she wondered if Lucia's wardrobe would offer something. When Lucia had left she had told her to feel free to use her discarded clothes.

Lucia's wardrobe had plenty to offer, and Ilona tried on two or three dresses before finally choosing the one she considered best suited her.

It was impossible to guess what Drake might think of it. He had implied that he wanted her to dress formally, so if she arrived in an outfit which suited Lucia's sophisticated tastes rather than her own and he objected to the choice, it would be his fault, not hers.

All the same, feeling that right was on her side did not give her the confidence which wearing such a dress demanded. It was styled in black velvet, with a halter neck which was fixed to a central point just below her throat. Her breasts were draped with two deeply separated pieces of material. These were joined only at the waist and at the loop from which the halter neck sprang. Thus an opening was formed which, as she moved, showed tantalisingly just a little more or a little less of the cleft between her breasts.

As for the rest of her body, it was wrapped around by

black velvet like a second skin, narrowing to her ankles. There was, perhaps, slightly less of Lucia than of herself, and in the skin-tightness of the dress, the difference in the vital measurements showed.

Since she did not possess the cosmetics to go with the dress, Ilona used only the make-up which lay half-used in her dressing-table drawer. She applied the merest touch of eye-shadow, a hint of cream foundation and a brush of lipstick.

Her hair did not let her down, shining and sparkling from the brushing she had given it. No, she did not look like a mouse now. She looked ... she turned from the mirror, finding no words within herself to describe the reflection that stared bemusedly back at her. It was not herself. It was another girl.

Another girl or not, Drake recognised her as he stood in the hallway of his large, impressively modern apartment. Ray had offered to take her, understanding her reason for attending the party, which was to promote her typing agency. His mud-splashed van had looked strange driving away round the semi-circular drive. As she had watched, Ilona felt that part of her went with him, back to the life she knew and loved.

Although Ilona sensed that her arrival had registered on Drake's consciousness—his eyebrows had lifted slowly—no concession in the form of a welcoming smile came her way. A maid, probably hired for the evening, took her coat and indicated the stairs in case she wanted to tidy her hair, but Ilona declined the invitation.

Even if her appearance had made no visible impression on Drake, his presence ten or twelve steps away stirred feelings so tumultuous that preventing them from showing was like putting a hand over an oil strike to stop the oil gushing out.

His hair seemed darker in the panelled hall, the blue eyes more inscrutable. One hand was pushed into a pocket of a sand-coloured silk suit, while the other hung at his side. His wide, sensual mouth and the hard set of his jaw gave a deep seriousness to his expression, as he scrutinised her, setting her nerve-ends tingling and her heart pumping madly.

He seemed so solid, his shoulders so broad, she wanted
to rush to him and plead with him to hold her safely in
his arms. Can't you see, she wanted to cry, how nervous I
am, how out of my depth, how strange I feel in such alien
surroundings?

With stiff fingers she gripped Lucia's black velvet evening
purse. On unsteady legs she stood in Lucia's sandals. The
whole of her, it seemed, had turned into Lucia, except for
her personality. But as before, while she had been working
for him and had dressed inconspicuously, Drake Warrick
saw only the misleading wrapping, and not the true
simplicity of the girl inside. But how different the wrapping
was this time! Did he like it any more than he had liked
what he had seen the first time he had noticed her?

He said, 'Thank you for coming,' adding, 'Won't you
come in?'

The room seemed to Ilona's dazed eyes to go on for ever.
When the moment of intense nervousness had passed, she
saw that the room was large, but not especially so. The
central area was sunken and there was a vague impression
of clear glass and chrome tables set with blue glass
tumblers, decanters and jugs; with silver cutlery and blue
woven place mats.

The background decor was white, as were the rugs. The
blue drapes were pulled back to reveal glass doors leading
to a patio. Beyond that were sun-loungers at the end of a
swimming pool which was glinting under the orange rays
of the setting sun.

Drake's hand came to rest on the bare skin of her back,
his fingers outspread as if to encompass the widest area
which his hand could span. His touch was gentle, almost
caressing. As she looked up at him, startled, he smiled as
if to say, 'There's no need to hide what you feel when any
part of our bodies make contact. I'm already aware of how
I affect you.'

His eyes moved to the smooth bareness of her shoulders,
finding at last the slit between her breasts and which, as
she moved, eased slightly to allow tantalising glimpses into
shadowed, enticing places. His hand slid under her hair to
the back of her neck. He whispered, close to her ear,

'I told you to dress, witch, not half-dress.'

Her cheeks grew pink. 'This gown isn't mine. It's Lucia's.'

'But you're wearing it, Mouse, and that makes all the difference.'

His familiar glance, hinting to whoever might be looking at a more intimate knowledge of her, had her confused and awkward. He said, his hand returning possessively to her back, 'Come, I'll make some introductions. I'll do my best. The rest is up to you.'

Yes, eyes had turned, one pair of eyes in particular. They belonged to a full-faced, florid-looking man, with a glass in his hand and malice in his gaze. Of course, she should have known Ron Bradwell would be here.

'Where's Diane?' Ilona ventured as they approached a group of men.

'She didn't feel well enough to come.' He spoke irritably, but Ilona felt impelled to say,

'Oh, dear, is she ill again? What——?'

'Ilona,' he cut her short, deliberately, she was sure, 'meet Philip and Mary Smart. Philip runs a hobby store in the town. Phil,' Drake's arm left Ilona's back and rested momentarily on his friend's shoulder, 'meet Ilona Bell. She runs a typing agency. I know you don't have any secretarial help, so if you have any letters you want typed——' his sarcastic glance bounced off Ilona's face, 'well typed, then this is the girl for you.'

Philip Smart's hand came out. 'You're just the lady I'm looking for,' he said. 'Give me your address and I'll send you a pile of correspondence. It would help me a heck of a lot if I could just rough out the replies on the letters and you could——'

'Write the replies from those?' she took him up. 'Easily, Mr Smart.'

'Drake, this is great. Why didn't you tell us you had this talented young lady tucked away?'

Ilona coloured slightly at the implication, but Drake took it in his stride, sliding his hand across Ilona's back. He answered with a broad smile, 'I like to keep the good things in my life to myself.'

Philip Smart laughed out loud and called, 'Kate, come and meet Drake's very nice young protégée. He's promoting the typing agency she's running. I'm sending her some of my correspondence. Miss Bell, my wife, Kate.'

'Thank goodness for that!' smiled Kate Smart, shaking Ilona's hand. 'Now he won't come bothering me to answer his letters. I'm so happy to meet you, Miss Bell. You don't know how happy!' There was general laughter.

With a slight pressure from Drake's hand, Ilona was propelled away and introduced to others. After half an hour of introductions, Ilona was delighted with the promise of work.

'You should have had some cards printed,' Drake advised. 'It would have saved you the bother of writing your address on all those pieces of paper.'

'I haven't had enough work to warrant having cards printed,' she confessed hesitantly. 'But now, thanks to you——'

'The thanks, Miss Bell,' his eye was drawn yet again to the opening in the fabric running from throat to waist, 'come later.'

'I wonder,' said a voice behind them, a voice Ilona hated and instinctively drew back from, 'what form they will take?'

At that moment Drake was called away. He glanced at his personnel manager and said, 'Take care of Ilona for a few minutes, Ron.'

'With pleasure,' Ron Bradwell answered to his employer's retreating figure. 'Doing well for yourself, little *mouse*,' he sneered. 'Got your ex-boss eating out of your hand.'

'I wouldn't have said so, Mr Bradwell,' she responded, head high. 'It's more likely that he's suffering from a guilty conscience at having fired me so unfairly. Not to mention, with your connivance, depriving me of getting another job through giving bad references.'

'Drake suffering from a guilty conscience where a *woman* is concerned? My dear little mouse——'

Irritated beyond tolerance by his use of the word which, used by Lucia, conveyed contempt, but when spoken by Drake carried a touch of indulgence and intimacy, she said, 'Don't call me that.'

He lifted a careless shoulder. 'If you don't like "mouse",

how about "cat"? In that dress, I'd say it was more fitting. As I was saying, the day our good friend Drake has a conscience about women, I'll be heir to the British throne. Which means never. He goes through the so-called gentler sex like fire through a wooden house. He sets them alight, gets all the goodies he can from them, then stands back and watches 'em burn to ashes. Finally, he walks away without even a stab of conscience.'

Ilona moistened her lips. Ron Bradwell might have been trying her out, observing her response to his provocative words. On the other hand, there might be more than a grain of truth in what he was saying.

There was no denying Drake's good looks, his proud bearing, the pulling power of his height, and some indefinable quality which made a woman want to give and give until he was satisfied—even if it was to her own cost.

'Made you think, have I?' Ron Bradwell jeered. 'You still love him, don't you? You haven't got him out of your system even though he fired you. I can tell you one thing, Miss Ilona Bell, you can put that man out of your mind. It may be his secretary he's chasing at the moment, but that won't last, any more than the others did. And I'll tell you something else, the next one won't be you.'

'Look, Mr Bradwell,' Ilona said a little too quickly, 'I've got a boy-friend, see? He's a farmer, a graduate in agriculture, good as they come—and they don't come like him often, so you can stop your taunting——'

Ron Bradwell looked pleased. 'If you regard what I've been saying as taunts, then the man must mean something to you, boy-friend or no boy-friend.'

'Oh, for goodness' sake!' She looked round, trying to find Drake. He was deep in a discussion with a crowd of men. 'I'm going home. Please say "thank you" to Drake.'

'Got a car outside?' Ron Bradwell asked.

She did not answer but pushed her way through the crowds of people and made it to the entrance hall. A telephone—surely there must be one! The maid appeared. 'Can I help you?' she asked.

'A telephone. Where is it, please?'

'Follow me, madam. There's one in Mr Warrick's private room.'

The private room presented a very different aspect of Drake Warrick's personality, but Ilona was in no mood to appreciate the fact. She dialled Ray's number and while it rang at his home, her eyes saw the comfortable armchairs, the dark oak furniture, the tall farmhouse-style dresser decorated with antique plates, bowls and jugs.

'Ray?' Ilona said when he spoke. 'You know you offered to come and collect me? Please, Ray, would you? Yes, I know it's early, but——' The door opened. 'What? You'll have to finish the job you're doing, then you'll be right over? Yes, yes, that's fine. Thanks a lot, Ray. See you soon.'

Ilona replaced the receiver and swung round. It was Ron Bradwell standing there, hands in pockets, head menacingly forward. 'So instead of accepting my offer of a lift, you run to the boy-friend.'

'You didn't offer me a lift.'

'I was about to. He can't come yet, eh?' He looked her up and down. 'I fancy you in that dress, honey-girl. It's one of Lucia's, isn't it? I recognise it.' He moved towards her spite in his eyes. 'Looks better on you. You're not so obvious as she is. Therefore you're more titillating.' His eyes roamed over her greedily. 'But you've still got that damned look of innocence that drives me mad.'

She was frightened now, backing away, 'What has your wife done to deserve a husband like you, Mr Bradwell?' she baited, striving to disguise her fear.

'Say something else *complimentary* about me, and I'll ruin your prospects.'

His meaning was beyond her, unless it was that he intended to rape her. If so, he could hardly do so there, in Drake's house. Or did he mean to harm her physically? Whatever it was, she knew she must get away from him as fast as possible. But he was between her and the door.

As she dived, so did he, catching her in a hold so tight she could scarcely breathe. His lips pressing on hers revolted her and she struggled so fiercely her dress became disarranged. As she tried to free her mouth to cry out, the door swung wide and their host stood watching them.

# CHAPTER SEVEN

RON BRADWELL let her go immediately, straightening his tie and widening his mouth in a smile that told of satisfaction and conquest.

'Darling,' he said, 'this is neither the time nor the place. You'll have to curb your very natural, very feminine instincts and wait until we're on our own.'

One glance at Drake told Ilona that he had read into Ron Bradwell's words everything the man intended. There was condemnation and contempt in his gaze and they were meant, not for the man who had been molesting her, but for herself.

Stiff with embarrassment, Ilona straightened her dress. It was useless trying to speak in her own defence. Drake was already so prejudiced against her he would not even listen.

'Bradwell,' Drake said sharply, 'I'd be obliged if you'd go back to the others and mingle. You,' to Ilona, 'I'm taking home. I've fulfilled the promise I made to introduce you to possible customers of your typing agency. There's no need for you to stay longer.'

Ron Bradwell lingered, smiling as Ilona said belligerently, 'It's not usual for a host to order a guest off his premises.'

'I can do what the hell I like in my own house!'

'All right, so you want me to go. But if you'd tell me what I've done, I could at least make some effort to defend myself.'

Ron Bradwell's laugh was spiteful. 'Next time you try to seduce me, darling, to get me to persuade Drake to let you have your job back, don't choose his home territory. There's always a risk of interruption.'

Her fury rose up and crashed like wild waves in a storm. Her hand reached out for something to hurl, grasped a pottery ornament and swung it high. A man dived and her wrist was gripped by fingers of steel. The ornament was prised from her hold, and two hands fastened round the bare flesh of her upper arms.

'By heaven, I'll tame that tigress in you yet,' Drake muttered between his teeth. 'If someone doesn't soon bring that temper of yours under control it will become ungovernable.' He jerked her into the hall, telling the waiting, wide-eyed maid to get Miss Bell's coat.

'You can't take me home,' Ilona protested, 'Ray's coming for me.'

Ron Bradwell said behind them, 'I caught her in your study phoning her boy-friend.'

'It's not your business, Mr Bradwell,' Ilona said furiously. 'Why don't you do as your puppet-master tells you and go back among the——'

A brutal hand was slapped over her mouth. 'What's the boy-friend's number?' Drake asked, removing his hand. When Ilona pursed her lips he said, 'All right, let him come for you unnecessarily.'

Ilona told him the number.

'I'll get the maid to call him and say I'm taking you back.' As the maid appeared, he took Ilona's coat, draped it round her shoulders and gave the maid Ray's number and the message.

The drive back was totally silent. It was when they stopped outside the cottage that Drake spoke. 'Well?' He looked at her, waiting. As she frowned he reminded her, 'Early this evening I said the thanks come later. Later is now.'

'Thanks for the lift. Thanks for the introductions. Goodnight.' She opened the door and was outside fumbling for her key, wishing there was a moon to help her find it.

Drake, moving quickly, was soon beside her. 'That's not what I meant, and you know it,' he said.

The key was in the lock and turning. If she could get into the cottage and close the door on him ... He must have anticipated her ruse, because it failed.

Light would help, light would take away the dangers which darkness held, the risk of broken-down barriers, of loss of restraint ... Her hand holding the lighted match shook so much that Drake took it from her and put it to the oil lamp. A soft glow filled the room.

'Too much to drink tonight?' he taunted. 'Or was it Ron Bradwell's lovemaking?' He sent the match spinning into the fireplace. 'Did my interruption of the big scene leave you frustrated and edgy and longing for the tumultuous finale?'

'Do you believe every single lie Ron Bradwell tells?' she counter-attacked.

'Lies? When I actually saw what was going on?'

She sank into the rocking chair, closing her eyes and moving gently to and fro. Her arms rested loosely on the wooden arms, her head drooped to one side. She had no more strength to argue. 'Believe what you like,' she mumbled. The evening wrap had fallen to the floor.

Drake was silent for so long Ilona's eyes came open out of sheer curiosity. He had been staring down at her, it seemed, but his gaze was inscrutable. With the lamp on the table throwing its light upwards, his face in its glow was angled satanically with shadows and half-lit hollows. He had been turned by the play of the lamplight into a man she did not know, who frightened yet excited, who held a mystique which tantalised yet fascinated and drew like some magnetic force.

He bent and caught her wrist, pulling her from the chair. Then he urged her slowly against him until her breasts were pressed against the hardness of him. His arms fastened like whipcord around her.

He said against her mouth, 'Ilona?'

'No, Drake.' She turned her head away. He did not try to turn it back.

Instead, the pressure eased and she thought he was releasing her. She was wrong. It seemed that the cunningly seductive design of Lucia's dress had done its work. While his left hand was outspread against the bare skin of her back, the other insinuated its way into the front opening. He caressed the provocative fullness of her breasts, murmuring,

'All evening you've tormented me. All evening I've been waiting to do what I'm doing now.'

She faced him slowly and his lips slid over hers, possessing her mouth. She melted into him, letting her feelings dictate her movements. Even if she had wanted to stop him, it was fast becoming beyond her power to do so.

Easing his mouth away, he murmured, 'I knew it

wouldn't take me long to soften that frigid manner.'

Unsure of his meaning, unwilling to believe that it was sarcasm and not tenderness which had prompted his remark, she remained submissive in his arms. He glanced up the stairs.

'Am I to get my reward?' She frowned, uncomprehending. 'I've done my best for you this evening among my business acquaintances. There should be enough work coming to your agency to help pay your rent for many months ahead.'

'You have my thanks,' she said quietly, 'my deepest thanks. What more can I do to convince you I'm grateful?'

Fingers lifted her chin. 'I surely don't have to put it into words?'

She stiffened and increased the distance between them. Reaction and an intense disappointment had her trembling. 'Is that the only reason you gave me help—for the "reward" at the end?' With a jerk, she was free. 'I'm sorry, but it's not a habit of mine to use my body as a "thank you" present.' She looked down at herself. 'Don't let this dress fool you. It's Lucia's and I've borrowed it. Remember that deep down I'm still just a mouse in a sophisticate's clothing.'

He reached out and caught her to him again. He looked her over, his eyes gleaming in the lamplight. 'When I'm in bed with a woman, clothing doesn't interest me. It's the essential female underneath that's of a paramount importance.'

Expertly his fingers trailed her shoulders and arms and his mouth homed in slowly to hers. Before her lips were imprisoned and her body brought to the point of surrender, she had to build a barrier between them.

If he chose to throw restraint to the winds and act as devilishly as the trick of the lamp's glow on his features suggested he might, she was totally at his mercy. It was dark, it was growing late. There was nowhere to run, nobody to run to. What frightened her most was that she was fast losing the wish to run from him at all.

Words were now her only protection from the final outcome of his lovemaking—and from her own clamouring desires. With trembling fingers she pushed away his lips,

trying to suppress the pleasurable shock that touching his
face aroused.

'You're an experienced man,' she fenced, hoping, by
forcing a laughing note into her voice, to conceal her growing dismay at her inability to deal with the situation. 'You
wouldn't enjoy taking an innocent, ignorant nonentity like
me to bed with you.'

His eyebrows rose and the lamplight gave a bronze fleck
to his eyes. 'You call yourself *innocent* after the way you
behaved this evening with Ron Bradwell? And now with
me, holding nothing back, in spite of the fact that you
have a devoted boy-friend in the background? Complete
submission to my demands wasn't far away just now, and
you can't deny it.'

It seemed she had succeeded only too well in driving a
wedge between them. He had freed her completely, thrust
her from him, withdrawn from her his warmth and his
enveloping desire, leaving her bereft, humiliated—and
alone.


Three days later, Ilona went with the charity committee
delivering leaflets advertising the fête.

Mrs Bryant, dressed as if she were about to attend a
royal garden party, set a fast pace, despite the plumpness
of her figure. Colonel Dainton, puffing and mopping his
brow, complained to his colleague's retreating back, but
she was out of earshot before he had finished the sentence.

Later, Ray took Ilona home. He locked the van and followed her into the cottage. Ilona made coffee, seating herself in the rocking chair, while Ray occupied the high-
backed chair at the living-room table.

'How's the agency going, love?' Ray asked.

'Ray, it's unbelievable! The work's rolling in.'

'That's great. What caused the up-turn in your fortunes,
as they say?'

'Well, you remember the other evening when you took
me to Drake's—Mr Warrick's house. The guests were business acquaintances and he told me he might be able to put
some typing my way. Well, everyone was very interested
and I got a whole lot of promises to send me work. And,'
she drank some coffee, 'they have sent me work, piles of it.

I can pay you back the money you lent me. And I can pay the rent man next time he comes.'

'So you're on your way? And it's all thanks to the man you used to work for?'

'True. The man who fired me.'

'And then, with his bad references, stopped you getting jobs?'

'Well, he did play a part in that, but——' Why was she bothering to defend Drake Warrick? He wouldn't have thanked her for it. 'His personnel manager was giving the written references.'

'All the same, Mr Warrick didn't exactly rush to help you get new employment.' She shook her head, hating to admit that the man she loved had done a great deal to stop her from getting a job.

'And now,' Ray went on, 'he's doing all this. What caused the change of heart?'

Ilona cursed the quick giveaway colour.

'So it's like that between you, is it, love?'

She looked down at her crossed ankles. 'Only on my side, Ray. I think that really he was sorry for me. Maybe he felt a twinge of conscience. He knew about the possibility of my being evicted from here because of rent arrears.'

'Thanks for telling me your secret, Ilona.' Her head lifted quickly and she smiled her thanks back at his understanding attitude. 'It's safe with me.' He rose to go, waiting patiently while Ilona wrote him a cheque for the money he had lent her. 'You needn't have bothered about this, you know. But,' with a twinkling smile, 'as our Mrs Bryant says, you're a "thoroughly nice girl with high principles".'

'Morals,' Ilona corrected him, laughing.

'What's the difference?' He caught her shoulders. 'Your heart might belong to another, but he won't miss this, will he?' He brushed her lips, left with a quick salute and drove away.

Ilona was busy typing next day when there was a knock at her door. Assuming it was Mrs Macey come to tell her she was wanted on the telephone, she hurried to open it.

Ron Bradwell stood leering at her. It was pure instinct

which made her begin to swing the door shut, only to en-
counter his foot in the way.

'Not so fast, little Mouse Bell.' He stepped inside and she
could do nothing to stop him. 'Don't get scared. Just a
friendly visit. I'm not a tomcat come to gobble you up.'

He looked at the typewriter, at the correspondence
spread over the table, at the three-tiered wire baskets full
of papers. 'So you're a successful businesswoman at last.
All this, yet no electricity, usually considered the essential
ingredients of a well-run office.'

'All I need is my typewriter, Mr Bradwell.'

'And what service are you providing for my revered boss,
Mr Drake Warrick?'

'You're making slanderous innuendoes, Mr Bradwell.'

He looked around with mock-furtiveness. 'No witnesses,
so you couldn't substantiate the accusation. And what big
words from Drake Warrick's girl-friend! What's he doing,
keeping you well supplied with cash?'

'Will you leave my cottage? I know that once it used to
be open house to you, but Lucia's no longer here to welcome you as her guest. And you're certainly not mine. Will
you please go, or I'll——'

'Yes?' He walked slowly towards her, a twisted, ugly
look in his eyes. 'What would you do? Call for help? Who's
to hear, eh?'

Terror was drying her mouth, stiffening her clenched
fingers. He fitted his hands round her neck. 'Who's to hear
you scream if I did this? And this?' His hands tightened
and she knew with a flash of intuition that only just
beneath this man's skin was a viciousness which might, in
the right circumstances, turn him into a near-criminal.
When his mouth pressed against hers, she stood stiff and
unyielding.

'Give, you little cat, give!'

'Get away from me!' she cried. 'Go back to your wife—
although I pity her with all my heart.'

'Any more insults and I'll——'

A car drew up and Ilona's head shot round. A van, Ray's
van! She broke away, raced to the door, flung it open and
as Ray got out, she threw herself into his arms. She stayed

there trembling, whispering, 'It's Ron Bradwell. He's threatening me ...'

'All right, love.' Ray's arms wrapped loosely about her. 'He's going now. Just stay where you are until he's gone.'

When she heard a car rev in the distance and leave, she moved away from Ray's arms, but the trembling lingered. 'Coffee, love,' said Ray, 'hot and sweet. That's what you need.'

They went together into the cottage.

'What did that man Bradwell want?' Ray asked as they drank coffee and Ilona returned slowly to her normal calmness.

'I wish I knew,' she said, frowning. 'Ray, that man frightens me. Once when Lucia lived here and I interrupted one of her parties, Ron Bradwell hit me and knocked me down. Just now he seemed to be threatening to choke me. Heaven knows what would have happened if you hadn't come along.'

Ray looked worried too, although he said, 'I doubt if he would have done anything really drastic. After all, he works for Drake Warrick and if anything had happened to you at Bradwell's hands ...'

Ilona said quickly, 'I mean nothing to Drake Warrick. He only helped me because his conscience made him do so.'

Ray looked round as Ron Bradwell had done. 'But Drake Warrick has helped you, hasn't he? As a result of his efforts, he's put you on your feet again financially. You can pay the rent and you know you won't be thrown out by the landlord.'

Ilona relaxed in the rocking chair. Ron Bradwell's unwelcome arrival at her home, his frightening attitude and his vicious threats were beginning to fade.

'Yes, it's true. Drake has been good,' she said. 'Somehow I feel I ought to thank him for everything he's done.'

'I agree,' said Ray.

'I've also got a feeling,' Ilona added thoughtfully, 'that I ought to thank him quickly, before Ron Bradwell tells him some more lies about me and pours poison in his ear.'

'Go and see Warrick,' Ray suggested.

'See him?' Ilona gasped. 'I don't think I——'

'Don't tell me you're frightened of the man?'

'Of course not, but——' No, she couldn't tell Ray how things were between herself and Drake Warrick. How every time they parted it seemed to be on a quarrel. She sighed. 'I suppose I shall have to try and see him somehow. It's no good phoning his office. Either he's not there, or he's in conference.'

'Surely you know him well enough by now,' said Ray, 'to telephone him at home. After all, all you're going to do is thank him.'

By the time Ray left it was early evening. The sun showed a marked reluctance to make its daily descent to the horizon and continued to shed its heat with a determined intensity. Ilona, however, hardly noticed the cloudless sky and was only partly aware of the warmth still penetrating the thin material of her summer dress.

As she walked along the track to Mrs Macey's cottage, she willed Drake Warrick to be out. It seemed that Mrs Macey was out, so Ilona searched in her handbag for her neighbour's key.

Drake was in. When Ilona told him who was calling, his laconic reply was, 'Is that so?'

So where did she go from there? Her hesitation made him speak again. 'If it's business, then let me tell you at once, I'm not dressed for it. In fact,' he drawled, 'I'm hardly dressed at all.'

Confusion made her say, 'W-were you in the bath? I'm sorry, I'll wait until——'

He laughed loudly. 'I did say "hardly". No, I'm wearing swimming briefs. We're sunbathing beside the pool.'

'We?'

'Yes. Diane's here.'

Why hadn't she guessed he wouldn't be alone? Of course his girl-friend would be beside him in his leisure time.

'Come and join us,' Drake invited.

'I wouldn't dream of it.' The sharpness crept in, surprising her. 'I wouldn't interrupt your enjoyment——'

'You'd be interrupting nothing. I'll expect you in half an hour. There's a bus you can catch in ten minutes. You see, I know the times of your very own local public transport—which proves what an astute businessman I am, doesn't it?' She replaced the receiver on his mocking words.

Ten minutes later, having changed into a button-up blouse which knotted at the waist, and pulled on a pair of metallic blue pants, she was on her way. As she watched the passing hedgerows through the windows of the bus, she couldn't help wishing that the journey to the town took more time. All too soon, she was walking along the street to Drake's apartment.

Drake opened the door. He had pulled on a short-sleeved shirt, but it was hanging free and unbuttoned, hiding little of his powerful physique. His smile was as usual tainted with cynicism.

'Brought a swimsuit?' Ilona shook her head. 'Pity.' He took her by the wrist, holding it loosely and leading her towards the living-room. 'Why did you want to see me?' he asked, standing still.

'To—to thank you for your help.' This was business and, as he had hinted on the telephone, quite out of place in the circumstances. 'The agency's doing well. I've been able to pay the rent and——' She had been going to add, 'Repay Ray's loan', but he stopped her.

'Good, good. Glad to have been of some help.' They continued on their way. His dismissal of the subject was cool and businesslike, despite his attire. The sight of the man, dressed as he was, might almost stop her heartbeats and infuse her with a longing to be back in his arms, but, she told herself, she must never forget that just below the surface of that easy manner lurked the ice-cold, level-headed tycoon.

'Ilona!' Diane half-turned in her seat.

She actually seems pleased to see me, Ilona thought, astonished. If I were in her place, I certainly wouldn't welcome the arrival of another woman on the scene. Diane wore a dazzlingly white two-piece swimsuit. Her figure was slender, her fair-to-gold hair swept sideways and fastened in a roll.

Everything about her caught and held the eye. With Diane as a rival, Ilona knew she stood no chance of gaining Drake's affections. What, to Drake Warrick, were a few kisses and caresses; a helping hand carelessly given and all strictly business anyway, as he had hinted a few moments before?

Drake motioned Ilona towards a sun-lounger, while he dropped into an upright chair. He pulled off his shirt and closed his eyes, as if luxuriating in the warmth of the sun. The pool sparkled, its blue depths invited.

'Have you been swimming?' Ilona asked Diane.

'No—didn't feel in the mood. Just sunbathing. Drake's been in.'

Ilona could almost feel the intimacy of their friendship. It was as though they had known each other for years and would continue to do so for many more.

'What about you, Ilona?' Drake's eyes were covered now by dark glasses. 'Be a devil and get yourself wet.'

'I told you, I haven't brought——'

'Why worry about that? I'm a big boy, my sweet.' How could he use such an endearment to another woman with his girl-friend at his side? 'I'm as used to seeing women in as many stages of undress as you can count on all your fingers and toes.'

'Drake!' Diane was laughing. 'You're embarrassing her.'

'I am?' His eyes turned towards her and Ilona wished she could see their expression. 'Good God, she's blushing! Miss Ilona "Free with her favours" Bell actually going pink at the mention of her nakedness!'

'Look out, Drake,' Diane joked. 'Any minute now there'll be a missile coming your way. She's mad at you.' Drake's smile broadened. 'Borrow my swimsuit, Ilona,' Diane offered.

'No, no, I won't be staying——'

'It's all right, I was going in to change anyway. Drake,' his head turned slowly, 'will you hate me if I say I'd rather not dine out tonight? I know you've booked a table, but——'

Drake's expression was serious. 'Not feeling too good?' Diane shook her head. 'I'm sorry about that, Diane. Of course I understand.' He transferred his gaze to Ilona. 'Ilona will act as your substitute.'

'Go out with you to dinner?' Ilona gasped. 'N——'

'*Please*, Ilona,' said Diane. 'Then I won't feel quite so bad at letting Drake down.' She rose. 'Won't be long changing.' She looked down at the white swimming bra and briefs. 'Our shapes are very similar. I'm sure these will fit you.'

'It's kind of you,' Ilona said, not wishing to hurt Diane's feelings.

When Diane had left them, they sat without speaking. Ilona felt too shy to address the remote man at her side. If she did, who would answer—the tall, handsome host who had welcomed her at the door, with his tough, sun-tanned body and his mocking eyes, or the aloof businessman who had so carelessly accepted and dismissed her gratitude?

The lack of verbal contact grew unnerving and Ilona hoped fervently that Drake would speak. However, he maintained his enigmatic silence and not a word passed between them. When Diane came through the glass doors to hand over the swimsuit, Ilona felt a tremendous feeling of relief.

'Don't see me out, Drake,' said Diane. When Drake told her he would take her home, she protested strongly.

'Please don't worry about me,' Ilona interposed in a small voice. 'I'll go. I only really came to thank you.'

'Stay right where you are,' Drake ordered. 'I'll be back in five or ten minutes. There's a cloakroom over there,' he pointed into the room, 'through that door and turn right, where you can change. Have a swim while I'm gone. Make yourself at home. Imagine all this is yours and that you've left behind the hardship of that primitive little cottage of yours for ever.'

'I don't want to leave my cottage for ever, thank you,' she said firmly, giving him what she hoped was a quelling look. He smiled in reply and put his arm around Diane's waist.

''Bye, Ilona,' Diane smiled. 'See you some time. Good luck with the typing agency—Drake's told me all about it.'

Ilona watched them go. So Drake discussed her affairs with the woman he loved! A few minutes later she crossed into the hall, looking for the cloakroom. On the doorstep, Drake pulled Diane close and kissed her cheek. 'See you in the morning, my dear.'

Diane nodded. 'It was kind of you to get me a taxi, Drake.'

'I have to take care of my secretary,' was the smiling reply.

Ilona shut herself in the cloakroom. She put on Diane's swimming briefs and bra, but the sunshine had gone out of the day. Had she really all this time been hoping that one day Drake Warrick might come to think of her as she thought of him? If so, she should have known better.

There was no mirror, but looking down at herself she saw that the briefs were a good fit—a little too good, taking the audience into consideration—and the top was adequate. It seemed that her figure and Diane's were not as similar as Diane had thought. It was the same with Lucia's dresses. It seemed that she, Ilona, possessed in shape just a little more than either of the other two women.

Drake was back in his seat when she walked self-consciously across the carpeted floor of the living-room and stepped barefooted on to the warm paving stones outside. He must have heard her coming, but he did not turn his head. Even when she came into view, he did not visibly react. With the sunglasses in place, his look was inscrutable.

For a few moments she stood beside the pool. If she had to swim alone, she would not enjoy it. Forcing a gaiety she did not feel, she asked,

'Are you going to join me, Drake?'

'I've been in,' was his only comment. Still she hesitated. 'Can't you swim?' The curt question surprised her. What had happened to his friendliness while Diane had been there?

'A little.'

'Little enough to need your chin held?'

It was spoken as a challenge and accepted as such. She clambered down the steps and dropped into the water. For a while she swam, conscious all the time of Drake's eyes, hidden by darkened glasses, watching her every move.

When she could not stand his scrutiny any longer, she clambered up the steps and looked around for a towel. Drake indicated one spread over a chair. She wrapped it around her, thankful for the slight protection it gave from his gaze.

From the moment she had appeared in Diane's swimsuit, Drake's eyes had never left her. Yet he had made not a single comment. Why was he treating her so coolly? Had Ron Bradwell contacted him in the short time that had elapsed since he had left her cottage and her arrival at Drake's house?

She shivered at the possibility and Drake said, 'The day doesn't last for ever. The temperature's dropping. Go and dress.'

'What about the swimsuit? Diane——'

'I'll give it back to her tomorrow.'

In the cloakroom, Ilona rubbed herself briskly and the towel dropped to the floor. In the few moments in which her fingers fumbled with the catch on the bra top, she noticed she had not locked the door. Since there was no one but Drake in the apartment she did not worry, because he would not follow her there.

But she was wrong. Even as she tried to unhook the unfamiliar fastening, the handle moved and the door opened. 'I'm not finished,' she called worriedly. 'Just a few more minutes ...'

Drake, however, stood there, gazing his fill, and she froze with her hands still behind her on the hook of the bra. He had pulled on slacks and pushed his shirt into place, although it remained unbuttoned.

Instead of retreating he approached slowly. She grew alarmed and her hands dropped away, leaving the swimming top in place. Small protection, but better than nothing ...

He did not speak, but his eyes, those blue eyes which could at times be icy and at others glinting, bronze-flecked in the lamplight, told her that he found in her an attraction which would not be ignored. He moved quickly and she was caught up in an iron-hard embrace.

'Has anyone ever told you,' he murmured, 'what a perfect body you have?'

'Drake, I—I'm trying to get dressed.'

'Why bother?' His mouth trailed the vulnerable areas on her throat, forcing her in her shivering pleasure to hang back her head. 'I want you, woman—and you know it. You know, too, that I watched you in the pool. Every movement you made made me want you more. Every twist and turn of that shape was made for my benefit. Tell me I'm right, my beauty.'

Her head came up to protest, but his mouth hit hers, fastening on to it, forcing it open, testing her, tasting her, arousing her until she had no willpower left. He had taken that over, along with her body. When his hands went to the fastening of the swimming top she did not protest, because she could not find within herself the willpower to do so.

All the longing for his love which had accumulated over the months in which she had known him more intimately than mere employer-employee burst like a many-coloured rocket in her mind. His mouth left hers and moved down, down to the womanly softness of her, until the very essence of her felt on fire.

'No, Drake, no. Please, *please!*' She twisted and struggled and he let her go. When she saw how much of her body was now revealed to him, the colour swept over her face. She grasped the top and tried to replace it, holding it against her.

He bent down, retrieved the towel and handed it to her. His face had altered and was a cold mask. His eyes, empty now of the passion he had displayed, had altered, too, resembling particles of frost.

Ilona flung the towel round her so that it enveloped her from shoulders to toes. She looked dazedly at the bra top which had fallen to the floor. 'Drake,' she whispered, 'what's wrong?'

'You want me to go on?'

She winced at the passionless question.

'Unless you wish me to, I'd rather not,' he went on. 'I've proved my point. Bradwell was right. A lift of the finger and you'd come at the call of any man.'

'So I was too late after all,' she said bitterly. 'I knew he'd go running to you with his lies, but I didn't think he'd be as quick off the mark as that!'

'Which is why you came this evening?' His eyebrows rose. 'Not really to thank me as you claimed, but to get *your* lies in first?'

'Why am I always in the wrong in your eyes?' she cried. 'Why is what I say lies, but what Ron Bradwell says the truth? Did he tell you he started assaulting me in my own

home today? Did he tell you how he nearly choked me—
literally—and probably would have done if Ray Hale
hadn't come unexpectedly?'

'Now I've heard both versions,' Drake commented, unmoved. 'Of the two, I'm afraid I prefer to believe Bradwell's. It's less—shall we say—inventive, less sensational
and theatrical.'

'All right,' she shouted, 'what if I tell you that I'm becoming so afraid of the man that I'm growing scared he
might break in one night and—and——' She could not
finish the sentence. The vision that shaped itself in her
mind of what he might do was too frightening to put into
words.

'He's vicious,' she went on, pulling the towel about her
in the hope that it would stop the trembling that was shaking her body, 'he hit me once so hard he knocked me down
—and that was in front of a crowd! He's got a good wife
and beautiful children—there's a picture of them on his
desk. He gives the impression of being a fine family man.
And you—you've fallen for it. You only see him as one man
sees another. Because I'm a woman, I've seen, and experienced, the other side, the bad side.'

Drake stayed where he was, leaning on his shoulder in
the doorway. It was impossible to tell from his expression
whether she had succeeded in persuading him to accept her
version of the incident with Ron Bradwell as the truth.

'I suppose,' Ilona went on, making one last attempt to
clear herself, 'he told you I ran from his arms into the arms
of my boy-friend?'

'Well, didn't you?' Drake's eyes were fixed on her face.

Her eyes fell before his. 'Yes.'

Drake shrugged as if there were no more to say.

The shivering was taking a stronger hold but she ignored
it, protesting, 'It was for protection. If someone had been
trying to choke you, wouldn't even you have to run to anyone who might save you? Not being a man and with
strength enough to match Ron Bradwell's, of course I ran
out to Ray.' His brief smile was so cynical she flared,

'You can accuse me, when you stand accused yourself.
Just now you were making passionate love to me, only

minutes after seeing Diane, your girl-friend, off the premises.'

'As I've said before,' he returned frigidly, 'my relationship with Diane is entirely my concern.'

He moved to the door, paused, turned back and said, 'By the way, you won't have to endure an evening with me. I've cancelled that table for two. But I'll run you home.'

'No, thank you, I'll go back the way I came. And don't bother to do what you did for Diane—call a cab. The bus is good enough for an *immoral* female like me!'

Her brown eyes darted a challenging look at him. For a few moments he watched her shivering under the towel. At the curious look in his eyes, Ilona's heart stumbled. Was he going to relent, wrap his arms about her and, by sharing with her the warmth of his body, help to end the spasms of shaking? It seemed not, because he gave a final shrug, said, 'please yourself,' and left her.

As she towelled herself into a calmer state and stepped into her clothes, she remembered Ron Bradwell's words when he had cornered her at Drake's party. *He goes through women like fire through a house. He sets them alight, gets all the goodies he can, then watches them burn to ashes. Then he walks away without even a stab of conscience.*

Those words, Ilona thought miserably, were surely the truest Ron Bradwell had ever spoken.

She emerged quietly from the cloakroom, hoping to slip unnoticed out of the apartment, but Drake, it seemed, had been waiting. He opened the door, gave an ironic bow and watched her pass outside into the golden evening.

# CHAPTER EIGHT

WHEN the letter came from the landlord's lawyers demanding vacant possession of the cottage, Ilona swayed and felt for a chair.

The letter went on, 'Not only are you not the legal tenant, since Mrs Lucia Wood is that, we have it on good authority that you are running a business from the premises, although a clause in the agreement which our client, Mr Moorley, exchanged with Mrs Wood prohibits this activity. On our client's behalf, we are therefore giving you one month's notice to quit.' The letter concluded, 'We are also instructing you to cease forthwith operating from the premises the business known as Bell's Typing Agency.'

Grasping the letter, Ilona made for the door and ran along the track to Mrs Macey's cottage. Mrs Macey opened the door, announced that she was about to make an early start and go shopping in the town—then saw Ilona's white face.

'My dear, come in. What's wrong? Sit down. Let me get you——'

Still stunned, Ilona shook her head, then told Mrs Macey about the contents of the solicitor's letter. Mrs Macey looked concerned, told Ilona that she could rely on her to help in any way possible and said,

'I have seven minutes to get the bus. I expect you'll want to do some telephoning. Do please feel free, my dear, to make as many calls as you like. After all,' she laughed, 'you do help me pay my telephone bill!'

She picked up her shopping bag, said she hoped everything would work out and started running along the track, waving as she went.

Ray was the second person who came into Ilona's mind. The first, she was convinced, would not help her. When she got through to Ray and poured the whole story out to him, he told her that if money was her chief worry he would willingly lend her some more. But as far as accommodating

115

her was concerned, there was nothing he could do.

'We've got a spare room,' he told her, 'but my sister and her husband and two kids are in the process of moving from one house to another. Jack's got himself a new job a few miles from here. They've sold their house but haven't yet found another. So my mother and father are having them here until they do.'

Ilona said she understood perfectly, and in any case, it hadn't occurred to her to ask them to take her in. 'It's still such a shock, Ray,' she said. 'I came straight to the phone to call you. I haven't even had time to think. Ray, I'll be without a job again. No money coming in, not even a home ...'

'Why don't you try Mr Warrick again, love?'

'I thought of him, but——'

'He helped you get the agency going. Maybe he'll have some idea on this, too.'

'Oh, Ray, I can't—I just can't ask Drake Warrick for any more help.'

'You'll have to, Ilona. Nothing else for it, is there?'

Not wishing to burden Ray too much with her troubles —and in any case, he seemed anxious to get away—Ilona made a noncommittal comment and said she supposed there was no alternative. 'Thanks for your offer of another loan, Ray.'

'As long as you take me up on it if you need it,' he answered, and she assured him that she would.

For some time she sat in one of Mrs Macey's upright chairs. Her fingers were spread over her face, her elbows rested on the table. She tried to think of a way round her problems, but her mind was so confused, she could work nothing out.

If Lucia would help ... As the legal tenant, if Lucia could persuade the landlord to allow her to pass on the tenancy ... Then she remembered the landlord's wish to sell the place.

Ilona's watch told her that it was still early enough for Lucia to be at home—if that was how she now regarded Colin Hardcastle's house. It was some time before the call was answered. Lucia's words were slurred as if she had been awoken from a deep sleep.

She grumbled, 'What do you want?'

'Your help.' Ilona told Lucia about the solicitor's letter. 'You're the real tenant, Lucia. The rent man's been kind enough to keep the fact that you've moved away a secret from the landlord, as long as I pay the rent each month. But now it looks as though someone—and I'm sure it wasn't the rent man—has told him everything, even about the typing agency.'

'Well, it wasn't me. I wouldn't have been such a fool. I'd have known you'd come whining to me, just like you've done. I certainly wouldn't have brought that on myself.'

'I wasn't accusing you of telling the landlord,' Ilona answered, exasperated.

'So what am I supposed to do about it?'

'I just thought you should know what was going on. After all, your name is still written down as being the tenant. The rent man, Mr Elson, told me it was in the agreement that only the tenant was allowed to live there, which means that now you've gone, I'm not really supposed to be occupying the cottage.'

'Now tell me some real news,' Lucia commented sarcastically. 'I was aware of that when I moved out. I only let you live there because you had nowhere else to go. You should be grateful to me that I didn't throw you out of the place the day I moved in here with Colin. I would have been within my rights to do so, and after all, I'm not a relative, just a family friend. Anyway, I'm living here now. As soon as Colin's divorce is through, I'm marrying him, so I've finished with the cottage. Whatever troubles you've got, you'll have to deal with them yourself.' There was a moment's silence. 'What about asking Drake for help?'

'I can't ask him!'

'Why not? I heard via the grapevine that he gave you a lot of assistance with getting the typing agency established. Try him again. Maybe he can give you advice on how to get out of the trouble he helped you get into.'

'You can't blame him,' Ilona answered. 'He didn't know any more than I did about the clause in the agreement about running a business. Anyway,' she finished lamely, 'I can't go to him for help any more. We're not really on speaking terms. Every time we meet we quarrel.'

Ilona heard Lucia's sigh. 'You're still not really grown-up, are you? You still can't handle a man. He's single, he's virile and very, very willing. I hear tell that he doesn't refuse any young, good-looking woman. If you let him know you're not only available but willing, too, he'd give you anything. You're twenty-four. You surely don't need your sister's friend to tell you how to go about getting yourself into bed with a——'

'That's not a habit of mine and you know it!'

'No? How about this fête where you're putting yourself up for auction? What's that if not offering——'

'That's different, and again you know it. And I'm *not* being auctioned. Anyway, there'll be no offering, whoever wins me.'

There was loud, high-pitched laughter from the other end, a jeering ''Bye, Ilona. Enjoy wallowing in your troubles. Maybe having to cope alone will help you grow up,' and a click as Lucia rang off.

More depressed than ever, Ilona sat at Mrs Macey's dining table, looking down at her own shadowy reflection in the highly-polished surface.

No one to help, nowhere to go ... She would have to gather her scattered wits and make her own plans for the future. Listlessly, she wandered round the cottage, which was a little larger than her own. The living-room was carpeted in a rust colour. The furniture was simple yet tasteful. On the windowsills were flowering bulbs, on the sideboard pottery vases were filled with flowers.

Electricity had been installed and in a corner stood a standard lamp with a large shade. In the kitchen was a stainless steel sink unit and double-drainer, complete with mixer tap. The old cooking stove remained, but room had been made for an electric cooker. On a flap-table hinged and fixed to the wall were the remains of Mrs Macey's quickly-eaten breakfast.

This, Ilona thought with a strange stirring of envy, was how her own cottage might have looked had Lucia cared to spend a little money in order to make it a real home. It was now that she realised that in choosing to live in such a primitive way, how much was missing from her life—not so much in the way of modern amenities as in the warm, welcoming atmosphere of a well-loved dwelling-place.

She checked her thoughts in dismay. What was the matter with her? Was she growing soft after visiting Drake Warrick's apartment and experiencing for an hour or two his luxurious way of life? An image of his home flashed into her mind but, she realised with relief, its comforts did not hold a lasting appeal. She wanted the simple pattern of her life to go on. Every day of living the way she had chosen to live was a challenge.

Again she looked around, seeing on a side table a woven basket containing fruit. Nearby there was a footstool. Mrs Macey was not young and needed these home comforts, Ilona decided. She herself was young and did not need them.

It was only when she caught sight of the solicitor's letter near the telephone that she remembered how, before very long, her life would have to change out of all recognition.

The telephone rang, jangling her nerves. Should she answer? The call might be for Mrs Macey. On the other hand, it might be a customer phoning about work.

'Ilona Bell here,' she said, and her heart turned over when she heard the clipped voice at the other end.

'I thought we weren't on speaking terms?'

'Who told you that?' she responded sharply. As if I didn't know, she thought.

'So every time we meet we quarrel? So you can't come to me for help any more?'

'What else did Lucia tell you?' she asked resignedly.

'That soon you'll be deprived of your home, not to mention your income.'

'They're both true,' said Ilona, 'but I'll manage somehow.'

'Contacted your sister?' Drake asked.

'Laura? She's just about to have a baby. Twins, in fact, or so the doctor's just informed them.'

'What about the boy-friend? Does he know about the landlord's threat?'

'You mean Ray Hale? Of course. He was the sec——'
She corrected herself quickly. 'He was the first person I thought of.'

There was a brief pause, then, 'Has he offered you a roof over your head, plus a room from which you could carry on your agency?'

'If he had, I wouldn't have called Lucia for help, would I?'

'So he's let you down? Some boy-friend!'

'Look, Mr Warrick, he lives with his parents. He couldn't help me in that way, even if he wanted to.'

'Couldn't he? Surely they'd welcome the chance to hold out a helping hand to their future daughter-in-law?'

'What are you talking about? I'm not engaged to any-one, and certainly not to Ray. We've never even discussed marriage.'

'So it's that sort of relationship?'

She said furiously, 'You can keep your insults to your-self. I didn't phone you. You called me, I haven't asked for your help. You see, I can remember the time I was in des-perate need of money to pay the rent and phoned you ask-ing if you could give me a job. Not only did you tell me "no", you insulted me by saying that if you ever did help me pay my rent, you'd want a lot more than a few kisses. You'd want the key to my cottage so that you could come and go whenever you liked.'

There was a slightly longer pause, then, 'In asking you to my house a short time ago and introducing you to a num-ber of business colleagues, I managed to put quite a lot of work your way. Enough in fact to get your typing agency going again *and pay your rent.*' In a deceptively silky voice, he added, 'Have I asked for the key to your cottage?'

She was forced to climb down. 'No. But,' she rallied, 'I don't want to put myself under any more obligations to you. So thanks for your interest, both past and present, in my business affairs. I won't keep you from your work any longer.' She put down the phone, glad he could not see her shaking hand.

Having lingered in Mrs Macey's cottage for a few minutes—would Drake ring back?—Ilona at last returned to her own. Depression hit her again as she unlocked the door. Soon all this would cease to be hers. The agency would have to close.

Soon she would have to scan the classified advertisements in the newspapers, looking for accommodation. But, and the thought made her hand fly to her forehead, how would she pay the rent for *any* place, bed-sitter, room with kitchen or even an apartment? Of course she would receive unemployment benefit, but she did not really want it. It was work she wanted, not hand-outs from the State. How long would Drake go on black-listing her as far as references were concerned?

It was a trap she was caught in, a trap of officialdom, of the law, of the prejudice of her former employer. Hadn't she, by her efficient running of the typing agency, yet proved her worth in Drake's eyes?

When the charity committee met again, the discussion ranged over the usual topics, but with a greater sense of finality. Preparations were well in hand for the supply of goods for the stalls.

Help for the fête had been offered from all quarters of the village community. Even the catering firm supplying teas and cold drinks were giving their services almost free of charge.

The item on the agenda which worried Ilona most was the question of the kind of clothing she would be expected to wear.

Mrs Bryant asked, 'Would you consider an evening dress suitable, Miss Bell?'

Ilona agreed with some relief, having dreaded that Colonel Dainton, with the interests of charity at heart, might suggest the wearing of a swimsuit.

'I know personally,' said Mrs Bryant, 'the lady who runs the little dress shop at the other end of the village. She would, I'm sure, be willing to lend you a dress, modest, but eye-catching enough to attract the men's attention. I'm certain she would regard the advertising of her business as sufficient reward for the loan of the dress.'

Ilona hesitated, wondering what was meant by 'eye-catching', but Ray nudged her. 'You've got to give a little, love. A dress which shows off your attractions would be acceptable, surely?'

It would have been unreasonable to refuse. Ilona said, with a sigh, 'I agree, just as long as it's not too eye-catching.'

'Would you want your hair done?' asked the vicar. 'My wife patronises a very good shop in the village. Again, I'm sure the hairdresser would, in the circumstances, give her services free.'

'Thank you, Mr Bushley,' said Ilona, agreeing now with every suggestion the committee made, since the whole matter seemed to be out of her hands. 'Would your wife make the appointment, or——?'

'Oh, I'm certain she will,' the vicar answered happily.

'Only two weeks to go,' boomed Colonel Dainton.

'We can only hope and pray the weather is kind to us,' murmured the vicar.

Ray turned to speak to his neighbour and Ilona sighed at Colonel Dainton's words. Two weeks! Where would she be, two weeks from now?

Refusing to be intimidated by events, Ilona closed her mind to the landlord's threats and to legal harassment and continued with the work which came with pleasing regularity through the letter-box.

Now and then, however, she could not prevent her thoughts from conjuring up pictures of herself trudging from one door to another, pleading for accommodation, only to have those doors slammed in her face.

She was sitting thus, gazing dismally out of the window early one evening, the typewriter before her on the table, when a figure passed the window. Its height, its breadth, its self-confident bearing, left her in no doubt as to the identity of the caller.

Already hammering, her heart lurched alarmingly at the rap of knuckles. As she opened the door, Drake nodded and entered. He saw the half-finished letter in the typewriter and looked at his watch. 'Working,' he queried, 'at this late hour?'

'It isn't late, and I work to suit myself.'

'Well and truly put in my place,' he mocked.

'The last time we met,' she challenged him, 'we had a violent quarrel, so why are you here?'

'So a quarrel is definitive, is it? It signifies "the end of everything"?' He smiled and folded his arms and she noticed how well his suit was cut to fit the lean outline of his body. 'Well, maybe I'm here because I like quarrelling with you. It happens so often, doesn't it? I seem to recall,' he rubbed a thumb thoughtfully round his chin, 'we quarrelled the time before that, and before that, stretching back into infinity. Interspersed, of course,' his eyes glinted wickedly, 'with tender love scenes and moments of passion!'

'Are you going to take your cynicism out of here?' she challenged, upset at the way he treated so lightly the kisses and lovemaking that had taken place between them. 'I should like to get on with my work.'

'I won't detain you long.' He looked her over for such a long moment she grew conscious of the careless way she was dressed. She wished her slacks were not so rumpled, that the wear and tear did not show so clearly in the round-necked top she had unthinkingly pulled over her head that morning. All day she had been too busy to care how she looked. And now this man was acting as a mirror and she wanted to turn her back on him and walk away from the reflection.

He went on, 'Are you in a good mood?'

'There's no doubting *your* strangely benevolent mood towards me!' she retorted.

He laughed loudly, then turned on her the full power of his vivid blue eyes. It was as if he knew that like laser beams they would melt her resistance, weaken her legs and make her want to run into his arms. He was playing, she was certain, on the feeling he knew she had for him. Hadn't Ron Bradwell told him long ago that she was in love with her boss, and hadn't she betrayed that love to Drake himself almost every time he had kissed her?

'There is no doubting,' he countered, smiling, 'your strange animosity towards me. Tell me, my love, what have I ever done to deserve your dislike?'

The endearment made the quick colour flare and he laughed uninhibitedly at her reaction. Anger burned in her just as quickly, and she retorted, 'What have you *done*? You fired me from my job on completely unfair grounds. All

along you've never believed a word I've said in my own defence. You've———'

His raised hand silenced her. 'You're in a good mood, remember?' He strolled towards her, linked his hands behind her waist and pulled her close enough for their legs
and hips to touch. 'Don't you think we know each other
well enough now,' he asked softly, 'to use the age-old
remedy for patching up our quarrels?'

'That's for married couples,' she parried, her hand straying to touch his tie, 'or for lovers.' Her eyes met his. 'We're
neither.'

'That could be easily remedied,' His smile, the unaccus-
tomed softening of his gaze, were almost her undoing.

She shook her head. 'No way.'

'I could—persuade you,' he murmured. 'More than once
we've been on the edge of abandoning the rest of the
world for a few hours of loving.'

'Loving,' he'd said, not 'love'. It was significant, it must
be remembered at all costs. But his nearness was a torment. She would not stand there encircled by his arms,
waiting tamely while he struck the match which set her
alight. Before her feelings flamed and seared, *she* would
be the one to walk away.

Swiftly she bent, ducked under his arms—and was free.
He seemed mildly annoyed, came after her, then changed
his mind. 'You think you're clever, don't you?' he contented himself with saying.

There was silence for a few moments and Ilona sat at
the table, hands in position over the typewriter keys. 'Can
I help you?' she asked sweetly.

He gave her a sardonic, sideways look, then said, pushing hands into pockets, 'Yes—provided you can spare the
time." She frowned and waited, hands clasped loosely in
her lap.

'At the moment I'm without a secretary.'

'Diane's away again?' The question shot out.

He inclined his head. 'Again.' He did not explain, but
Ilona persisted,

'Is she ill, then?'

'She's ill, in hospital. I'm on my way to visit her.'

At his words, the vitality drained from Ilona's body, the

pleasure of Drake's presence evaporated. She was left pierced and empty, like a discarded Coke tin. She could not go on like this, letting him kick her feelings around, then leave her on the emotional garbage heap, when all the while he cared deeply and exclusively for another.

'I'm sorry to hear she's ill,' she said, 'very sorry.' She knew better than to ask him what was wrong with Diane. If anyone knew how to hand out a rebuff, it was Drake Warrick. 'You said I could help you?'

'I have a couple of letters which must be answered to-night. The girl who took my dictation today left work the moment the clock reached five-thirty. Everyone else had gone, so I came to the only person who I knew would help me out.'

Which, Ilona thought with sad resignation, explained his visit explicitly. She searched for her notepad, found it and said, 'Dictate, Mr Warrick.'

He gathered a handful of her hair, tugged it twice in spite of her protest and smiled. 'Just like old times. Me, boss. You, slave.' He made his way to the rocking chair, settled in it and moved gently back and forwards. For a few moments he was silent, then the words flowed. Once again Ilona discovered that she could easily keep pace with his dictation. Now and then he glanced at her, but each time she was waiting, pencil poised, for him to resume.

When the dictation was over, she asked for two pieces of the company's headed paper. 'Have you——'

'Forgotten?' He smiled. 'No. I'm as efficient a boss as you are a secretary.' He raked in his pocket and pulled out his car keys, holding them up. 'Would you? They're in my briefcase on the back seat.'

'You're trusting me to go over your briefcase?'

'My sweet girl,' he lounged back in the chair, gently rocking it, 'a man in my job has to learn to know whom he can trust. I trust you. Got it?'

She smiled down at him impishly. 'A mouse has to be grateful for small mercies,' she said, and backed away as he made to lunge at her.

It took a few minutes to walk to Drake's car, unlock it and search through the briefcase for the company's headed letter paper. When she returned to the cottage, Drake was emerging from the room which Lucia had occupied.

Surprised, she asked, 'What were you doing in there?'

He shrugged. 'Just prowling. You need an odd-job man about the house. There are various things that need fixing.'

'I know. I'll have to ask Ray some time.'

'The boy-friend? All right,' his raised hand checked her correction of the description, 'call him what you like. I was going to say, is he the one you run to when the window catch stops functioning or a pane of glass is broken?'

'Or the stove smokes badly,' she took him up, 'filling the kitchen. Or the tap outside freezes and I'm left without a water supply. Or the rain gets in my bedroom upstairs. Or when birds make a nest in the thatch and cause near-havoc. Yes.' Her wide smile was turned on him again.

Their smiles reached out, catching at each other like outstretched hands. Ilona's breath came quickly and she dreaded that her love for him, her wish to be in physical contact with him, showed in her eyes.

'Brown eyes, big eyes,' he said, 'you need a husband. Why aren't the men falling over themselves to be first past the post with you?'

Her smile faded. 'You're a man, you should know. I must lack what it takes to entangle a man's heart, mustn't I?'

'Must you?' He had moved nearer and she retreated towards the table.

'I'm happy alone.' Did her voice contain an element of defiance, coloured by the merest tint of doubt?

'You really like living here in these conditions? No water laid on, no electricity, no comforts, no central heating?'

At the last phrase she shivered. 'I wouldn't exchange a series of aloof radiators for the fire that burns in that grate over there when the snow's on the ground. It licks its way through logs, enormous chunks of coal, fallen branches, even cardboard boxes. Anything you care to feed it with, in fact. And the heat it throws out has to be felt to be believed.' Her face lifted defiantly. 'You can keep your central heating.'

'And you're under notice to quit?'

Her cheeks were warm, as though she had been sitting in front of that imaginary blazing fire. At his reminder, the warmth faded.

'I'm under notice to quit.' She sank into the upright chair. Her eyes, despondent now, sought his. 'How long do you think I've got here? I mean, how long will it be before the final notice comes?'

Drake wandered to the window which overlooked the field at the back of the cottage. 'As I see it,' he said, with his back to her, 'you should be all right for a month or so. You see, to get you out, the landlord would have to obtain a court order for possession from the County Court. The court always takes its time, especially in cases of this kind—they have their human side, believe it or not, and they don't really like making people homeless. So the best thing you can do,' he faced her and rested against the high sill, 'is to hang on here as long as the law allows.'

'But what about the agency?' She motioned towards the typewriter.

'Carry on with that, too, until you're told officially to stop. Bearing in mind, of course, that at any moment you'll have to write hurried letters to your customers explaining that you've been forced to close the agency.'

'Thanks, Drake. Thanks for your advice. I've been worrying about it, you see ...'

He said nothing and she inserted the paper into the machine. While she typed the letters he had dictated, Drake wandered around again. He went into the kitchen, and was there for some time. He emerged and looked up the wooden stairs. 'May I?' he asked, explaining, 'Just want to count how many young birds there are in that nest you mentioned.'

Ilona laughed. 'They make enough noise in the early morning to wake me better than an alarm clock!'

When he came down, the letters were waiting for his signature. He said, 'Clean and tidy up there, but stark. Don't you wish sometimes for a carpet to step on to, for polished floorboards down here, for *any* creature comforts?'

Ilona paused before answering, remembering her reaction to the warmth and colour in Mrs Macey's cottage. 'Maybe,' she replied, staring unseeingly at the opposite wall, 'now and then. But if they were installed, what else would follow? That's what frightens me. Everything, eventually, all the trappings of twentieth-century torment, in the way of gadgets and switches. All the things that detract from the dignity and self-confidence of the individual by doing things for him—and her—which he, or she, would be happier doing with their own hands. And,' she transferred her gaze to his expressionless face, 'as I've told you before, I've got privacy of mind and body. Here, I can shut out the world.'

'Yet soon, if the landlord has his way, you'll be pitch-forked headlong into modern-world reality. What are you going to do then? How will you adjust?'

'I——' she moistened her lips and smiled faintly. 'I think I'll stuff my essential belongings into a rucksack, carry it on my back and become a happy wanderer. I'll—I'll see the world—in *my* way, live in *my* way, eating and sleeping and working wherever I can. Young people are doing that all the time these days,' she said, the defiance creeping back.

She went on, 'They look upon the world as their "village". They're opting out of climbing the status ladder. A lot of them just want to be happy, coming and going whenever they want, not "company" men and women striving to reach the top jobs, with the stress and responsibilities that go with them.' She gazed up at him earnestly. 'They want to do their own thing *their* way. You do understand me, don't you?'

He considered her for a long time and she wished she could read his thoughts. 'I'm ten years older than you,' he said at last, bending down to sign the letters. 'Just ten years, yet a chasm yawns between our ways of thinking.'

Ilona folded the letters and placed them in the envelopes. He took them from her.

She said, her heart sinking inexplicably, 'It's only natural, isn't it, that you don't see it my way. You're already in the top job.'

He smiled wryly. 'That despised "top job"! But I climbed no ladder. I started my own company. It was darned hard work, although I'm not complaining.'

For a moment, Ilona was silent, studying the typewriter keys as if trying to make some sense of them. At last she said, rising. 'One day you'll see my point of view, and all

young people's. Everyone will see it. They'll have to, because the way young people are thinking is the future, and
the future's with us now.'

His hands came out and caught at her arms, pulling her
against him. 'You, my sweet, elusive, maddening Miss Bell,
are the most extraordinary female I've ever met.' His
mouth came down in a breathtakingly possessive, almost
angry, kiss. When he let her go, she said, eyes brilliant,

'I'm *not* extraordinary. I'm just representative of a growing number of my generation. One day older people will
understand and agree with us.'

'So I'm one of those "older people"?' He went to the
door.

'I didn't say so,' she called after him with dismay.

'Nevertheless,' his voice was cold, 'we're on different
sides of a very high fence.' His eyes were not cold. They
gleamed with a strange kind of anger. 'I think I'll go and
visit Diane. Somehow, I understand her language.'

'Which,' Ilona thought, sinking despairingly into the
rocking chair and hearing the car drive away, 'puts me,
totally and unequivocally, out of Drake Warrick's world. It
also puts him right out of mine.' Tears welled and she
whispered, 'Message concluded. Over and out.'

The following day the rent man called. Ilona paid him, then
asked, 'Mr Elson, how much longer will I be allowed to
stay here?'

The question brought a curious anxiety to his expression.
He scratched behind his ear with his pencil. 'Difficult to
say, miss.' He would not meet her eyes. 'Never can tell with
these notice to quit cases. One thing I must warn you
about, though. The landlord himself told me to tell you.
You know he wants to sell the place after you've left?
Well, to get a good price, he wants to make a few alterations and improvements.'

It took a few moments for the information to register,
then Ilona burst out, 'What sort of alterations?'

'Er—let me see.' Mr Elson looked around, found the
mains tap in the front garden and said, 'Well, for a start—
as far as I know, mind—he wants running water in the

kitchen. He wants a sink unit with double drainer.' He thought a moment. 'Oh, yes, and round the back he wants a proper—er—you-know-what——'

'Toilet,' said Ilona, feeling the tension growing with the rent man's every word.

'That's it,' he evaded her eyes, embarrassed, 'toilet put in. Oh, and a door knocked through for access from the cottage.'

'Any more?' asked Ilona, tight-lipped.

'Um—yes.' He eyed her nervously. 'Electricity. He wants that put in.'

'*Electricity?*' she gasped. '*In this cottage?*'

'I don't see what's wrong with that, miss. Should have thought you'd be delighted.'

'Well, I am *not* delighted. I don't want electricity installed. Nor do I want running water in the kitchen. Nor do I want anything that other people would say made life easier. I don't want my life made "easier". Tell my precious landlord that!'

'If I may say so, miss, I don't really think it's for you to say. You're under notice to quit, so it shouldn't trouble you much longer, this place, should it?'

'I've been told about that,' Ilona said, scarcely able to contain her anger. 'I know it can take quite a long time obtaining an order for possession, two to three months sometimes. I want the time I've got left here to be peaceful and the way I want it. Can't he wait until I've gone? Must he——'

'Not my business, miss,' said Mr Elson, plainly anxious to leave. 'I've done my duty. I've told you what's going to happen. My responsibility ends there.'

'Mr Elson,' she pleaded, changing her tone, 'please will you give me the landlord's address? I'll go and see him. I'll—I'll appeal to his better nature. I'll *make* him see my point of view.'

Mr Elson's shake of the head was emphatic. 'He won't see none of his tenants, miss, and that's final. He won't have anything to do with them. Strict instructions from the man himself.'

'But, Mr Elson, he can't sack you. You're not employed by him, are you? You're employed by a firm of rent collectors. So what have you got to lose if you give me his address? Just whisper, Mr Elson, that's all I want. I won't give you away.'

'No fear, miss. It'd be the end of my job if I betrayed a confidence. *He* may not sack me, but my boss would. No, miss,' he walked away, 'I'm not telling. Sorry, miss.' He swung a leg over his bicycle and was away as fast as the wheels would carry him.

It was next morning that a builder's van drew up outside the cottage, followed by a small open truck containing building materials.

Ilona stared in disbelief. The landlord certainly hadn't wasted any time in carrying out his decision to make improvements.

While her breakfast stood on the table, she ran out and confronted the man climbing out of the driver's cab. ''Morning, miss,' he said cheerfully. 'Hope we're not too early.'

'Too early for what?' Ilona demanded.

'To start work, miss.'

'Work? On what?'

The man was becoming puzzled by her attitude. 'Don't you know about it, miss? The sink unit. We're going to start on the installation work today. It means clearing a space, removing whatever's in the way, and so on. We've got the measurements——'

'Who gave you the measurements?'

'Why, the——' the man was growing bewildered, 'the landlord, miss.'

'How does he know? He hasn't been here.'

'Well, far as I know, miss, he knows this cottage like the back of his hand. When he bought the place——'

'All right,' Ilona accepted sharply. Of course Mr Moorley knew his own property. He might even have lived there, using it perhaps as a weekend cottage, before letting it out to tenants. 'But you're not starting work, Mr——' she looked at the name on the side of the van. Huntley and Grantham, it said. 'Mr Huntley.'

'Grantham,' the man said.

'You see, Mr Grantham,' she searched about in her mind,

'there's—there's a dispute going on between myself and the landlord. I'm——' another search for a reason, 'I'm going to ask him if he'd mind postponing the improvements until—well, until I've vacated the place. You see, I run a business from here, and the upheaval of having builders around would interfere with my work and—and I'd lose a lot of money not being able to fulfil my commitments. So you see, I'm sorry, but you can't start today.'

'I'm sorry too, miss, because you see, we've had our orders. Start today, they said, so we've rearranged our work schedule so that we could start today.'

'Mr Grantham,' Ilona said, angry now, not with the man but with the situation which seemed to be slipping from her control, 'would you kindly give me the address of the man—my landlord, Mr Moorley—who gave you these instructions?' She waited, holding her breath. Now she would get the information she wanted so much.

But Mr Grantham said, 'That wasn't the name of the person who gave the instructions. It was a firm of solicitors. Can't remember the exact name——'

Ilona sighed exasperatedly. 'If only you could, Mr Grantham, you'd really be doing me a kindness. If—if I showed you a phone book, would that help? The lady who lives at the cottage along there, she's on the phone. She'd have a directory. *Please* try and remember, Mr Grantham. You see, I *must* see the landlord. We've got to get everything sorted out. I can't—I *cannot* have any kind of up-heaval——'

'We wouldn't make a mess, miss. We'll be most care-ful——'

'Would you please go away?' she pleaded. 'Would you please take your van and lorry and go? I absolutely refuse to let you put one step into my cottage. No offence, Mr Grantham, nothing personal. But would you please convey that message to the firm of solicitors who told you to come here, and they can pass it on to their *client*!'

She returned to the cottage, slammed the door and put her whole weight against it. However, no one tried to force an entry. A few minutes later, after a discussion among the workmen, the two vehicles drove away.

Ilona sank into the rocking chair as exhausted as if she

had fought a hand-to-hand battle like an ancient warrior.

So the time was nearly here for her world to start falling apart. She shook her head, then held it. Twentieth century, she thought bitterly, here you come!

## CHAPTER NINE

For most of the day Ilona wandered about the cottage, savouring all the old familiar things which, before very long, she would be forced to leave behind for ever.

Beyond their surface importance, they signified so much —her freedom from pursuit by the outside world, her ability to do things the way she wanted, her personal privacy which she cherished like other women their jewels.

How long would she be able to keep at bay the invasion of all she had run from? How many times could she turn away those building contractors? How soon before they ignored her wishes and carried out the landlord's instructions?

She had just finished washing the dishes next morning when Mrs Macey came hurrying towards the front door. Ilona stood at the window and Mrs Macey mouthed, 'Telephone!'

Ilona hurried after her. Could it be Ray? Colonel Dainton about the fête? *The solicitors about the alterations?*

'Ilona?' The voice was brisk and familiar, and her heart gave its usual lurch. 'I need help, your help, if you could oblige. I told you that Diane is in hospital. Well, the girl who was deputising is up to her eyes in the work I gave her yesterday. The others are fully occupied. Is it possible for you to come in, just for the day, and give me a hand?'

'I'd like to, Drake, but——'

'I know how busy you are, but just a few hours, Ilona? If necessary, I could put things right with whoever has to wait for their work. I know them all——'

Ilona sighed loudly enough for him to hear, but he could not see the brightening of her eyes, nor the way the colour of excitement crept into her cheeks. A day working for Drake! 'All right,' she conceded slowly. 'I'll come as soon as I can, but there isn't a bus due yet.'

'I'll send a cab for you. I can't wait on the whims and fancies of public transport. It'll be there in ten minutes. Right?'

There was no arguing with that tone. 'Yes,' she said, affecting another sigh.

'Good. When you arrive, come straight to my office. Oh, and—thanks.'

As she took the lift to the executive offices, Ilona found it strange to be back. She met no one on the way to Drake's room. She passed the closed doors of the offices occupied by the managers of the various departments. One, however, stood open. It led to the office which belonged to Ron Bradwell. As she approached, she grew worried in case the occupant saw her and came out, detaining her. The room, however, was empty, the desk at which he sat cleared of everything except a telephone.

When she tapped on Drake's door, he answered at once. His smile was touched with a certain warmth, as were his eyes, which flicked quickly over her. Ilona was glad she had chosen her dress with care. It was a deep blue with touches of white, and she wore sandals to match. For once, it was one of her own dresses. None of Lucia's hanging in the bedroom cupboard was as unpretentious as this.

Her hair was soft from its washing the evening before, and swung free to her shoulders. Her make-up was light, her head high, her swinging step hinting at a confidence which was only skin deep. Nothing, however, could take from her lips the curve of pleasure at seeing Drake again. Nor could it dull the bright light in her eyes as they absorbed the overpowering attraction of his personality and his heartbreaking good looks. Yes, they *were* heartbreaking —didn't he walk away at the end of each relationship with a woman?

Momentarily, Drake rose, a politeness she had not expected from him. He commented, 'Every centimetre the young business woman.' If the statement contained mockery, it was slight. 'Thanks for coming to my rescue, Ilona.'

'I'm in your debt, anyway.'

He frowned. 'How so?'

'All the work you've put my way.'

'Oh, that!'

'Why, what did you think I meant?'

His shoulders lifted and he smiled. 'I was racking my brains. To be truthful, I couldn't remember a single time when I had been kind to you.'

They laughed together and he motioned her to the secretary's chair beside him. Ilona delighted in being so near. For a few hours, he was her boss again. Did he know that she would do almost anything he wanted? Almost? she questioned herself, flicking the pages of the notepad he had pushed towards her.

No, the answer was not 'almost'. Everything, *anything* he asked of her. Having thus, in her mind, committed herself totally and for life to the man she loved, she picked up a pencil and prepared herself mentally for work. It came, fast and furious. The words flowed from his lips. He knew her capabilities well enough by now to go at the speed which came naturally to him. He showed her no consideration. At the end of each sentence, she was ready, poised and waiting.

So the morning passed. It seemed that in Diane's absence, lack of really skilled help had caused the correspondence to pile up. With a girl by his side who was efficient to her finger-tips, it seemed that he revelled in composing answers to the technical questions contained in the letters.

Since they had not even paused for morning coffee, Ilona was experiencing a fatigue which she wished at all costs to hide. It was lunchtime before Drake stopped. It seemed that even he could not deny his body the nourishment for which it craved.

He halted in his striding about the room, wheeled round and came to stand in front of her. He took away the notepad and pencil, and bent forward gripping her chin with forefinger and thumb.

He gazed into her eyes and the tension within her which had mounted as the morning had progressed, increased even more. 'Deny you're tired,' he murmured.

'I do deny it.'

He released her. 'Stand. Come on, demonstrate your two slender legs are in a fit state to support you.'

Too quickly she obeyed his command, and swayed. He caught her against him, and her forehead found his shoulder. They stood quietly for a few moments until he said softly, his lips against her hair, 'I've worked you to a standstill, haven't I?'

She shook her head against him. She wanted him never to let her go.

'You're magnificent, my love.' Her heart pounded at the murmured caress. 'What mad urge made me fire you?'

She lifted her head, finding his piercingly blue eyes. 'My typing errors, Mr Warrick, sir?'

His fist bunched under her chin. 'Impudent puss!'

It was so wonderful not to be quarrelling with him, she wanted the moment to go on for ever. Her lips parted of their own accord and it was as if he could not resist. His mouth placed a swift, brushing caress on them. 'Don't tempt me in office hours, Miss Bell.'

A joke, but sufficient to remind her of the time, the place and the man's status relative to her own. 'I have a lunch engagement, damn it, otherwise I'd take you out somewhere. I may be back late, too. If there are callers, tell them to contact me tomorrow.' He went to the door and turned. 'This evening I'm visiting Diane at the hospital. Will you come with me? I'm sure a fresh face would brighten her up.'

Put that way, she could hardly refuse. 'What time?'

'I can go when I choose. Stay on instead of going home and I'll come in for you. Use Diane's office.' He half closed the door, opened it again and said, 'Have I told you how grateful I am to you for giving up a day to help me? By the way, I intend to pay you for it.'

'Please don't bother. I——'

'If you do it for nothing, I can't ask you to help me out again, can I?' A brief smile and he was gone.

Throughout the afternoon the girls with whom she used to work called in to see her. One of them was Mary.

'Heard about Ron Bradwell?' she asked.

'I was wondering about him,' Ilona admitted. 'I haven't seen him since I came this morning, and his office has been empty each time I've passed it.'

'He's gone. One day he didn't come in and he hasn't been in since. So we've all assumed he's been sacked.'

'But why?' Ilona asked. 'I didn't like him as a man, but as a personnel manager, he was quite effective.'

Mary shrugged. 'Don't ask me why. We're mystified. None of us liked him, either, A new man's starting Monday.' She yawned. 'Thank goodness it's Friday! Mr Warrick's been working me off my feet. He thinks so fast, I just can't keep up with him. Odd, isn't it, how you always were the only one—Diane apart—who could match his pace, yet you were the one he fired? Talking of Diane, she's been away for some time now. He's been like a bear with a sore foot, biting everyone's head off. We think he's worried stiff about her. Oh, well, must get back to the prison without bars.'

Ilona smiled. 'Is that what they call the general office now?'

'Well, it's not that bad. But you know Mr Warrick—a perfectionist if there ever was one. You must come up to his standard, though.'

Ilona tried to shrug off the compliment. 'Great for me!'

Mary caught the sarcasm, but could not see the flash of pleasure which shot through Ilona's body at her words.


Drake did not return until it was time to go home. He kept his promise and walked into Diane's office as Ilona was holding up her powder compact.

'Don't bother with that. We're going to my place first.'

Her compact snapped shut. 'Why?'

'Food, that's why.' He strolled towards her. 'Did you think I had in mind one of those "tender love scenes" with which our cat-and-dog relationship seems highlighted?'

His cynicism about their relationship hurt. 'Surely you mean haunted?' she hit back.

'Are you trying to tell me you don't enjoy my kisses?' he demanded.

There was a knock at his door and he cursed under his breath.

'Shall I see who it is?' she asked.

'I'll go. I don't need to be over-protected by my stand-in secretary, even if she is a mouse with the aggression-potential of a tigress guarding her cubs.' The knock was repeated. 'I wouldn't like anyone calling on me, whether employee or visitor, to be torn to pieces by her before my very eyes.'

'Don't be silly,' she said.

'Arrogant I may be,' was his reply as he walked towards the connecting door, 'but *never* silly. Remember that in our future relationship, Miss Bell.'

Ilona frowned. Future relationship? Try as she might, to her sorrow she could see none where she and Drake Warrick were concerned.


When Drake stood back to allow her to enter his apartment, he asked, 'Where shall we go—to the large room, my study or,' with a glinting smile, 'the kitchen? In which place would you feel happiest?'

'I've never seen your kitchen.' She flashed him a smile. 'Since it's almost certainly full of modern equipment, which I couldn't stand——'

'Technological gadgetry you once called it,' he interrupted. 'Well, I assure you it is.'

'Then your study, please. But, Drake, I'm not really hungry. Honest.' She smiled at his frown.

'Would you prefer a snack? Sandwiches and coffee?'

'Just right.'

Soon they were sitting in armchairs facing each other, eating sandwiches from plates on small tables beside them. Drake poured the coffee and as they drank it, he asked, 'Sure you've had enough to eat?'

'Absolutely sure. I have a small appetite.'

He leant forward and his expression brought the colour sweeping over her cheeks. 'For food—or love?'

'For the first, of course. The second——' She shook her head shyly.

'I suppose only your boy-friend could answer that?'

It was a question which called for either denial or agreement. She could not agree because it would not be truthful. If she denied it, he would believe her as little now as he had before, so she sighed instead and muttered, 'Maybe.'

He rose slowly and came to stand in front of her. 'Maybe,' he echoed mockingly. 'Maybe I should ask myself. I've behaved to you like a lover many times in the past weeks, haven't I? And wasn't it only this afternoon in Diane's office that you had the audacity to tell me you didn't enjoy my kisses?'

She grew confused by his words, his proximity. 'I—I didn't say that. I——' His arms went round her and she was pulled against him. She strained away. 'I didn't mean that I did . . .'

He ignored her resistance and his mouth found her ear, nuzzling it and leaving it throbbing as he explored her throat revealed by her thrown-back head.

'The hospital,' she murmured indistinctly. 'Drake, we must go——'

'Soon,' he murmured, 'soon.' His lips brushed her eyes, her cheeks, her chin. He said against her mouth, 'Tell me something,' but what it was he wanted her to know, he did not explain. His mouth teased hers until her lips parted and his came over them, possessing her mouth deeply. His hands were possessive, too, running over her and tracing the sensual enticements of her body.

Her fingers found his shoulders and she clung to their solidity, gaining strength from his strength to reinforce her weakening limbs. She could not have made it plainer if she had tried how much she welcomed and enjoyed his kisses. If her yielding, joyful response was the answer to his question, then he must know by now without a trace of doubt the message she was trying to convey.

'My sweet one,' he murmured, burying his face in the hollow of her neck, 'your appetite for love can no longer be in doubt. I need no other man to tell me that about you.'

No other man could, she was going to say, but his lips over hers again prevented it. 'Drake,' she whispered, her heart pounding, 'we must stop.'

'Yes, yes.' He put her an arm's length away. Contact was cut. The action and the trace of irritation—or was it self-reproach?—in his tone made her feel strangely cold and apprehensive.

They had been behaving like lovers, but lovers they most decidedly were not. In a moment they would be on their way to see the woman he really loved. So why, she asked herself tormentedly as she tried to tidy her hair and watched as he pulled on the jacket he had discarded, has he made such passionate love to me?

Diane looked pale. Around her shoulders was a bedjacket, a

delicate shade of pink which echoed her fragile femininity.

A book was open in front of her, but it was doubtful if she had been reading it. Drake entered the ward first. Ilona, behind him, watched as Diane's face came to life when he walked in.

'Oh, my dear,' she said, a flush tinting the white cheeks, 'how kind of you——' Ilona came into view and she exclaimed, 'How good to see you both! Not just one, but two friends.'

Ilona felt her empty-handedness intensely and apologised, starting to explain the reason. Drake interrupted, 'Put all the blame on me. The poor girl came to my rescue at short notice today and I've worked her to a standstill. She hardly had a chance to blink, let alone go out and buy flowers.'

'Don't worry, Ilona,' Diane urged. 'Drake sends me so many the room is like a florist's shop. Not to mention paying for all this . . .' Her arm indicated the privacy, the comfort that only money could buy.

So, Ilona thought hopelessly, he pays for her private treatment, as well as lavishing money on gifts. And no doubt, also pays her salary. He might make love to me, but his heart is, without doubt, reserved for this young widow in the hospital bed.

'Sit here,' Diane told Ilona, 'and you, Drake, here,' indicating the chair at the other side of her bed. 'Now I can look at you both. You bring with you the freshness and vitality of the outside world. Somehow,' she frowned, and a passing sadness clouded her still-beautiful face, 'in here, it recedes.' Her head went back against the pillows. 'Sometimes I wonder if I'll ever see it again.'

Drake did not look concerned at her words, nor did he utter the usual placebos. He merely said, 'There's no doubt about that. It's only a matter of time and patience.'

Her hand reached out and his covered hers. 'How long will you keep my job open for me, Drake?'

'For ever, if necessary,' he said simply.

Ilona thought, I shouldn't be here . . .

Then Diane, perhaps in her weakened state more sensitive to changes of mood, seemed to know of her discomfiture. 'Tell me all about yourself, Ilona. How's the agency going?'

'Fine at the moment but, unfortunately, its future is doomed.' Ilona tried to speak lightly. 'I'm under notice to quit the cottage. I'll have to find somewhere else to work. Perhaps I could move in here?'

Diane laughed, then became serious. 'So you'll be without a home?' Ilona nodded. 'That's terrible. Drake, can't you do anything? You seem to have the magic touch where getting people out of difficulties is concerned.'

Across the bed Ilona's eyes met Drake's. His brows lifted. 'I doubt,' he said, 'if Ilona would agree with you. She seems to regard me as the devil in person.'

Ilona saw that his hand still covered Diane's and said, 'It doesn't really matter, does it, how I regard you?'

A nurse knocked and entered. 'Time?' asked Drake, rising at once.

'Two visitors today, Mrs Ayrton?' said the nurse, smiling.

Diane nodded. 'A pleasant surprise. Drake,' Diane's arms reached up to curl round his neck. The nurse went out. Drake bent down and Diane said, 'I want to thank you again and again, Drake, for all this, for—for everything.' Her forehead went against his cheek and Ilona could hear the suppressed sob.

'My dear,' he whispered, 'you must be happy. You're getting better now.'

She nodded, then whispered some words into his ear, her moist eyes lighting up. Ilona could not bear to look at them. She called softly, ' 'Bye, Diane. All the best.'

'Please come again,' Diane's voice drifted after her.

A few moments later Drake joined Ilona in the corridor. His eyes were serious, but his expression could not be interpreted. His arm went automatically round Ilona's waist. No lover now, this man. It was the gesture of a friend.

'I'll take you home,' was all he said.

They spoke little on the way. Drake seemed preoccupied. Ilona stared out at the darkness, thinking ... thinking suddenly of what Mary had told her.

'What happened to Ron Bradwell, Drake?' she asked.

He frowned, as if his thoughts had been far away. Back at the hospital, probably, Ilona thought.

'Bradwell? I fired him.' A moment's silence, then, 'He betrayed a confidence.' Drake stopped and after some time went on, 'If you want to know, he told your landlord you were not the real tenant, a fact he had learned from Lucia, and that you were running a business from the cottage. He was instrumental in your being given notice to quit.'

'But why fire him on my account? If he's hurt me— which he has—what difference does it make to you? I mean nothing to you, so why should his betrayal of me cause you to dismiss him?'

'If you were to think calmly, instead of rushing for some inexplicable reason to the man's defence, you'd realise that if he can betray someone like you simply out of spite, he's hardly a reliable person for me to employ in such an important post as personnel manager.'

Ilona had to admit that what he said was true. His firing of Ron Bradwell had no real connection with her. However, all she said was, 'I wasn't rushing to the man's defence. I hate him. He frightens me.' Then she remembered all the things Ron Bradwell had told Drake about her. 'Now perhaps you'll believe me when I tell you how much the man has lied about me.'

'Yes,' he said tonelessly. 'Even the story he told me about the little "mouse" who loved her boss was a lie.' He waited, and she wondered why. Was he expecting her to say, 'No, it wasn't a lie' 'It was true,' Drake went on, 'But was it also a lie that when he went to your cottage, you ran into your boy-friend's arms?'

'No,' she was forced to admit dully, 'I ran to Ray, of course I did. What else did you expect me to do when I'd nearly been throttled?'

Drake turned left on to the narrow single-lane road, then left again to drive along the track which led to the cottage. He braked. There was silence and darkness all round.

'Ilona?' She looked at him. 'Thanks for today, for your help, for coming with me to see Diane.'

'It was nothing. Well, good——'

Her shoulders were caught by strong hands which ran upwards to settle round her neck. The fingers moved, pressing against the pulse which throbbed madly under the touch of those hands. The world drifted away. 'Throttled,' she had just said. This man she loved ... she wouldn't have minded ... whatever he chose to do to her, she didn't care

... Not even about the way he kissed her so deeply as if slaking his thirst, the way his hands invaded so intimately the neckline of her dress, finding the firm curve of her breast. Not even the way he was using her to assuage his masculine desires which were so thwarted at present by the illness of the woman he loved.

He said thickly, releasing her, 'I think we'd better go in.'

'No need for you to come,' she said, emerging reluctantly from the dreamlike state into which his lovemaking had taken her. 'I can see myself in.'

He ignored her words and got out. Ilona walked carefully in the darkness, aided by the flashlight which Drake had brought from the car. She stopped, gazed at the path, then at the area around the tap in the front garden.

'Strange,' she said. 'It's damp, as though someone's been running it. I've been away all day, so who——?' She looked around. 'There's something not quite right. I can't pinpoint it ... Drake,' she was frightened now, glad he was with her, 'can't you feel it?'

He did not reply, but flashed the light at the lock. She turned the key and stepped into the living-room. 'Please, Drake,' her courage was leaving her, 'will you light the lamp?'

He did so, and as the light increased, picking up shadows and throwing them around, her eyes swung to the kitchen door. She caught her breath. Someone *had* been there. There was a trail of dust on the carpet from the front door to the kitchen. A fainthearted attempt had been made to clean the place.

'The builders,' she cried, 'they came after all! Someone must have given them a key.' She swung towards Drake. 'The landlord—that was who! Yesterday I sent the workmen away. Today they must have called, found me out and gone for a key to start their work.'

She ran into the kitchen. 'They've installed it,' she cried with a touch of hysteria, 'they've put in the sink unit!' She turned a tap. 'No water—at least I've been spared that.' The trail of dust seemed to go towards the back bedroom. Ilona followed it and found footmarks on the carpet leading up to the rear wall. 'They've been in here, too. But what have they done?' She peered out of the window into the darkness. 'There's something there.'

She rushed past a silent Drake and out of the front door. Round the back she saw a sight that made her go cold. Stacked neatly against the wall of the cottage were builders' implements, bags of cement, a wheelbarrow and an extending ladder. Jutting out from the cottage walls was a raised area of newly-laid concrete. One day it would be the basis of a floor, an extension leading off the back bedroom. The cement which glistened wetly in the light from the semi-circle of moon, was kept in place by three planks of wood resting on their edges.

It was the way the fourth side nestled against the cottage, as though it actually belonged, that roused Ilona to an uncontainable fury. She ran to the building implements, seized a spade, ran back to the cement and swung the spade high.

It slashed down in a swooping arc, sliding its way through the painstakingly levelled surface. As she lifted the spade to make another attack, some of the cement came with it, making it just a little heavier. She was not deterred.

Down the spade came again, digging deeply; again and again until all over it were holes and dents and slashes. Cement sprayed everywhere, leaping on to her hair, spattering her dress and coating her shoes. But she was unaware of everything except that the area of half set concrete in front of her now more resembled a lumpy, stirred-up bowl of porridge rather than the meticulously-flattened, professionally-finished basis of a floor.

Footsteps came running and a voice shouted, 'Stop that, do you hear? Drop it, drop that spade! What the blazes do you think you're doing? Stop it, you little fool!'

One more lift, one more vicious slash and concrete spurted again, splashing her face. The spade was torn from her hands and thrown down. Her shoulders were caught in a vice and she was shaken with a violence which set her teeth chattering. She gasped, fighting for the breath she had expended during her few mad moments of devouring revenge.

The shaking stopped at last. Drake grasped her wrist, pushing her in front of him round the side of the cottage to the front and in through the door.

'You destructive, crazy idiot!' he shouted. 'You've undone hours of diligent work. By your arrant stupidity, you've thrown away time, money, planning and labour.'

'Why should you worry?' she shrieked back, breaking free. 'It's not *your* money or *your* time. It's the landlord's.' She found a handkerchief and tried to wipe away the cement which was caking her cheeks. 'I'm going to Mrs Macey's cottage and I'm going to phone the rent man, Mr Elson. I'm going to demand that he tells me the telephone number of the landlord, Mr Moorley. Then I'm going to phone Mr Moorley and tell him exactly what I think of him and his improvements. Then I'm coming back and I'm going to do to that sink unit what I did to that concrete floor. And this time you're not going to stop me!'

She turned to open the front door, but found her way barred. Drake was there, his back to the door, arms folded, legs apart. 'Try to get past me and see what happens, Miss Ilona Bell.'

Her eyes opened wider, challenging. 'You can't stop me. You can't prevent me from calling my landlord and——'

'You're speaking to your landlord right now, Miss Bell. Tell me, what else do you want to say to him?'

# CHAPTER TEN

ILONA stared, hand to her throat. *'You're* my landlord? But you can't be!'

'Although it dismays you to know it,' he said coldly, 'I'm telling you the truth. I bought the cottage for next to nothing. I reminded the former owner, Mr Moorley, of the poor state of the cottage, the absence of the most elementary amenities and so on.'

Ilona remembered how Drake had often wandered round the cottage, but she still found it difficult to take in his words. 'The alterations—did you give instructions to have them done?' Drake nodded. 'Even though you knew I didn't want them?'

He smiled faintly. 'Even though I knew. Your opinion isn't the only one that counts any more, is it? If,' his eyes goaded, 'at all.'

The words excluded her. Was that what he intended? 'Now I see,' she said, her eyes staring dazedly, 'why you got me out of the way today, by asking for my help. It was to enable the builders to work without interruption from me.' He did not deny it. 'It was a miserable trick,' she accused. He did not deny that statement, either. 'Are you,' she rallied, 'going to have me thrown out?'

He took his time, eyeing her, seeing the cement splashes, the air of fear which had taken the place of the wild anger. It seemed he had decided to play on that fear. 'It depends,' he said at last.

'On what?'

'On whether you can learn to tolerate my presence here, day and—maybe—night.'

This was worse, much worse than she had imagined. 'You're actually going to *live* here?'

'It sounds as though the idea horrifies you.'

How could she tell him, The idea of having you take up residence here frightens me more than anything I've ever known. It frightens me because we would be in constant

147

contact by day and you'd only be a few dozen paces away
from me at night. It would wreck my sleep in the long dark
hours and take away my peace of mind every waking
moment. She sidetracked to deflect him, saying belligerently,

'These changes you're intending to inflict on me, how far
would you go?'

'Didn't Mr Elson tell you?'

'So he was in on this, too?'

'Of course. He had to know about the change of ownership. But I swore him to secrecy.' His hands slipped into
his pockets. 'I figured that if you knew I had become your
landlord, you'd pack your bags and go, making yourself
into a homeless, rootless roamer of the world quite
pointlessly, and purely out of pique.'

He had, as usual, guessed right. If she went, it would
not be because she wanted to, but out of a kind of twisted
spite.

'Mr Elson told me the landlord wanted electricity and
water laid on,' Ilona said. 'Also a proper toilet.' She recalled other things Mr Elson had said. Her eyes widened
as the fear returned. 'He also told me that the landlord
wanted me out in order to sell the place. You're the new
landlord. Does that mean *you* want me out?'

'As I've already said,' his tone was indifferent, 'that's
entirely up to you. Actually, Elson was talking about two
different landlords. The first—Mr Moorley—did give you
notice to quit, because he discovered via Ron Bradwell
what was going on. He decided to sell. I bought the place
from him, and that made me the second landlord. I was the
one who wanted the alterations.' He added quietly, 'I intend to carry them out, Ilona.'

Again she panicked. Her world was crumbling, her
privacy, her simple, uncomplicated way of life was slipping
out of reach like a child running into a road full of traffic.
There had to be a way to save it, to pull it back from complete extinction by the relentless build-up of Drake's
sophisticated, expensive, twenty-first century manner of
living.

She cried in anguish, 'By installing these so-called improvements, you're violating my personal liberty, and tak-

ing away my freedom to choose how I conduct my life.'

'Nonsense,' he dismissed. His brutal overriding of her objections showed how little he understood of her way of thinking. 'Instead of complaining,' he said briskly, 'count the blessings I'm bestowing on you. Just consider ... I'm giving you back your security of tenure—no fear any more of being made homeless. There will be no need for you to trek across the world in search of a personal, unattainable, undefined dream. Also, I'll be easing your life by freeing you from the drudgery you've had to endure.'

'The life I lead isn't drudgery to me,' she retaliated. 'Doing things with your own two hands is far more satisfying than filling a machine, switching on and walking away.'

He shook his head as though irritated by her lack of comprehension.

'You know my views on modern technological aids,' she persisted, 'yet you propose to wreck this cottage, its atmosphere, its very soul, by introducing them one by one. You also seem to be intending to deprive me of my privacy, and you know how much I cherish that.'

'Isn't privacy something you can share?'

'I love my solitude, too, and no one can share that.'

His lips thinned at her stubborn attitude. 'You'll become reconciled,' he said tersely.

'No, never!' she cried.

He drew a sharp breath. His anger surfaced now and he went closer, grasping her shoulders. 'I could shake you, woman. Can't you see I'm on the level?'

'When you bought the place without telling me? I don't call that being honest.'

'Don't you see,' he said, his grip tightening, 'that my action was not entirely selfish? That I bought it partly to help you? Though God knows why, in view of your lack of gratitude. I haven't yet turned you out——'

'But the time might come,' she interrupted, 'as I'm sure it will. What about Diane? When she recovers, you'll want to bring her here. Do you expect me to share with you *both*?'

He pushed her away. 'If and when the time comes to discuss that particular subject, we shall do so. Anyway, your boy-friend won't be prepared to wait for you for ever.

The time will come when you'll gladly give all this up to run into his waiting arms.'

'Let's keep Ray Hale out of this,' she snapped. 'If you refuse to talk about Diane, then I won't talk about Ray.'

Drake's shoulders lifted and fell, reflecting his indifference.

She taunted, 'You'll never adjust to a life of simplicity. Not only are you used to comfort, but luxury as well. I've seen that with my own eyes. You yourself said there's an unbridgeable chasm between us.'

He walked to the window and looked out at the fields behind the cottage. It was silvered by moonlight. 'Did I?' he said tonelessly.

There was a long silence. Ilona sat in the rocking chair, its movement no longer soothing but becoming part of her agitation. 'What about the rent?' she asked. 'In view of the so-called improvements, will you increase it?'

'I will not increase it. The cheque should be made payable to me personally and sent to me by post.'

His formality hurt her. He was acting the high-handed landlord and she longed to goad him in revenge. She affected a yawn. 'I'm tired—I've had a long day. Thank you for bringing me home.'

He did not move but said to the window pane, 'As broad a set of hints as I've ever received.'

She would end his amusement. 'What did you expect,' she asked cuttingly, 'an invitation to join me in my bed? After all, it wouldn't be out of place, really, would it?' He swung round at last and inwardly she shrank from his coldness. 'You've used me this evening,' she persisted nonetheless, 'and countless other times, to assuage your suppressed sexual desire in the absence of Diane, the woman you really love.'

His jaw gritted. 'You,' he rasped, 'are a sour-tongued, embittered little prig!'

He strode to the door and left her alone.

It was during a restless night that Ilona heard a disturbing noise. It seemed to come from below her window at the rear of the cottage.

There were muffled footsteps, the rustle of the hedge

although there was no wind, the faint clang of something metallic. There were, she knew, the building contractors'' implements stacked against the cottage wall. She wondered angrily if Drake had contacted the builders and asked them to come while she slept and inspect the damage she had caused to the wet cement.

She opened the window wider. The noise must have warned whoever it was—if indeed there was anyone—and they must have slipped away, because although Ilona listened intently, there were no more noises.

The incident, however, both annoyed and worried her. In all the weeks she had spent there alone, not once had she felt fear. Now she was aware of a thrust of anxiety, and it had not entirely left her by morning.

Still annoyed, she decided, before having her breakfast, to take action to prevent a second disturbed night being forced on her. Hurrying to Mrs Macey's cottage, she used the spare key to open the door. She called out, letting Mrs Macey know she was there, and received a cheerful reply from upstairs. 'Carry on and use the phone, dear,' the voice called. 'Just having my morning cup of tea.'

Ilona dialled and waited. When the call was answered, she did not apologise for disturbing Drake so early, or for not waiting until he was at the office. He sounded brisk enough to have been up and about for hours.

'Would you call off your spies?' she demanded, on the offensive at once.

'What spies?'

'You know very well,' she stormed. 'The builders, that's who, the ones you told to come and look at the damage I caused. Someone sneaked there in the night to have a look —I heard them. They picked up the shovel I used. They certainly made a noise, although it sounded as though they tried to be quiet so I wouldn't hear.'

There was a brief silence, then, 'Thanks for telling me.'

'As if you didn't know!' she cried, but heard in reply the sound of his receiver hitting its cradle.

After breakfast, Ilona walked to Ray's father's farm. Ray was there, as usual going through the books. 'Hi, love,' he said, his smile warm. 'Getting yourself in the right mood for Saturday?'

'For Sat——? Oh, the fête.' Only a few hours to the afternoon she was dreading!

'Don't forget the offer of making use of Mrs Bryant's favourite dress shop. And the services of the vicar's wife's hairdresser.'

'Oh, Ray, I don't know . . .'

Sensing a threatened change of heart, Ray took Ilona's hands. 'You can't back out now. The tickets are selling like bottles of vintage wine!' He squeezed her fingers. 'Promise you won't back out?'

She sighed. 'All right. But that's not what I came about.' She sank into a chair at the table and he sat down again. 'Ray, I've got a new landlord.' Her voice faltered. 'It's Drake Warrick. He's bought the cottage from Mr Moorley.'

Ray rubbed his forehead in a slightly harassed gesture. 'I did hear something about that. But it's good from your point of view, surely? At least you won't be turned out.'

'I haven't decided whether or not to stay.'

He looked at her incredulously. 'You wouldn't leave just because there's been a change of landlord—and for the better, too? I know how much you love the place——'

'As it is, yes, but not as Drake Warrick plans to alter it.'

'You don't know till it's done, now do you?'

'So you're on Drake's side? All right,' as Ray grew agitated, 'I'll probably stay. But Ray, last night something, or someone, disturbed me. I was asleep and there was this noise. I've never been afraid being alone before, but——'

'I'm glad you told me, love. To be honest,' he looked a little uncomfortable, 'Mr Warrick did advise me to keep an eye on you. If it happens again, scoot along to Mrs Macey's —doesn't matter what time—and ring me from there. You've got a key, haven't you? Tell her today what it's all about, then she won't think someone's breaking into her place.'

Ilona nodded, thanked him for his advice and left. She went straight along to Mrs Macey's cottage, but there was no answer to her knock.

As she walked away, she recalled Ray's reminder about Mrs Bryant's offer. Since the fête was the next day but one, it occurred to her that she should contact Mrs Bryant.

The call was answered with Mrs Bryant's usual precision

and clear articulation. 'I should be delighted to accompany you, Miss Bell. Mrs Sanders has an excellent eye for the style which best matches the personality, and I'm sure she will be only too pleased to lend you a dress for the occasion. Shall we say this afternoon at three o'clock? About your hair—do you wish me to make an appointment for you with the hairdresser?' Eagerly Ilona agreed. It would save her the trouble, she said, and meant it.

'Saturday morning at, shall we say, eleven-thirty?' Mrs Bryant suggested. 'Washed and set? Just a simple style, I think, don't you?'

Again Ilona agreed, glad for once to go along with Mrs Bryant's rather managing manner and sighing with relief at having the matter taken out of her hands.

It took Mrs Sanders exactly an hour to find the dress which suited exactly both the occasion and, as she called it, Ilona's 'refreshingly innocent' personality. The dress was of pale cream silk jersey, the neckline reaching high, almost to her chin.

The skirt was ankle-length, the sleeves were long, the material clinging chastely yet provocatively to her slender shape. When Ilona said she would do her best to return the dress in a near-perfect condition, Mrs Sanders said,

'Oh, keep it, dear. Look upon it as an act of charity— not to you, but towards the fund for which you are undertaking this—well,' she laughed, 'speaking as a woman, I can only call "self-sacrifice"!'

'Oh, I wouldn't say that,' said Mrs Bryant. 'Miss Bell is a thoroughly nice girl. Nothing terrible could *ever* happen to her because she just doesn't invite trouble—not like some girls.'

The two women nodded and spent their time while Ilona changed into her own clothes commenting on the low moral standards of people today. Mrs Sanders folded the dress with loving care and Mrs Bryant drove Ilona home. She reminded Ilona of her appointment with the hairdresser and drove away.

Admiring the dress, Ilona hung it in the cupboard in her bedroom, then she went downstairs to the room which was once Lucia's. Among the shoes which had been left behind was a pair of white evening sandals. To Ilona's surprise, she discovered that they fitted her own feet, plus or minus a little discomfort.

Having settled the matter, Ilona looked at her face in Lucia's old dressing-table mirror. She was not particularly pleased with the reflection which gazed back so critically. She shrugged. Whoever 'won' her would only have to endure looking at that face for a few hours, and he—she had acknowledged with resignation that it would be a man —would hardly have time to wonder about any blemishes which might lie behind the layer of make-up she would apply.

Feeling hungry, she decided to have an earlier supper. The fire which heated the cooking stove was low, so she stoked it with the small amount of coal in the bucket, and went round to the back of the cottage to refill it from the coal shed.

She noticed in passing that the builders had not been back to resume their work, nor to repair the damage. This was strange, she reflected, in view of their nocturnal inspection which had awoken her. She supposed Drake must have contacted the builders, instructing them not to return until he could be certain that its occupant would not again damage their work beyond repair once they had gone away. In other words, she thought, he doesn't trust me. But after her action the night before, could she blame him?

The fire burned with a satisfactory crackle when replenished with more coal. Ilona put into the stove the cheese pudding she had made, then peeled a couple of potatoes, slicing them into long, thin pieces. It was while she was frying them that a key turned in the lock. Afraid, she froze, in her hand a scoopful of fried potatoes hovering over the pan.

It was not imagination, nor was it a ghost who walked in. It was Drake. He came to stand at the kitchen door and their eyes met. Hers were wide with disbelief. His were cool and steady. At last he said, motioning with his hand, 'They'll all burn if you don't lift them out of the fat.' Then he turned away.

Quickly she removed the last of the fried potatoes from the pan. Piling them on a dish, she pushed them on to the lowest shelf of the stove to keep warm underneath the cheese pudding which was bubbling and almost ready.

She left the kitchen, and looked round the living-room, expecting to find him there. The room was empty, so she hurried into Lucia's old room. He was there, his suitcase was flung wide. He had found some empty drawers and was proceeding to fill them with clothes.

Ilona choked, 'What are you doing here? You can't stay. This is *my*——'

'Home?' he broke in. 'Ah, but,' his smile was a little twisted, 'it's *my* cottage, which means I have the right to come and go at will. I did warn you. Or am I,' he looked round the room, 'occupying someone else's territory?'

As frigidly as she could, she asked, 'What exactly do you mean?'

'The boy-friend? Maybe he comes here sometimes, stays the night? Is that why you're so put out at my appearance?'

Bringing her teeth together with a sharp snap, she reached out. There was a glass ornament on the chest of drawers next to the door. Her fingers gripped it, her arm lifted—and Drake lunged at her, wrenching the ornament away and twisting her arm behind her back.

'My word, you need a strong hand, you fiery, vicious little she-dragon! "Mouse" did they call you once? Never was a word more misapplied!'

'You're hurting me,' she choked.

'Say you're sorry and I'll let you go.'

'No, I'm not sorry,' she flung back, writhing with the pain. 'You threw insults at me, so I'm justified in throwing things at you. Let me go!'

After a few tantalising seconds of maintaining his savage hold, he released her. 'All right, so I throw insults at you. But at least they're only words. Yet you try and chuck back something which, on target, could be lethal.'

She rubbed her arm and shoulder. 'H-how can I type,' she asked with a catch in her voice, 'if you turn brutal and immobilise my arm? How can I carry on my agency if my arm hurts so much I can't work?'

He said nothing. With his fists on his hips, he looked her over. Ilona returned the compliment, noting his polo-necked green shirt and his brown jacket with buttoned pockets and long zip-fastener, the dark pants that fitted so casually yet so well.

Ilona pushed back her brown hair, revealing flushed cheeks.

Her large brown eyes held his. 'I'm cooking my supper. Do you want some?'

'No, thanks. I'm going out.'

'To see Diane?'

'To the hospital, yes, but this time to take Diane home.'

In spite of a stab of jealousy, Ilona's face brightened. 'She's well enough to go home?'

Noncommittally he answered, 'She's well enough to be discharged. She's been walking about the ward for a day or two now. I'll eat at her place.' He turned back to his task.

Ilona knew he was dismissing her, but she had to ask, 'Drake, you can't be intending to live here?'

He carried on unpacking. 'I've already told you, I'm free to come and go as I like.'

She whispered, 'You're coming back here tonight? To *sleep*?'

He turned to her, eyebrow lifted. 'Why, can you think of something better we could do?'

She swung away. 'I'm hungry,' she snapped.

'So am I,' he called after her tauntingly, 'but food wouldn't satisfy *my* hunger.'

At ten o'clock, Ilona thought of going to bed. She had realised with a sinking heart that there would be complications.

In normal circumstances she would bring in pails of water, heating it in pans. Then she would wash in the kitchen, since it saved her the trouble of carrying heavy containers of water upstairs. Now she could not do that. Any moment Drake might come in and make for the kitchen to heat milk, or toast bread at the fire.

Everything would change while he was there. Her privacy would go, her peace of mind melt away ...

Moments later he came in. Ilona stayed in the rocking chair, moving gently, watching him with big, apprehensive eyes. In his hand was a shopping bag. He held it up.

'My food, not to be confused with yours. Where shall I
put it?'

'In the kitchen, I suppose.'

He was in there some time. When she crept across the
room to see what he was doing, he was writing on the
paper around the tins or the boxes of food he had bought.

'Writing "X, my mark"?' she asked sarcastically.

He swung round and lifted his arm, grasping the tin on
which he had been scribbling. She ducked as he had done
earlier when she had threatened to throw an ornament
at him.

'You see,' he said with hard eyes, 'two can play at that
game.' Slowly his arm lowered. 'You're an impudent little
minx, aren't you? "X, my mark"!' He repeated her jeering
words.

' "Mouse",' she prompted.

His head shook slowly. 'Oh no, not mouse, not any
more. You've got an aggressive streak in you I've never
ever encountered in a female before.'

'And you've known a lot of "females"?'

He concentrated on writing his initials. 'A few. Here and
there.'

'M'm. Ron Bradwell told me.' He looked at her and the
coldness was back. His eyebrows lifted questioningly.
'About you and women.' She paused, considering, then
decided to take the plunge. 'That you set them alight, get
everything from them you wanted, then stood back and
watched them burn.'

'Do go on.'

'Then you would walk away without a stab of conscience.' He regarded her levelly, saying nothing. 'I know
one thing,' she finished defiantly, her heart pounding, 'you
won't set fire to me and watch me burn.'

'I shouldn't bet on that if I were you,' was his cool
response, then his back was turned on her.

Ilona wandered away, sat down and rocked aimlessly in
the chair. That she was deeply disturbed by his presence she
could not deny, but how to overcome her troubled
emotions sufficiently to relax and sleep that night? Knowing he was there below her? Hearing him move in his bed
as she had heard Lucia? Unable to sleep, creeping round

her room and making the floorboards creak above his head?

He came out of the kitchen, looked at her, then at his watch. 'What time do you go to bed?'

'When I feel tired.'

A lift of his shoulders, then, 'Fair enough.' He looked around. 'Isn't there another comfortable chair in the place?'

'Sorry, only the ones at the table.' She pushed herself upright. 'Have the rocking chair.'

'No, thanks. You seem to need its movement to calm your shattered nerves. Have no fear, my love, I won't lay a finger on you. Unless I'm invited.' The last phrase was spoken with a mildly derisive smile.

Ilona rocked back and forth furiously and he laughed out loud. 'You seem to want to hit me.' He bent over her, supporting himself with his hands on the arms of the rocking chair, stilling its movement. 'Carry on. Hit me.'

The challenge in his cool blue eyes and the derision playing about his lips were without doubt meant to goad. Her hand lifted quickly, but it was a defensive, not an offensive action. To her consternation it did make contact with his cheek, but not to hurt. She found it resting there, against the shadow which, even at that hour, pricked against her palm. Involuntarily, the hand began to trace the outline of his jaw—then it stopped abruptly as if surprised at its own presumptuous action.

As she jerked her hand to her lap, he whispered, 'No, no, don't lose contact,' lowering his lips until they rested on hers. Her head turned sideways so suddenly his lips trailed her cheek to settle on her ear, but she pressed her palms against his chest, putting a distance between them.

He was only playing with her. There must be something she could say to hurt him. 'If you want love, go back to Diane.'

He straightened, removing his jacket and throwing it across the table. A simple action, but to Ilona it represented an incontestable statement of his claim to ownership.

He folded his arms and looked down at her, the warmly

caressing look quite gone. 'Alas for you, my insubordinate, unruly tenant, Diane is the last person I can go to. I'm able to go for "love", as you put it, to Diane as much as I can go to that empty fireplace for warmth. From now on, as far as I'm concerned, *love* from Diane is out, extinguished, totally quenched.'

'So,' she flared, 'Ron Bradwell was right. You got what you wanted from her, let her burn, then walked away.'

Her words did not stir his anger as she anticipated. Instead, he said, 'It's ironic. I stop believing in Ron Bradwell's lies, so you jump to the opposite side of the fence and start believing them.' He hitched a thigh on to the corner of the table. 'Now I'll put you in the picture. Diane's been suffering over the past eleven or twelve months from a serious blood disorder.'

'Which is why she's been away so much?'

'Correct.' He hooked his thumbs around the belt at his waist. 'However, thanks to the strides forward made in medical science, and the devotion of the doctors she's consulted, she's slowly and, we hope, surely, fighting the disease. What's more,' he shifted and walked about the room, pausing to look out of the back window at the fading colours of the summer sunset, 'as an unscientific but potent aid to her further recovery, she's also fallen in love —with one of the doctors attending her. He returns her love.'

It took a few moments for the information to make an impression, then Ilona said hoarsely, 'But you've done so much for her. Sent her gifts, helped her financially by continuing to pay her salary ...'

'Yes.' There was a long pause. The sun had slipped below the horizon. 'While Diane was Brian's patient, they had to keep their love a secret. Which was why she whispered the news to me the day you came to visit her at the hospital. Now she's wearing his ring. It's official.'

'I see. I also see it's soured you. For once in your life you've been rejected by a woman and it hurts.' Ilona's voice was still husky. 'I also see why you're coming to me for love.' He gave no response. 'Because you're frustrated,' Ilona added. At last there was a reaction.

- In a few strides he was across the room. Every line of his face was hard. 'If I were you,' he snarled, 'I'd go to bed, while I let you go to bed—alone.'

He went into his bedroom and closed the door.

Washing was not the difficult procedure Ilona had imagined. She brought in the water and heated it. Drake remained in his room.

However, Ilona was taking no chances. Not only did she fasten a notice to the other side of the kitchen door—'Washing in progress. Please keep out'—she pushed boxes and bins against the door so that anyone attempting to enter would find that there was a certain amount of resistance to overcome.

Drake did not even try to come in. Ilona heard him wandering around the living-room. Once there was a noise of amused disgust, the result she assumed, of his having read her notice.

She had to come out of the kitchen in order to go upstairs. She was prepared for that, having brought, besides her nightdress, her bathrobe. He was there, hands slid into the waistband of his pants, watching the kitchen door ease open and watching her creeping out.

He smiled sardonically. 'You disappoint me. I'd expected at least a semi-strip show.' He nodded towards the notice. 'If ever anything was designed to titillate a man's lustful inclinations, it's that.'

'I'm sorry, I didn't mean to—I mean, I've never lived with—lived *in*—the same house as a strange man before, so I——'

He stood stock still. 'Strange man? You call *me* a "strange man"? When you've been in my arms countless times, when I know almost as much about you as a man knows about his woman? When I know the feel of your skin—its delectable smoothness—as well as I know the roughness of my own?'

She gave up expecting him to understand. 'Why are you pretending you don't know what I really mean? Goodnight.'

As she climbed the stairs, she felt his eyes on her all the way.

*

Ilona, however, did not have a 'good night'. There seemed to be no sleep in her. Instead, there was a twisting, turning restlessness which no amount of sheep-counting could overcome.

If only Drake weren't there, she would go downstairs, stir the fire and heat some milk. Half an hour later she decided that, Drake or no Drake, she would have that milk. She crept down the stairs, looked around the empty living-room and went into the kitchen. Filling a cup with milk, she took down a saucepan—and promptly dropped it. The clatter it made in the night silence was enough to wake half the village.

It certainly woke Drake. He came from his room, eyes heavy, hair untidy and, to Ilona's puzzlement, still wearing his dark pants, with a deep blue shirt unbuttoned and hanging free. So he had not undressed. She could not think why.

He ran his fingers through his hair and said touchily, 'Anything wrong?'

'Just—thirsty. Thought I'd heat myself some milk.'

He looked around. 'What on?' She pointed. 'That thing?' He felt it. 'It's cold. The fire's out.'

'No. Damped down for the night.' Ilona pushed a poker through the bars and slowly the fire kindled.

'It'll take hours on that,' he commented.

'What if it does? I didn't ask you to get up.'

'I was only half asleep anyway. And don't tell me *you* were dreaming sweet dreams. Your constant writhing in sleepless agony was enough to keep a log of wood awake.'

The milk *was* taking a long time to heat.

'I can't help it if I can't sleep.'

'Can't you?' He wandered to stand beside her and she held herself taut. In his untidy, heavy-eyed state, with his strong-muscled, dangerously attractive body within reach, her responses leapt into life like the fire at which she was staring. 'I can think,' he went on, his eyes gleaming with an inward fire, 'of a well-tried, entirely satisfactory way to help us both on the long journey to the land of dreams.'

'For heaven's sake,' she said in as bored a voice as she could manufacture, 'you're so frustrated you'd even patron-ise a——'

A hand clapped over her mouth, another gripped like an iron band around her waist. Her mouth was freed, only to be imprisoned again by two brutal lips prising hers apart. His free hand, impatient of her robe and gown, forced its way to the silk-smooth, rounded softness beneath.

Her arms, creeping round his neck, locked together. As the potency of his lovemaking broke down her barriers with relentless sureness, the ecstasy aroused by his skilled manipulation of her emotions made her pull him closer, yielding more willingly with every stroking touch.

There was a warning, bubbling noise, followed by a pungent smell. 'The milk!' Ilona cried, trying to fight free of Drake's arms. 'It's boiling over.' His hold loosened and she twisted round to lift the saucepan high.

'A cloth,' she said, 'anything to mop up this mess before it burns on hard.'

He looked around, his face like a storm about to break. He tore a handful of paper towels from a roll on the wall and handed them to her. The fire was by now burning so brightly the milk had almost dried of its own accord.

He said, with ill-concealed impatience, handing her the half-filled cup, 'Drink your milk, or what's left of it. Then we can finish what we've started. Maybe after that we shall both be able to get some sleep.'

She stared at him. 'You can't mean it?'

He folded his arms and looked her over, dishevelled as she was from his lovemaking. 'I've never meant anything more sincerely in my life. You've allowed me to progress thus far with you. You're surely woman enough not to be squeamish or surprised when I say I want to continue to the ultimate and most satisfying conclusion?'

The milk slid down her throat and was gone. It did not help at all. Drake had aroused her to such a state that, short of complying with his suggestion, she would have to scrub the cottage from top to bottom to work off the longings and desires which were by now screaming to get out.

He took the empty cup and pulled her back into his arms, but she knew that if his lips so much as brushed hers, she would have to fight him like a tigress.

To avoid such a conflict, she struggled free. 'First you treat me as if I were some kind of tramp, then you suggest using me as a—a therapeutic outlet for your thwarted passions!'

She moved past him into the living-room, drawing herself in to avoid touching him. The slightest contact would have had her innermost longings crying out to be satisfied and there was no other place in the whole world in which that would be accomplished except back in his arms.

Facing him, she challenged, 'What makes you think I'd agree to sleep with you?'

'What was that vibrant, glowing woman doing in my arms in there if not asking to be taken into my bed?'

Asking, pleading—no, crying out for your love, your expression of love in words as well as deeds, for a positive commitment on your part that there would be, could be, no other woman for you *ever* until the day you ... No, it was impossible to speak those words to him, either now or at any other time.

All right, so Diane's heart was not for him, she'd given it to another. But for Drake there would be other women, many others. He would make them his and walk away. Hadn't she been warned? Her subconscious mind obliterated at that particular moment just who had given the warning.

Her head drooped as she gazed blankly into the enormously empty grate. 'Reflex action,' she mumbled, answering his question. 'The spontaneous reaction of my body to the stimulus you were providing and over which I had no control.'

'As scientific an explanation,' he scoffed, 'of a woman saying "yes" without words as any I've yet heard.'

'All right, so you don't believe me.' She was going to have to fight him—and herself—harder, because when she looked at him, seeing the soft hairs on his chest against which her yielding body had been pressed; the lean waist and hips, the hard thighs which had entangled with hers, her legs turned to water and her limbs were filled with a primitive, bewildering desire.

She forced herself to continue, 'But this you'll have to believe. Your intrusion into my sanctuary, which is how I look on this cottage, has knocked my world sideways. You're stealing everything from me.'

The blue of his eyes had deepened, and in the lamp's glow looked colder than an Arctic wilderness. He lounged against the table, legs crossed, hands resting, palms down on the table top. 'Tell me a few.'

'How could I put into words intangibles like—like the things I've told you before? I said once we were worlds apart. Your coming to live here doesn't alter anything. You've simply transposed your ways, your different level of thinking and behaving to a lower plane, an inferior environment.'

She paused to choose her words. 'To you living here is probably just a kind of adventure, an enduring of primitive living for the sake of it so that you can return in a few days to "civilisation" and boast to your friends and colleagues about how you roughed it—and of course,' with sarcasm, 'thoroughly enjoyed roughing it, in your country cottage. Don't you understand,' she cried, her passions rising, 'this is my home, whereas to you, it's merely a playground?'

'I'm sure there's more to come.'

'Your cynicism sickens me,' she flung at him. 'My aim in life is to live as unpretentiously as possible. I told you *that* before too. I also said I thought that *your* aim in life was to make as much money as possible for yourself. I still think so.'

'You certainly know how to flatter. But carry on.'

'You're—you're a threat to everything I hold dear.'

It's not true, her other self was screaming. *He* is everything I hold dear. Where he is, there's my happiness, security and peace of mind. All the same, she contradicted herself, everything I'm telling him is true. If we ever came together it would be on the physical plane, she agonised, not the mental, and then only for a few ecstatic weeks or months. It wouldn't work, it just wouldn't work.

She went on, with urgency, 'I don't want your twentieth century gadgets. I don't want to turn a switch and let a machine do what I now take delight in doing by hand. I don't want modern technology to make my presence redundant. I don't want it to make me feel I've got time on my hands and then feel so lost I don't know what to do with it, so I wander off and watch television and just sit and sit ... and sit. Forgetting even what my limbs are for, what my hands are for, what my brain is for.'

His silence was unnerving.

'Do you understand now?' she finished weakly, sinking exhausted into the rocking chair. She closed her eyes and let her head droop to one side.

When arms lifted her, holding her to a hard chest, she did not resist. When lips whispered, so near she could feel the breath coming through them, 'I understand. I understand far more than you think.' She was being carried across the room, then up the staircase.

As Drake put her full-length on her bed, he said, 'But something I must and will say, something you've forgotten. I gave you back this cottage. I kept a roof over your head, the roof of the "sanctuary" you love so much. Goodnight, my love of the night. The kisses were sweet, even if the girl I kissed was not.'

# CHAPTER ELEVEN

WHEN Ilona came down in the morning, her robe trailing behind her on the stairs, she found Drake stripped to the waist and washing vigorously in the kitchen.

'Cold water,' he said, soaping his arms.

'I told you,' she said, 'I heat it in pans on the fire.'

'Fire's out.' He lathered his face, moving to his neck and re-soaping his hands for all the rest of his body which was uncovered.

'But I—oh!' Her hands flew to her mouth. She remembered how, instead of refilling the fire with coal after heating the milk, she had become so exhausted Drake had carried her upstairs.

'Sorry,' she said, watching Drake wash at the new sink unit which he had filled with cold water from a bucket. She was fascinated by the ripple of muscle as he moved, rinsing away the soap, reaching blindly for the towel and drying himself.

'Good grief,' he exclaimed, opening one eye and gazing at her, 'you have to be a hardy animal to live in these conditions! Much more of this and I'll soon become so primitive I'll drag my woman by the hair into my secret lair and ravish her!' He opened the other eye, rubbing his neck. 'You—I mean, serf.' He strolled towards her, towel flung over his shoulder. 'Do you realise that as your landlord, I could throw you out any time, unless you do my bidding?' His damp hands came to rest on her shoulders. She was propelled forwards and his lips found hers. 'Yes,' he said, lifting his head, 'as sweet as in the early hours. Is your temper any sweeter, I wonder?'

Irritably, she struggled free. His careless kiss had brought her fires leaping to life. 'I'm best avoided first thing in the morning,' she snapped.

'That,' he said, grinning, 'is because you wake up alone.'

'Maybe it's because I prefer to.'

An eyebrow lifted and the smile was cynical. 'Are you kidding?'

She swung away, partly to express irritation, but mostly to get the tantalising sight of him out of her line of vision. As she crouched at the fire, removing the grating and raking the dead ashes, she felt herself pushed aside.

'Believe it or not—and you won't—I'm an expert fire-maker,' Drake said.

Ilona stayed crouched beside him. 'So I've been told.' She grinned impishly. 'In other ways, I mean.'

He turned, his curled fingers raised threateningly. 'My primitive instincts have been aroused enough by the surroundings, woman, without you adding fuel to the flames.'

She grinned again. 'You have to get the fire started first.'

He reached for her. 'That's as good an invitation as any man could want.' But his hands never caught her. She sprang away, squealing at the coal dust which had already blackened his fingers.

He looked up at her. 'By heaven, if I hadn't got a day's work in front of me ...'

Her body tensed for the chase, but he did not rise. Instead, all his attention was centred on clearing the grate and re-laying the fire. He took sticks and coal from the half-empty bucket and as she watched, her eyes strayed yet again to his body. The shoulders were broad, there was strength even in his shoulder blades, in the bones of his spine down which she longed to run her fingers.

She wanted to kneel behind him, slip her arms around that lean waist and rest her cheek against the tough, sinewy flesh of his back.

He looked up quickly and caught her eyes on him. The colour stained her cheeks and he said with surprising abruptness, 'If you really don't want me to take you to bed, I'd strongly advise you to go upstairs and get some more clothes on.'

With that taunt in her ears, Ilona scampered upstairs and did as he suggested.

When Drake had gone to work, wearing a suit which he must have brought in his suitcase and hung in the wardrobe, the cottage seemed unbearably lonely. It was a loneliness which frightened Ilona, because until now she had never wanted anyone's company but her own.

Drake had left for the day and she did not even know when—or if—he would be back. He might, having staked his claim to come and go, decide not to return for weeks. The fact that he had brought with him a few clothes meant nothing, except that he would have a change of outfit whenever he chose to visit the place and maybe stay a night or two.

After working through the morning, Ilona cooked her lunch, wishing for the first time that she was not eating alone. It was useless telling herself she was being foolish, because all day she was haunted by the sense of being incomplete.

Towards the end of the afternoon, she prepared her evening meal, putting peeled vegetables and cubes of beef into a covered dish and placing it on the lower shelf of the stove. Later, as she continued to work, she could hear the casserole bubbling noisily.

Tiring of typing, she stretched and wandered to the window. Once again the workmen had stayed away and she wondered why. Did Drake still not trust her not to damage their work when they had gone? If so, when *would* he trust her? Did he have it in mind eventually to turn her out, then ask the contractors to return?

The thought chilled her and she shivered. The sky was cloudy and she wondered if the weather would be kind for the fête tomorrow. It would be a pity if it rained, but no doubt Colonel Dainton would have prepared for the possibility and cleared his grand entrance hall of valuables and prized carpets, so that the stalls could be erected there instead of in the extensive grounds.

She remembered the dress she would wear for the raffle. It hung, somewhat neglected, upstairs in her cupboard. Now, when she was alone, would be a good time to try it on again. There was no full-length mirror in which to study her image, but looking down at herself, she saw how well it fitted.

There was a knock at the door and her heart bounced like a dog welcoming its master. But Drake had a key and would have used it. The knock was repeated and she knew by the rhythm that it was a friend.

'Hi there,' said Ray, then, 'Wow! A girl from my dreams

greets me on the doorstep. Wearing that tomorrow? You'll be a riot, love. Can I come in?'

The door creaked wider. 'Why not?' As Ray looked round, Ilona said, 'It's all right, I'm alone. But it wouldn't have mattered if I hadn't been. You know Drake's been staying here for a couple of days?'

'I did know, and it wasn't idle gossip that told me. But don't worry, not many people are aware of the fact. Although they know he owns the place now.'

Ilona frowned. 'I'm not *worrying*, Ray. He's the landlord —that's his room, where Lucia used to sleep—and I'm the tenant and,' pointing upwards, 'that, as you know, is where I sleep.'

His hand squeezed her shoulder. 'It's all right, love,' he reassured her. 'I know you, the whole village knows you. I might have laughed at Mrs Bryant's description of your character—"high moral fibre" and all that, but what she said was perfectly true. By the way, I met Mrs Macey just now hurrying along the lane. She's gone to stay with her sister in Brighton for the weekend. Apparently she's not too well. Mrs Macey asked me to tell you.'

'Thanks. So you like the dress? Good, so maybe the person who "wins" me will like it, too.' She frowned. 'Ray, I'm scared. I wish I'd never agreed——'

He sat sideways on the chair in front of the typewriter. 'Look, love, just quit worrying, will you? Everything's going to turn out all right. I know it will.'

Ilona frowned. 'How do you know? Is it you who's going to "win" me, or Colonel Dainton? I wish it were. I'd feel a lot safer——'

'Thanks,' said Ray, smiling crookedly. 'It boosts my manly confidence no end when a girl says she feels "safe" with me!'

'Sorry, Ray, I didn't mean it that way.'

'I know you didn't. I've just got a feeling, and you know these feelings. They're often proved right, aren't they?'

Ilona shrugged. 'Maybe. Would you like a cup of tea? My supper's not ready yet.'

'Wouldn't mind a quick one. Then I must get back. Father wants my help with the correspondence.'

Ilona put the kettle on the fire and put out two cups and

saucers. 'Ray,' she said at the kitchen door, 'I don't want
to spoil this dress by spilling something on it. Mind if I go
up and change it? Won't be more than a few minutes.'

'Okay by me, love. I'll pass the time reading the letters
you've been typing!'

She laughed and sped up the stairs. In a few moments
the dress was off. With care she slipped it on to a hanger
and hung it in the cupboard. As she turned to get her jeans,
she heard voices downstairs. For a moment she was
petrified, then she crept on to the small landing outside her
room and gazed down.

Drake was at the foot of the stairs looking up at her.
When she saw the icy contempt in his eyes, it came to her
what he was thinking. There she was, upstairs in her bra
and briefs, while downstairs a young man waited.

'Drake!' she croaked, and dashed back into her bedroom.

' 'Bye, Ilona love,' Ray called. 'See you tomorrow at the
fête. Hope the right man wins you!' And he was gone.

By the time Drake reached her bedroom door, she had
just had time to pull on her jeans, but nothing else. He
folded his arms and was unsparing in his scrutiny.

'So what did I interrupt?' he gritted. 'Or maybe you were
getting ready and I spoilt your fun even before things had
got going?'

'I don't know what you're talking about,' she retorted,
trying to cover her bare midriff by wrapping her arms
across herself. 'All I was doing was changing from the dress
I'm going to wear at the fête tomorrow. I didn't want to
spoil the dress by spilling things on it . . .'

Her voice tailed off as she realised he wasn't even listening.

'So despite everything you've said to the contrary,' he
went on, 'Ray Hale is your boy-friend. No wonder he calls
you "love", since he's your lover. And no wonder you
objected so strongly when I came here and occupied the
spare bedroom. I asked you at the time if you were expecting company. You denied it.'

'Of course I denied it, and I still deny it.'

'I suppose that's reasonable,' he drawled. 'The "friend"
you entertain would sleep up here, not down there. I must

admit, I'm not usually so naïve. I must have been completely taken in by that look of innocence about you.' He walked towards her. 'That damned, infuriating look of innocence! Every time I see it, it draws me but at the same time holds me off. It's plain now that I was the world's biggest fool not to realise it was a complete illusion.'

'You're wrong, so wrong!' she cried, backing away and coming up against her bed. 'You're basing your assumptions on purely circumstantial evidence. Ray came to have a word with me about tomorrow. I'd put the kettle on to make some tea, then came upstairs to change out of that dress.'

He continued to move forwards, knuckles on hips, until their bodies made contact. She felt her longing for the touch of him grow until it became a pain. Her fists lifted and pressed against his chest to push him away to a reasonable distance.

Drake continued to regard her coldly. Close as he was— the length of her arms—he was remote, detached, almost a stranger. It was at that moment that she despaired of ever reaching him, of ever crossing that 'chasm' or of overcoming that 'high fence' which he had once declared divided them. Then she heard a murmur in her mind, Couldn't love overcome barriers, heal breaches, close chasms, bring opposites together?

She pulled her hands away. *Love?* she thought. What's the use of one-sided love? Before Drake could touch her again, she took up her striped top and pulled it over her head. There was one answer to the problem created by this enforced proximity. One of them had to go and, she had to face it, it would have to be the tenant, not the landlord.

Her rucksack was on top of the cupboard. She reached up and tugged it down, coughing and closing her eyes as the dust came with it. A few pats with the hand removed most of the dust. She went to the chest of drawers and opened one drawer after another, pulling out clothes and stuffing them into the rucksack.

Drake watched in silence, hands in his pants pockets, the jacket of his suit draped over his wrists. His tie was a dark red, the white of his shirt broken by narrow, dark-red stripes. He was the picture of an immensely successful,

overwhelmingly confident businessman. He was also so
attractive as a man that it hurt Ilona to look at him.

When she proceeded to tie a pair of walking boots to the
rucksack by their laces, he asked, his voice quiet and a little
bemused,

'Will you tell me what you're doing?'

All the fury which she had held back, all the resentment
against life that had crazily placed the man she loved so
desperately so out of her reach that he might as well be
orbiting in a space station erupted and spilt over.

'It's plain,' she stormed, 'that there's only one thing I
can do to please you, and that is, get myself out of your
life. I told you once that if I ever left this cottage I'd stuff
my rucksack with my belongings and become a h-happy
wanderer.'

Happy? she thought, suppressing the threatening tears.
I'll never be happy again . . .

'I said I'd see the world, living and eating and sleeping
and working *my* way. Well, I'm doing what young people
all over the world are doing, I'm opting out. I want to be
h-happy,' how that word stuck, 'not criticised and falsely
accused and imposed upon. Not having things forced on me
I don't want, a way of life I don't want, a m-man I d-don't
want . . .'

It was no use, she could not sustain the anger. There
was no alternative but to go down the stairs and walk out
of Drake Warrick's life. As she descended, she heard him
follow, but he made no attempt to detain her.

As she opened the door, she thought, One word, just one
word would keep me here . . .

'Ilona, before you go, shall I tell you something?' He
stood on the doorstep, shoulders pushed back, his long legs
stiff, his eyes without expression. He was, without knowing it, every inch the landlord. 'I, too, have a rucksack.
Like yours, it's a little dusty through disuse, but like yours
also, it bears signs of wear and tear. When I go on vaca-
tion, I don't act the rich man-playboy. I use my limbs—
my legs to get me places, my shoulders to carry the weight
of the pack, my hands to put up a tent for the night. Our
worlds are not as different as you believe.'

Uncertain now, Ilona lingered. Had *she* put up the

barriers? No, not all of them. Drake had contributed, too. He had said that day—she remembered it so clearly—that he'd go and visit Diane, because she spoke his language. Diane, the woman he had loved and lost.

Was he, by this explanation, hoping to persuade her to postpone her departure and give him her company a little longer? In order, maybe, to try to forget his love for Diane, or—the thought was almost too painful to allow—sublimate it by using her?

Their eyes held and to her dismay a hard light crept into his. 'Maybe I'm being naïve again. Maybe all this talk of roaming the world is a blind, and instead you're going to join your boy-friend, Ray Hale, at some secret assignation?'

The aroma of cooking wafted out to her. It was strong and compelling and revealed to her a gnawing hunger in her stomach. It also told her that her beef casserole was almost certainly spilling over and staining the inside of her stove. Her stove, her kitchen, her cottage, her world ... She couldn't leave them, any more than she could walk away from the man who filled that world of hers with meaning!

Anxiously, her eyes sought his. In them was a cold contempt. She caught her breath. Had he read her thoughts? Did he know she wouldn't want to live without him?

Slowly she walked back along the path and he moved to allow her to re-enter. The rucksack hit the floor and they stood looking at each other.

'So I was right in my assumption of your destination—Ray Hale, and not the wide open spaces of the world?'

Her lips parted to speak in her own defence, but she changed her mind and pressed them together. What was the use of trying to explain the complexities of the internal arguments which had led her to the decision to remain?

She shrugged, sighed and said, 'It smells as though supper's ready. Do you want to share?'

'If there's enough.' His voice remained hard and unforgiving.

She removed her jacket and threw it across to the rocking chair which swayed busily under the impact. In the kitchen, she opened the stove door and with pot-holders to protect her hands, took out the bubbling casserole and transferred it to the top of the stove.

Drake stood at the door, watching her. 'Want any help?'

A piece of hair fell across her eyes and she shook it back. 'Can you set the table?'

He smiled tightly. 'This will surprise you. I not only can, but will.' He turned, scanning the living-room. 'Table-cloth?'

'Place mats there,' she pointed, 'cutlery in that drawer. Salt, pepper and so on, in the sideboard.'

Three minutes later he returned to the kitchen. 'Mission accomplished. You see,' he mocked, lifting his hands, 'these have a use other than signing letters and contracts, picking up the telephone and making love to women.'

'Oh!' Ilona said flatly, and handed him his plate.

They ate their meal in almost total silence. Ilona was unnerved by it. It was impossible to tell whether Drake maintained it on purpose to express his condemnation of what he considered her lie about her true destination after leaving the cottage, or whether his work occupied his mind to the exclusion of everything else.

Ilona had had no time before Drake's unexpected return to prepare a second course, so she offered him cheese and biscuits or fresh fruit. He took an apple from the dish, carried it to his mouth, then checked himself. He inspected the apple and asked, mockery deepening the blue of his eyes, 'Has it been washed?' Ilona nodded. 'Under the tap outside in the garden?' Again she nodded. 'And dried on a paper towel?'

She guessed then that he was laughing at her and she replied, colouring a little, 'All right, so you've had your little joke. You won't be happy until you get that tap working in the kitchen on the sink unit, will you?'

He bit hugely into the apple, leaning forwards, elbows on table. 'I don't know,' he said, chewing. 'There are ways—and ways—of being happy, if you get my meaning?'

She said slowly, incredulously, 'Are you saying that you might eventually get to like my way of living? That you could adjust to living the hard way—and actually be *happy*?'

His switch of mood, his hint of acceptance of her manner of living made her pulse rate as staccato as Morse code.

'Scratch the surface, lady, and you'll find primitive man lurking under my veneer of sophistication. Given the right environment and enticement, he'll leap out and take you by storm. Does that answer your question?' His eyes glittered, teasing her.

'In a roundabout way.' When would her heartbeats settle down?

He finished the apple and as they drank coffee, Drake leaned back.

'Looking forward to tomorrow?' he asked.

'I'm dreading it.'

'If you feel as strongly as that, why did you agree to the idea?'

Ilona shrugged. 'One of the committee members made the suggestion and everybody looked at me.'

'Couldn't they also see that you weren't the right type of girl? You're hardly the kind of female who brazenly displays her attractions, then watches a line of people form to buy tickets to win her.'

'All right,' she snapped, toying with a piece of bread, 'your message is loud and clear. I just don't have the necessary glamour, looks, charm. But if I wear that dress I've been given, and smile a bit, that should be enough. It's for charity, and that's all that matters, really. If the man who wins me is disappointed, he can always dump me and give me the fare home. Because I know one thing, I'm going to fight like crazy if any man tries to—to——'

A broad grin preceded the mocking comment, 'To take you to bed?'

'Yes.'

'Am *I* intended to take that as a warning? Because if so, I warn *you* that if I should decide to take you there myself, you can bite and scratch to your heart's content, I'd be the one to win.'

She rose quickly, scraping her chair. 'I have to get some water in to heat on the stove for washing the dishes. Please excuse me.'

'Give me the container. I'll get the water in.'

It was a tone she could not disobey. Drake took the plastic bucket from her and she heard water running into it from the tap outside. When he brought the water in, he said, 'How have you managed to carry this heavy weight into the cottage a dozen or more times a day? You could have done yourself a serious injury.'

'Well, so far I haven't.' She heard a murmured sarcastic 'Lucky you' as he carried the pail into the kitchen.

'Is this the pan?' he called. 'How long does it take to heat—a couple of hours?' The sarcasm persisted. 'I can think of faster ways. A stove fired by portable containers of fuel, for instance. A method which not even you could refuse on the grounds that it constitutes a luxury.'

'Buy a stove like that,' she retorted. 'Install it. I can't stop you. You're the owner now, as you keep repeating.'

'I might. I might well do that.'

Together they washed and dried the dishes and Ilona could not fault Drake on his meticulous care. She wanted to tell him so, but was too shy. Also she knew that only sarcasm would come her way if she praised him.

Slowly, very slowly, her opinion of his capabilities was undergoing a change. There could be no doubting his ability to adapt to her kind of environment. The thought even occurred to her—and after all the insults she had thrown at him, it made her blush—that he might be much more adept at truly roughing it, and in a far less secure environment, than she was. Was his 'life of luxury', therefore, a product of her own prejudiced imagination?

But she remembered that it had been he who had referred to the 'deep chasm' between them. Had he meant of mind rather than, as she had assumed, physical stamina, in contending with a tough, austere environment?

The dishes were washed and dried in silence, and her heart leapt in anticipation as she wondered what the evening held in store in the way of conversation and togetherness. The answer was immediate. When the dishes were stacked away, Drake went into the bedroom which had now become his and put a match to the lamp in there.

Since he did not close the door at once, Ilona went across and said, in an effort to make some kind of contact, 'I'm sorry there are still so many of Lucia's clothes hanging on the rail.'

'I thought they were yours.'

'No, I don't wear dresses like that—except one, once.' Her colour deepened when she remembered the effect which that particular black dress had had on him. 'Shall I move them?'

He shrugged as if he did not care. For a few more moments she stood her ground, but as he opened a document case and proceeded to spread papers over the bed, she felt as though she were a junior clerk back in the office, and he was the boss pointedly dismissing her.

Well, she was no longer one of his employees. She would not be so easily dismissed. 'Your car isn't outside, Drake. Where have you parked it?'

'I didn't come in my car. A friend gave me a lift.'

'Oh.' A pause, then, 'How will you get back tomorrow?'

'Tomorrow is Saturday. I don't work Saturdays.' With an irritated frown, he returned to his reading. 'Anyway,' he looked up again, 'if I need a car I'll call a taxi. Where's the nearest telephone?'

'Mrs Macey's. She's away at the moment, but I've got a key.'

His nod was so abrupt she could not ignore it, so she retreated, leaving the door ajar. Moments later, it was snapped shut and remained so all evening.

At about ten o'clock, Ilona gave up trying to read. Drake had been so quiet it was as though she had been alone. There was simply nothing else to do but wash and go to bed. While the water heated, she went upstairs, removing sufficient garments to give herself a thorough wash. Pulling on her bathrobe, she went down the stairs. The living-room was still empty.

Since she refused to risk another dismissal and ask permission to open Drake's door, she was unable to tell him of her intention. There was no alternative, therefore, but to put up the 'Please keep out' notice which had so offended him the evening before.

In order to wash the top half of herself while keeping the lower half covered, Ilona slipped her arms from the robe and let it hang loosely from the tie belt at her waist. She was soaping her neck when the kitchen door burst open. Drake stood there, his blue eyes piercing, his lips thinned.

In his hand was the torn-down notice. Holding it out,

he said, 'Were you trying to *provoke* me into seducing you? I told you last night the effect such a notice had on a male man, and I, my girl, am a male man, a fact you should at least have some inkling of by now.'

Horrified by his sudden appearance, Ilona had paused in the act of washing. When his eyes started to roam over her, lingering on her piquant, alluring shape, on the glistening, damp skin of her arms, neck and face—and when those eyes began to burn with a growing desire—she groped for the towel and flung it round her.

He did not laugh at her embarrassment. It seemed to anger him more. 'If your boy-friend is allowed to take all the liberties in the world with you—which is plain that he is, by his presence here today when I returned—why should you deny me the sight, and not only the sight, of your beautiful body?'

In three strides he was beside her. The towel was thrown aside. His hands ran down her arms and back again to her shoulders, moving easily over the soaped skin. Then her neck knew his touch, her back, her midriff and, last and most sublimely of all, her breasts. But even as her ecstasy grew and her head drooped back to rest against him, he moved away, drying his palms on the hips of the tightly-fitting pants he now wore.

With a smothered expletive, he swung round and was gone.

## CHAPTER TWELVE

IT was about one o'clock when Ilona gave up trying to sleep and began walking round the room. She was not aware of the creaking boards, of the chill breeze from the open window. She knew only that downstairs was the man she loved so completely she wanted to throw caution, convention and even pride to the winds and run down to him.

But each of these sides of her personality had, as a result of her firm upbringing, too secure a hold for her to bypass them now. So she trod the thin carpet, backwards and forwards, hands clenched in her robe pockets, enduring the pain of unindulged longing and unreturned love.

In her agitated state, she had not given thought to the next day, the fête, the raffling of herself as a prized companion for some man for the length of a day. It had not occurred to her how the sleepless hours might affect her looks and her energies, to see the day through to the end without flagging. Nor, in her restless wanderings, did she hear the approach of footsteps. She therefore had no warning of the door being opened to reveal, the tall, broad-shouldered figure of her landlord.

His hair was ruffled as if impatient fingers had been thrust through it. His eyes were shadowed, yet he was fully clothed and wore a thick, deep blue high-necked sweater. It looked as if he had no intention of going to bed that night.

'Anything wrong?' he asked abruptly.

'Just—just can't sleep.' There was a prolonged pause. While Ilona felt her own tension intensifying, she saw in the folded arms, serious face and firm-muscled legs of the man standing before her the relaxation for which she craved.

He was a few steps distant, yet they were in reality far apart. There might just as well have been a desk between them as there had been in the past, the chasm of status separating them as there had been when she was his

179

employee. In spite of the intimacies which had, on occasion, moulded them as one, she had come no nearer to the quintessence of the man than when she was a mere typist in the general office of his company.

There had to be a way of bridging the gulf. The healing words came spontaneously. 'Drake?' He did not move, just continued regarding her pale, drawn face. 'I'm sorry for everything I've done.' He did not seem to understand. 'Like —like smashing up that concrete outside. It was fear that made me do it, a—a kind of primitive wish to destroy anything that—that threatened the simplicity of my way of life.' There was no reaction.

'I'm sorry, too,' she went on, 'for all my insults. I didn't mean them really.'

As her tension grew, so his relaxed state seemed to deepen.

'This afternoon, I wasn't really going any place—certainly not to Ray's. There's a girl in the town he likes. He's not my boy-friend.' Her knuckles showed white. 'If—if I was going anywhere, it was—well, back here, I suppose. I just couldn't have left this cottage.'

If only he would say something!

'Drake,' she whispered, 'I don't dislike having you here. I like it, really.'

His lips parted. At last he was going to respond ... 'I suppose it makes you feel more secure having a man about the place?' It was sarcasm, not the forgiveness she had longed for.

She shook her head, but did not reply to the question. 'I understand how you feel, Drake. I know you love Diane and have lost her to someone else.' He had returned to silence. His arms were still dauntingly in place across his chest. His blue eyes glowed in the lamplight, while the angles of his face had hardened. Lack of sleep? Lack of sympathy? Condemnation of her morals and behaviour despite her attempt to heal the wounds she had inflicted on him?

She persisted haltingly, 'She told me once, "It won't be long now." I thought she meant before she married you.'

'She thought she was dying, and in so doing, that she'd soon "rejoin" her husband.'

The solemn words aroused grief, compassion—and a

strange relief. So Diane had not returned Drake's love?

Ilona held her head. 'Part of *me* is dying,' she thought. 'You're drifting even farther away, instead of coming nearer. I'm losing you, Drake ...' Of its own accord, her hand came out, reaching towards him.

Fatigue, plus a profound, instinctive need to establish a friendly relationship, if nothing else, had overcome at last the deep-rooted inhibitions left over from her early years.

'Drake, please help me. I'm worried—about tomorrow, about what I'm going to do, and what's going to be expected of me——'

His arms dropped to his sides. He had not yielded in any way. 'You went into it with your eyes open. Work out your own problems.' He went out, closing the door.

The bed was a refuge as she threw herself upon it, the pillow something to cling to, the sobs that racked her both a pain and a release from the terrible tension.

It must have been an hour later that she heard the noise outside—the grit of footsteps on gravel, the sound of builders' implements being disturbed. Sleep had not come, although she had slipped into a dazed, dreamlike state which brought no relief. *Had* she dreamt the sounds? Slowly she lifted her tired body from the bed, to sit on its side.

When the head and shoulders of a man appeared at the open window, she held her cheeks. Eyes wide, mouth open, she tried to scream, but nothing would come. It wasn't Drake, he would have come up the stairs. It wasn't Ray. This man was solidly built ...

She stood, hands to her mouth, wanting to run but immobilised by terror. A foot came over the sill, then the other. At that moment her limbs loosened and she dived for the door. She had delayed a fraction too long.

The man was on to her, arms like a vice round her waist. She could not see him. It was dark and her back was to him.

'Come quietly,' a voice said, 'or I'll knock you cold. I said I'd get you one day, and this is it. I'll wipe that innocence from your pretty face. It won't be so pretty by the time I've finished with you ...'

The voice was frighteningly familiar. She said desperately, 'Have you gone mad, Mr Bradwell? I'm——'

No, she wouldn't tell him that she was not alone. With no tell-tale car outside, he might not know Drake was there, downstairs—sleeping? She hoped not, oh, she hoped not ...

'You're Ilona Bell, my sweetie, and I'm going to take you —in every way, do you understand? In every possible way, my lady. I'll bring you down, you little vixen, I'll bring you down until you grovel!'

Her body went slack and she said in as simpering a voice as she could manage, 'Mr Bradwell, you haven't come to tell me—and *show* me—the facts of life! Oh ...' she choked as his arm hooked round her neck. With a super-human effort she turned, gripped his hand and clawed at his face, fighting him crazily, frantically and screaming, 'Drake, *Dr-a-ke*!'

Footsteps pounded upwards, and there was an answering shout. Ron Bradwell cursed and mumbled, 'My God, she's not alone!' He turned on her, as if determined to do some damage before he escaped. He hit her face with his palm, then the back of his hand, one, twice, three times. Delaying no longer, he threw her to the floor and made for the window.

The door was flung open and Drake was on to him. 'Run, Ilona, if you're able to,' Drake shouted, 'go next door, call the police, emergency. I'll knock this bastard cold and get him locked up, if it kills me!'

Ilona struggled to her feet. She swayed and held her head, dazed by the impact of the floorboards. But fear for Drake's wellbeing, his life even, as he writhed and wrestled with the interloper, gave wings to her feet. She raced downstairs, slid the bolts, seized Mrs Macey's key from the hook and ran barefoot over the hard, stone-scattered track to the cottage along the lane.

Ilona sat at the table, her head lying on her folded arms. Drained, exhausted beyond expression, she listened to the drone of voices from her bedroom.

Ron Bradwell was out, cold, which he had threatened would be her own fate. Drake had done it to him, Drake who at times she had as good as accused of not knowing a twig from a log of wood. There was hidden within him the strength of an athlete, the muscular power and control of a mountain climber.

Her face still stung from the impact of Ron Bradwell's hand, her head still throbbed from the hardness of the floor as she had fallen full-length. Her feet ached from the abrasions inflicted by the race along the track.

But the police car's engine purred outside and Ron Bradwell lay senseless in the back seat. There had been a brief and sympathetic interview with the two policemen. He had used the builders' stepladder, they told her, to make the entry. Also, he was not completely sober, they could tell by his breath.

The policemen were coming down now. With an effort she raised her head. One of them paused at the table. 'Like a lift to the hospital, miss, for a check-up, just in case?'

Vigorously, Ilona shook her head. She was all right, she assured them. Just tired, very tired.

'I'll look after her cuts and bruises,' Drake assured them, as he saw the policeman out. The door was half open and Drake's words drifted in.

*Came to stay for a night or two on purpose, expected an attack some time. When I fired him, he threatened to beat her up, saying she was the cause of him losing his job. Completely untrue. He'd told the landlord about her living on here after the legal tenant had gone. Now I own the place and she's my tenant.*

Now, Ilona thought wearily, I know it all. That was why he had come to stay. Not for me, not for the simple life, not for anything but to catch Ron Bradwell ...

Five minutes later, Drake found her still in the same position. She did not look up. Her eyes were open, staring at nothing.

'I know now,' she muttered. 'I know why you came. Well, you've caught Ron Bradwell. You can go. I'll be as safe alone as I ever was.'

The man at her side answered quietly, 'Yes, I did come here to catch him—before he caught you. I came to protect you.'

Ilona stirred but stayed as she was.

'He told me he'd get you, and when he did, you wouldn't

have a pretty face any more. He'd make it so that you'd be in such a mess you wouldn't be "saleable" in the fête raffle. Which is why I was especially alert tonight.'

Slowly her head lifted and her heavy eyes dwelt on his fully-clothed state. 'Which is why you didn't go to bed.'

'Right. And also why I became disturbed when I heard you walking about upstairs. I was listening all the time. You see, I thought he'd try and break in by the front door. What I didn't guess was that he'd make use of that ladder. I could kick myself for being so obtuse in not calculating that he'd choose the most direct route to you.'

'So when I heard a noise the other night and thought it was the builder inspecting the damage I'd caused, it must have been Ron Bradwell?'

Drake nodded. 'Reconnoitring. When you phoned and told me what you'd heard, I guessed at once who it must be, which is why I came here, prepared to stay as long as necessary.'

'Well,' she watched her own fingers pleating her handkerchief, 'you've finished acting as my security guard. Thank you very much,' she finished tonelessly. 'You can go. Your own home's waiting for you.'

He did not move, except to slip his hands into his pockets.

'Why,' she asked to fill the silence, 'did you tell the builders not to come again?'

'I decided to await events.'

She looked up at him, puzzled by the look in his eyes. 'What events?'

'The appropriate moment to consult you, to discover what you'd like brought into your home.'

*But it's your home as well!* The words trembled on her lips, but she managed to hold them back.

Her eyes widened. '*You* consult *me*? You're the owner, so you make the decisions.'

He moved nearer, hands in pockets. A smile that was not a smile played over his lips. 'You're the one who's going to live here, so you must make the final choice.' He bent over her to support himself with his hand on the table. 'Do you want this cottage to remain just a place to live in, or do you want it made into a home?'

A picture tuned in to her mind of Mrs Macey's cottage, with its rugs and polished table, its flowers and comfortable chairs, its little touches of simple, yet natural, luxury ... Anybody of any age appreciated a home, not just someone at Mrs Macey's stage in life. A home ... She discovered she had spoken aloud.

'A home? A home you shall have.'

She looked up wonderingly at his tone. A hand lifted her face, and the blue eyes narrowed. 'He hit you, that swine.' She rubbed the back of her head and his hand followed. 'A bump. Yet another he's inflicted on you.'

'Yes, and the day after that first time, you fired me. Why, Drake, why, when I told you the truth?'

He lifted his shoulders. 'The reasons are too complex to analyse here and now. I thought you went to the party voluntarily, and were lying to me. Remember I was encouraged to think so by Bradwell, whom I trusted at that time. I thought you were pretending to be the quiet type, when in reality you were the other kind. Also, in my work I'm a perfectionist.'

'Ruthless,' she put in.

He smiled. 'Maybe, but I've had to be in my business life. You understand that?'

'And in your personal life.'

'Not true, my love. But perfectionist, maybe.' His lips lowered and fleeting kisses touched her cheeks where Ron Bradwell had hit her. 'I've found the perfect companion, the woman who, I hope, will go through life by my side.'

Her heart began to race. 'Please tell me who she is, Drake,' she whispered.

He took her hands and pulled her up to face him. 'With words, my love, or with actions?'

She whispered in his ear, standing on tiptoe, 'With kisses, Drake, with kisses.'

'Willingly, my darling. I, Drake Warrick, will kiss thee, Ilona Bell, to your—and my—heart's content.'

Some time later, they pulled apart and he lowered her into the rocking chair. 'I have something to show you. And to give you.' He went into his bedroom and emerged holding two boxes and a piece of paper. This he smoothed out and held up for her inspection. 'A special licence. To-morrow, we shall be married.'

She stood quickly. 'But you haven't asked me!'

He rubbed his chin, affecting a frown. 'Surely I haven't forgotten? Ilona Bell, will you marry me?'

'Yes, Drake Warrick, I will,' she answered, laughing, her shadowed eyes brilliant with happiness.

'Good, but then I never did doubt it. I was told weeks ago that a certain member of my staff loved her boss.' He dodged the hand which lifted playfully to hit him. 'Incidentally, that was about the only truthful thing Ron Bradwell ever told me.' He opened a ring box. 'The wedding ring. Try it. No, no, you put it on. That will be my privilege tomorrow.'

It fitted perfectly. Drake opened another box, revealing a two-stone diamond and platinum ring. Ilona gasped. 'But, Drake ...' He lifted her hand and pushed the ring into place.

'A little too big,' Drake said. 'We must get it adjusted.'

'Not yet,' said Ilona, hugging it to her. 'Oh, Drake, I——'

He held up his hand. 'Don't tempt me, sweetheart. Here,' he caught her up and sat with her on his lap in the rocking-chair, 'we can talk.' There was a contented silence for a few moments, then he said, 'About those alterations——' Ilona's head lifted from his shoulder, but he pushed it back. 'Only those you approve of will be carried out, my love. I have no intention of spoiling the simplicity of our life. And I promise to learn it from you. I'll be an enthusiastic student. In fact, I'm more than half-way there already!'

She gazed up at him delightedly, then her expression changed to one of horror. 'Tomorrow,' she gasped, 'the fête, the raffle! How can we possibly be married? Lots of people have bought tickets and it wouldn't be fair to whoever "won" me——'

He said, smiling blandly, 'A certain Mr Drake Warrick will "win" you, Miss Bell.' At her astonished stare he laughed loudly. 'No, I'm not out of my mind. Put yourself in my place. I couldn't stand by, could I, and see the girl I loved being handed on a plate, as it were, to some other man, whatever his age? So I "bought" you in advance.'

'But that's cheating, Mr Warrick!'

He rubbed his cheek. 'That's one way of putting it, Miss Bell. *Ruthlessly* determined to keep my wife-to-be to myself would be the other!' His glowing eyes mocked her gently.

'But,' she said with a frown, 'when did all this take place?'

'The ticket-buying? Oh, some days ago. I went to see Colonel Dainton and we arranged it between us. I waved a cheque for a substantial amount in front of him, money to be added to the charity fund—on one condition: that the girl being raffled would become "mine".'

'But, Drake, there's still tomorrow, and drawing the tickets from the hat. So how———?'

He looked down into her large, tired eyes. 'Ah, now there I might be upsetting your principles. There'll be two sets of tickets———'

'Pink and yellow. But the colours have no significance.'

'Now there you're wrong. *I* have bought all the pink ones. Don't worry, the yellow tickets will be in the hat, but at the bottom. All the pink tickets will be placed on top. Since Colonel Dainton's wife is making the draw, he has been able to instruct her to take the topmost ticket. Thus, even without seeing what she's taking, we know in advance it will be pink.'

'Drake Warrick, you're———'

'Ruthless. I know. Afterwards, when you're "mine", we have an appointment with the registrar. A little after four o'clock tomorrow, we shall become man and wife. A few friends have agreed to attend a small reception at the Royal Hotel———'

'Whose friends?'

'Yours and mine. Colonel Dainton and his wife, for instance. Ray Hale, a certain colourful lady called Mrs Bryant. My friends, too. Does that suit you?' Contentedly she nodded. 'Then we shall return here to our home, cut off from the world. Any objections?'

'None whatsoever.'

'Any questions?'

'Yes. Will there be time for me to change into a suitable dress for our wedding?'

'Why bother? From all I've heard, the dress you'll already be wearing will be ideal.'

After a moment's thought, Ilona agreed. 'One more question, Drake.' She found herself unable to meet his eyes. 'Did—did Diane ever mean anything to you?'

'You mean was I in love with her? No, I was not. She had lost a dearly-loved husband. Then she discovered she had a serious illness. I was so sorry for her I kept her on the payroll and she came to work whenever she could. I sent her gifts to cheer her up. I took her out to give her something to live for. I paid, when necessary, for her medical treatment. When I heard she was getting better and, what was more, had fallen in love with someone else—thus easing her unhappiness over her late husband—I was delighted.'

'So,' Ilona whispered, closing her eyes with relief, 'she never meant anything to you?'

'My darling, how could she when my heart was caught in a trap by you? A trap, moreover, from which I never wanted to escape.'

'I was trapped, too—by my boss! I hated quarrelling with you. I hated fighting you.'

'And you're a little liar,' he murmured, putting his lips to her neck. 'You gloried in our battles, both physical and verbal.'

'Last night, when I was washing and you——'

'Started to make love to you? I wanted to go on, and on, but I checked myself. When I heard you walking about and came up to your room, I could see the love in your eyes inviting me to stay. I wanted to stay and possess you there and then, but circumstances, and the knowledge that in less than twenty-four hours' time you would be my wife, stopped me.'

'A girl for a day, we were going to call the raffle,' she mused.

Drake shook his head, pulling aside her robe and burying his face in the hollows of her neck, making her curl her toes and fingers. 'My woman for the rest of my life. Tomorrow will be just the beginning. My day of possession,' he said softly.

She pulled back his sleeve and looked at his watch. 'Tomorrow is today already, darling,' she whispered, lifting shining eyes to his.

His eyes grew dark with desire and understanding. 'My love,' he murmured huskily, 'oh, my love.'

He lifted her, extinguished the lamp and by the light of the moon, carried her up the stairs.

# *Harlequin* |Plus|

## A WORD ABOUT THE AUTHOR

Born in London and raised in North Essex, a county in eastern England, Lilian Peake grew to love the countryside, going for long rambling walks and filling a journal with all she observed. She became secretary to a local mystery writer, then embarked upon a journalism career.

From fashion writer with a London magazine, she moved on to a position as advice columnist with yet another magazine, both of which jobs, she feels, contributed to a greater understanding of people.

Until almost the moment she started writing her first novel, Lilian believed that she could not do it. "Then I read a book that challenged me," she said. "I remember thinking, *I could write like that!* So I did."

Today, Lilian Peake is the wife of a college principal. Her interests vary, but reading and listening to music top the list. "And as I do the housework," she admits, "I think about my characters and my plots."

# Take these 4 best-selling novels FREE

*as advertised on TV*

That's right! FOUR first-rate Harlequin romance novels by four world renowned authors, FREE, as your introduction to the Harlequin Presents Subscription Plan. Be swept along by these FOUR exciting, poignant and sophisticated novels . . . . Travel to the Mediterranean island of Cyprus in *Anne Hampson*'s "Gates of Steel" . . . to Portugal for *Anne Mather*'s "Sweet Revenge" . . . to France and *Violet Winspear*'s "Devil in a Silver Room" . . . and the sprawling state of Texas for *Janet Dailey*'s "No Quarter Asked."

  **The very finest in romantic fiction**

Join the millions of avid Harlequin readers all over the world who delight in the magic of a really exciting novel. SIX great NEW titles published EACH MONTH! Each month you will get to know exciting, interesting, true-to-life people . . . . You'll be swept to distant lands you've dreamed of visiting . . . . Intrigue, adventure, romance, and the destiny of many lives will thrill you through each Harlequin Presents novel.

*Get all the latest books before they're sold out!*
As a Harlequin subscriber you actually receive your personal copies of the latest Presents novels immediately after they come off the press, so you're sure of getting all 6 each month.

*Cancel your subscription whenever you wish!*
You don't have to buy any minimum number of books. Whenever you decide to stop your subscription just let us know and we'll cancel all further shipments.

*Your* **FREE gift** *includes*

*Sweet Revenge* by **Anne Mather**
*Devil in a Silver Room* by **Violet Winspear**
*Gates of Steel* by **Anne Hampson**
*No Quarter Asked* by **Janet Dailey**

# FREE Gift Certificate
## and subscription reservation

**Mail this coupon today!**

In the U.S.A.
1440 South Priest Drive
Tempe, AZ 85281

In Canada
649 Ontario Street
Stratford, Ontario N5A 6W2

**Harlequin Reader Service:**

Please send me my 4 Harlequin Presents books free. Also, reserve a subscription to the 6 new Harlequin Presents novels published each month. Each month I will receive 6 new Presents novels at the low price of $1.75 each [*Total – $10.50 a month*]. There are no shipping and handling or any other hidden charges. I am free to cancel at any time, but even if I do, these first 4 books are still mine to keep absolutely FREE without any obligation.

NAME                    (PLEASE PRINT)

ADDRESS

CITY            STATE / PROV.        ZIP / POSTAL CODE

Offer expires October 31, 1982                    SB496
Offer not valid to present subscribers

Prices subject to change without notice.